I0686897

LITTLE TURTLE ISLAND

೫

LINDA JOHNSON

A GARDEN GATE FARM PUBLICATION

Published by Garden Gate Farm 2017

Copyright © 2017 by Garden Gate Farm

All rights reserved. No part of this book may be used or reproduced in any manner whatsoever without written permission from the publisher, except in the case of brief quotations embodied in critical articles and reviews.

First Edition: June 2017

Library of Congress Control Number: 2017949420

ISBN 978-0-692-90947-8

Little Turtle Island is a work of historical fiction written and designed by Linda Johnson. Any inaccuracies or misrepresentations are the responsibility of the author alone. Any references to historical events, real people, or real places are used fictitiously. Other names, characters, places, and events are products of the author's imagination.

This book is set in Requiem, a typeface designed in 1992 by Jonathan Hoefler of Hoefler & Co. inspired by an illustration in a sixteenth-century writing manual.

www.at-the-garden-gate.com

— ALSO BY LINDA JOHNSON —

Yellow Bird

— DEDICATION —

to
Dave

— IN MEMORY —

of
Evelyn

"Johnson (*Yellow Bird*, 2010) writes in a meditatively poetic style, full of emotion and depth: 'Then you came. This strange man, all alone. I saw then how large the universe is, and how many secrets it holds. I could see the whole world spinning under the heavens.' Both characters' stories are powerful enough to stand alone, and the author dexterously weaves them into one coherent narrative....A moving story about cultural alienation and familial identity."

—KIRKUS REVIEWS

᚛

I have been a multitude of shapes,
Before I assumed a consistent form.
I have been a sword, narrow, variegated,
I have been a tear in the air,
I have been in the dullest of stars.
I have been a word among letters,
I have been a book in the origin.

TALIESIN, SIX-CENTURY WELSH POET

NUSHÈMAKW

❧

1518 CE

MIDWINTER MOON

It was Honarha's turn to speak, and for once she didn't know what to say. Her mind felt like an empty shell. Last night her dream came again. Only this time it invaded with such strength that, before retreating, it filled her every pore with its crystalline light and sharp edges, an ebbing tide scraping clean her very soul, leaving behind only its hard implacable imprint, a message too fathomless to describe.

They all sat around the fire waiting for her to speak. It was the first evening of the Midwinter Ceremony, and the women were tired. The Thanksgiving prayers had been recited, the meals had been prepared and blessed and eaten, and later that night they would rejoin the men for the sacred dances.

But now it was time for dream guessing. Onondaga Turtle Clan mother started them off. "In my dream," she began.

Honarha knew it would be an easy dream to guess. It was how Clan Mother always started the ceremony. "In my dream, I was in a field, lush and beautiful, and in the distance on top of three fertile mounds, something tall was blowing in the breeze."

"Maize!" called out Keguenha who was sitting across from Honarha. "Grandmother, your dream was about maize!"

"Very good," she said. "Yes, I dreamed that the rains came early this year, and the maize grew strong. A gift from Earth Mother."

Honarha sat to the right of Clan Mother, which meant it was her turn now. Everyone was waiting, and the silence became heavy. The only sound was that of the fire snapping and popping and sending little bursts of sparks into the darkening sky. She closed her eyes against all of their staring faces.

"What is it, daughter? It's not like you to hold back your dreams. What's wrong?"

Honarha folded her hands across her swollen belly. "Look how restless the baby is, Grandmother. I'm worn out by all of her kicking. She never stops." As soon as she said it, the baby quieted.

Clan Mother laughed. "I think she heard you, daughter. Maybe she's waiting for you to tell your dream, just as we are. Why don't you try?" Clan Mother took Honarha's hand.

Honarha sat a little straighter. "It's more than a dream, Grandmother. It's a nightmare." She looked across the fire to her waiting sisters. "Who will guess it?"

"Is it about the baby?" ventured one of the women.

"Yes."

"A girl?"

"Yes."

"Did you dream that something was wrong with the baby?" Keguenha asked. "Was the baby born sick?"

Honarha shook her head and closed her eyes again.

"That's enough guessing for now," Clan Mother said. She turned to Honarha "Tell us about this nightmare."

All of her sisters and aunts and mothers leaned in, and the firelight glowed on their faces.

"No, sister. In my dream, my baby girl was born healthy and strong. It was the birthing that scared me." She was relieved to have started. Her shoulders relaxed as she continued.

"I was in the wiktut, and the pains were coming. They kept coming and coming, getting worse and worse, bearing down, pulling and pulling and telling the baby it was time to come into this world. But she refused to be born. It was tearing us both to pieces, and still she wouldn't come." Honarha stopped and her eyes filled with tears.

"It's all right, Honarha. Keep going," encouraged Clan Mother who squeezed her hand.

Honarha wiped her eyes. "My baby," she continued, "my daughter said to me, 'Mama, I cannot be born, because the moment I enter this world, I will lose my name. I will lose who I am. I will lose everything. Mama, I will even lose you.' And then I woke up."

There. She said it. And yes, she felt better. "Grandmother," she asked into the thickening night, "what do you think it means?"

The stars winked down on them. It would be cold tonight. The frost had already settled over the village, but they were spared its bite inside the warm ring of fire. Clan Mother pulled her bearskin cloak under her chin. "I'm not sure. It could be a lot of things. I wonder if it means something other than you think."

"Like what?"

"On the one hand, a dream can be a premonition, a vision of what's to come. It may be true that the birth will be difficult. Unless the baby turns soon, it surely will be. But don't forget, many of your aunts and sisters are healers, especially Kedgiens who is ready to help you when your time comes."

The elderly woman smiled and nodded from across the fire.

"Think about that when you sleep. It may quiet your nightmare." Clan Mother continued. "On the other hand, a dream can go deeper and get at something else, something that you have had trouble coming to terms with."

"Like what?"

"Like Achimwis, for example."

"What about Achimwis?" Honarha said too loudly.

"You've never talked about the problems he's caused you, and will cause again once the baby is born."

Honarha's face grew hot. She pulled her hand away from Clan Mother's. "What do you mean? My Achimwis is a good man. He loves me and he loves our baby. He'll be a good father!"

"I know, I know," Clan Mother comforted, "Everyone can see how much he loves you. You're right. Achimwis has helped all of us. He's kind and considerate. So we welcome him like our own. But still, that doesn't change the fact that he's Lenapé. His Unami People Down the River are neither Onondaga nor Haudenosaunee, and now we'll soon have a baby who is all of these."

Keguenha elbowed Honarha. "Is that what's bothering you? Is

that why you dreamed the baby would lose her name?"

Honarha's heart started to race. "I don't know."

"Remember," Clan Mother consoled, "your baby will be Onondaga no matter what happens. That's the way it's been since time began. Look around you. These women are your family, your baby's family. These are the baby's sisters and aunts and mothers. At the edge of the forest sit her brothers and uncles and fathers," she said, pointing to where the men were gathered. "These are the people who love you. Your baby is Onondaga. She always will be."

Honarha looked at the sky. The Star Path blazed above her, and she could feel the truth in Clan Mother's words. She was surrounded by her people. Above, her ancestors were looking down, caring about her, and caring about the baby. Clan Mother was right. It *had* always been this way. She took Clan Mother's hand and placed it on her belly. The kicking started up again.

"See. She never stops. I know she's Onondaga. I know she always will be. But this child is different. Can't you feel it? We need to help her. I know she'll be forever tied to our Onondaga Turtle Clan, but the truth is, she'll be more like her father than me. She'll look Lenapé and act like her father. Achimwis—the dreamer, the storyteller, the traveler, the interpreter, the emissary. All the things that I love about him, she will possess too. And like Achimwis, she'll be a stranger among her own people. What will that mean for a little girl?"

Keguenha began to answer but Clan Mother held up her hand.

"She'll need something more," Honarha continued, scratching the ground with the toe of her moccasin. "She'll need another name."

"What do you mean, another name?" asked Clan Mother.

"At her naming ceremony during the Green Corn Moon, she'll receive her Onondaga name with all the other babies?"

"That's right."

She turned to Clan Mother. "I'm asking you to give her another name, too. Promise me that you'll also give this baby a Lenapé name."

"Why would I do that?"

"Because she'll need it. She told me so. She said she'll need her Lenapé name."

"The baby told you her Lenapé name?"

"Yes, in the dream. She told me her name is Nushèmakw."

And as soon as Honarha said it, the baby fell asleep.

1518 CE

FISHING MOON

"It can't be my time. Not now. Not so soon."

Nushèmakw held onto all that was her mother. The warm comfort of her womb. The sound of her heart. Her mother's blood, her blood. Life pulsing through them both. She was safe here.

But now the wind began to blow. Blow and blow. A steady gust sweeping around her, lifting and pulling with its strange darkness. It tugged at her arms and yanked on her legs. Now it turned her upside down and thrust its weight upon her.

"I won't go," she said.

It began to hurt. The wind whipping, the womb bearing down, pinching and pressing. Now the wind began to spin and whirl above her, gaining speed, cutting at her ankles and pushing her down into her mother's birth canal.

Then she heard her mother's heart stop beating.

"Take me with you, Mother," she pleaded. "Take me with you to the Star Path of our ancestors. I want no part of this world!"

Her mother was silent as her spirit slipped away.

Then Nushèmakw saw it. A light. A column of light before her. A steady glow: red, then yellow, now white. "Take me," the light said to her. "Take me with you into the world."

Nushèmakw held the light in her little fist and pressed it against her heart. "Now I will go."

1530 CE

FRESH MOON

It was chilly when Nushèmakw entered the forest, but as the morning wore on, the air warmed and her hike along the deer path was pleasant. Her basket was filled with the beechnuts and acorns she had collected along the way, and she sat to rest on a warm rock bathed in autumn light.

She traveled the route on the ridge along the east side of their village. From there, she could see the longhouse with its two ribbons of smoke rising from the roof holes. Some of the women were busy grinding corn, while others rendered grease in a cook pot over the fire. The men had just returned from a long and productive hunting expedition, and they sat in small groups to rest and exchange stories.

The other side of the ridge was engulfed in endless forest, a spectacular canopy of color stretching out before her, the orange glow of the sugar maple against the darker red of oak and deep green of pine. The yellow leaves of beech were shining throughout, their translucent leaves catching the breeze, tossing and turning like a million tiny flames.

A noise blasted through the deep woods and Nushèmakw jumped. It came again, an echo more than a noise. She shook her head thinking she had imagined it. It came again. A screech and then a roar. The hairs on her neck stood on end.

She was used to the strangeness of the forest, especially when she was alone. The wind through the trees spoke to her in hushed tones. The crows watched her with their pokeberry eyes. Even the bobcat who appeared on the top of the cliffs never frightened her. But she was afraid of this. This terrible sound.

She dropped her basket and the nuts went everywhere. She pressed her hands over her ears and closed her eyes to block it out, the way she always did when she was afraid. She was paralyzed. Then deep within she found that companion of light who had been with her from the beginning—that trusted and unwavering presence.

"Help me," she said, and there it was. She opened her eyes and breathed again. The cool and cleansing air filled her lungs and her fear fell away. "We go together," she reminded herself.

For all of her twelve years, the light and Nushèmakw were inseparable. She had only to still herself to see it, to remember that the light was the one reason she was alive – it was life, wasn't it?

Go now and take care of this, it said to her.

So she entered the forest, picking her way through the underbrush as quietly as she could. Halfway down the rocky slope, she squatted on an outcropping and peered into a ravine that stretched out below. Beyond it was a clearing where the flickering sun played on her eyes and made it hard to see.

Again, she heard the unearthly roar. It was the sound of pain and rage and sorrow, and it kept coming.

She heard a boy. That voice. Was he singing or was he laughing? She moved in closer and caught a glimpse through the maze of trees. It was Guiarasi, Clan Mother's grandnephew! He was one of several boys in line to be the next chief. What was he doing? It filled her with dread.

She slipped further down the hillside until she could see everything. Guiarasi was singing and dancing around a black bear he had tethered to a tree. A sow, not very old, but strong. He circled the tree and chanted. Every time he passed the bear he barbed her with his knife until she screamed and roared.

This can't be happening, she thought. But it was happening. The sow roared again. Nushèmakw felt something die inside. A precious seed, a germ of life, her hope that the world would be better than this.

Her attention flew to the murmurs and mews that came from the other side of the clearing. Three little cubs were huddled in a netted snare. They were watching it all.

A bolt of rage exploded inside Nushèmakw, and she flew down the bluff and across the clearing. The sow raised her head, and their eyes met. Nushèmakw saw the look of both courage and despair. Round and round went Guiarasi, consumed by his chanting, oblivious to her approach. She had seen the ritual dances of her uncles. This was nothing like them. This was a frightening thing that gained momentum with each pass round the tree. It grew and grew, gaining a life of its own. The force hovered over her cousin, and would soon consume them all. It was blue and cold and deadly, like the crackling light of thunderheads.

Take care of this.

Nushèmakw picked up a stone and waited for her cousin to pass behind the tree and cross to the other side. When he lifted his knife, she hurled the stone as hard as she could. It hit Guiarasi squarely on the temple and he fell to the ground.

Her eyes widened. "I've killed him!"

A thin bead of blood trickled from the wound in his head. She ran over and placed her hand under his nose. He was breathing. Two fingers on his neck showed her that his heart was beating strong.

She grabbed his knife and began cutting at the netting that held the terrorized cubs. "Come, little ones," she whispered. "I won't hurt you. No one will hurt you now." They refused to move and pressed harder against each other, whimpering and shivering. So she began to sing to them the way Aunt Sarhak did when she was a baby. Soon they stopped trembling. She held out her hand. They crawled up to her and sniffed, curious about this new stranger.

Nushèmakw turned to the mother bear, knowing full well what a bear could do to anyone who stood between her and her cubs. When she saw the wounds through the sow's black coat, she no longer cared what might happen to her or her cousin.

"You're beautiful," Nushèmakw whispered, moving closer still. "I want to set you free. Will you let me?" The bear eyed her. "I mean no harm, but we must hurry. My cousin will wake up soon. Look. I've released your cubs. Let me cut you loose, too." She reached for the bear's shackled forepaw and cut away the strap. She could feel the sow staring down at her, but the bear made no move to hurt her. One by one, Nushèmakw cut the lashes until the bear was free.

Nushèmakw stepped back and the bear stood up. On hind legs, she was an overpowering sight, taller than Nushèmakw, taller than her cousin. The cubs came running and climbed all over their mother, licking her fur and clinging to her limbs. She took another long look at Nushèmakw and then at Guiarasi lying on the ground. She showed her teeth and growled long and low. A warning. Without another sound, she swept up her cubs and disappeared into the forest.

Nushèmakw turned to Guiarasi, his body prone and motionless. She would return the knife where she found it. He would never know she was there. Soundless step after soundless step, she crept toward him. Ever so slowly she lowered the knife.

Guiarasi's eyes flew open and he grabbed her.

"You think I don't know what you're doing?" he hissed, squeezing her arm until she thought it would break.

"You tell me," she shouted defiantly, but still her legs trembled. "What am I doing, cousin?"

"You're trying to destroy me."

"I am not!" she said. "Let me go."

"What have you seen?"

"Let go of me and maybe I'll tell you."

Guiarasi let go and before she had time to think, she flung the knife across the clearing and into the brush.

Guiarasi watched it fly. "You think I'd kill you? My own cousin? A girl?" The blood on his face etched a dark line along his jaw. "Maybe I should. I'd be within my rights to kill anyone interrupting a hunt." He looked around, and she could feel the anger building in him. "You've let them go. All of them. Why?"

"You know why. This was no hunt. All you wanted to do is hurt and torture them. You could've killed them quickly, and they wouldn't have suffered, but you chose to do this instead. Our uncles would never act this way. You're not a hunter. You're a monster!"

She'd gone too far. What scared her now was his silence. Finally he spoke, but with a smile that unnerved her. "You say I'm a monster. I say you're delirious. You're seeing things again, cousin. Like you always do. Things that aren't there. I'm not a monster, and I'm not cruel. You know nothing about hunting or about a warrior's rituals, and you shouldn't pretend to."

"I know enough. I'll tell Clan Mother what I've seen. Turtle Chief, too. Let's hear what they have to say about this. About you!"

Guiarasi's smile disappeared. "Go ahead and tell them. I've already proven myself to them. They know I'm a capable hunter and that I'll soon be a warrior to reckon with."

That strange light appeared over him again and was gaining strength as he spoke. "They see me for what I am. A boy who is a real Onondaga with an Onondaga name. A boy soon to be a man worthy and able to take over as Turtle Chief when my time comes."

Nushèmakw backed away.

"Go ahead. Run. Run and tell them what you saw."

She did run, but before she reached the edge of the woods, he called out to her. "They know who you really are, Nushèmakw," he said, spitting out her name. "They know you're not a real Onondaga girl, but just a girl afraid of her own shadow. A girl who dreams dreams no one believes."

Nushèmakw ran as fast as she could across the ravine, up the bank, and over the ridge. She had to make it home before her cousin did. Surely they would believe her. Clan Mother knew she wouldn't lie. She reached the village out of breath, her lungs about to burst.

"Oh no!" She looked across the village yard. Guiarasi had beaten her there and was already talking to Clan Mother. She raced toward them and Clan Mother held up her hand.

"Quiet, Nushèmakw. Come with me."

Nushèmakw cringed. She passed her smirking cousin and followed Clan Mother to the longhouse where a large pot of cold water sat next to the cooking stone. *Good,* thought Nushèmakw, *maybe now I can tell my side of the story.*

Clan Mother dipped her hand into the pot and splashed water all over Nushèmakw's face.

She stood there with her face dripping wet. How could Clan Mother embarrass her this way? She had never felt so humiliated.

"But Grandmother," her voice was shaking, and she tried her hardest not to cry. Guiarasi was taunting her behind Clan Mother's back. She would not give him the satisfaction of seeing tears. "What have I done wrong?"

"Your cousin was hunting. Not just any hunt. He was practicing for his coming of age passage. You knew this."

Nushèmakw's eyes widened. All the boys who had turned thirteen since the Midwinter Moon were training. Yet in that terrible moment, that spectacle of cruelty, she'd forgotten.

"How could you interrupt the hunt? Your cousin must master his skills if he's to become a man and a warrior. Have you no concern for our traditions and the honor of your cousin?"

She stood looking at the ground, unable to answer.

"Your cousin says you released his catch—a sow and her three cubs. Is this true?"

"Yes, Grandmother, it's true."

"Do you understand that this is not just about you or about your cousin. It's about the Clan. Those bearskins would have kept your brothers and sisters warm this winter. Now they will go without cloaks unless our men are able to trap more. What in the world were you thinking?"

The silence hung miserably around her while Clan Mother waited for an answer. Guiarasi stepped between them. "She should be punished! She has dishonored me," he said shaking his finger at her. "The Chief will have something to say about this sacrilege. It's unforgivable!"

Nushèmakw couldn't believe this was happening.

Speak. You must speak.

She gathered her courage and looked the boy in the eye. "What is unforgivable, my cousin, is to torture a mother bear while her helpless cubs watch."

Clan Mother turned to Guiarasi, and he looked away.

"You may go, my daughter. We'll talk more about this later."

※

1530 CE

HARVEST MOON

"Grandfather has sent me," the young scout said to Clan Mother. "He's ready to leave."

Clan Mother nodded. Word came to Turtle Chief only days ago that the Onondaga Firekeeper, Tadodaho, had called a meeting of the Grand Council of Five Nations to take place at the new moon. If they were to make it in time, they must get moving. Nushèmakw carefully packed the last of the acorn biscuits between layers of pigweed to keep them from crumbling. Her uncles handed Clan Mother their stashes of tobacco, and she and Nushèmakw placed them in a large basket that held the sacred objects they would need for the Condolence Ceremony.

It was a short half-day trek westward to the greater Onondaga village, but it could take longer depending on how swollen the creek was. Getting their provisions as well as the elders over the water always took time, especially if the weather turned cold.

"Grandfather is waiting," the scout repeated.

"Yes," said Clan Mother, aware that she should not keep Turtle Chief waiting. "You may go now and tell him I'm coming."

"Sarhak!" she called. "Nushèmakw will be going with us." She nudged Nushèmakw toward her aunt.

With a respectful nod toward Clan Mother, Sarhak took Nushèmakw's hand. "We've got to hurry," said her aunt, the woman who had raised Nushèmakw since the day she was born—the day her mother died. They left quickly to prepare for the trip.

The scouts moved out first. They would cross the creek at the headwater south of the falls and press west through the forest. They would wait there for the rest of the Clan to catch up with them. The warriors left next, spreading out deep into the woods to guard the tribe from ambush. Turtle Chief took his place at the head of the Clan, and the elder fathers followed. Clan Mother and the other senior women lined up behind them. Sarhak, Nushèmakw, and the other young women brought up the rear. Those who didn't carry babies fastened to cradleboards had strapped large packs of supplies on their backs.

"How many Grand Councils have you been to?" Nushèmakw asked her aunt.

"A few. Most years I've stayed home to look after the children and help gather what's left of the harvest. There's always maize and squash left to pick and dry this time of year. You've seen all the crows and squirrels, Nushèmakw? They're just waiting for us to leave so they can eat up everything," Sarhak teased.

Nushèmakw. Her name sounded beautiful when her aunt said it. "How'd you learn to pronounce my name? Grandmother has a terrible time with it. Sounds like she's got pebbles in her mouth when she says it."

Her aunt laughed. "That's because I heard it from the source. Your father taught it to me."

A chevron of geese passed above them, honking their signals to each other as they headed southward. The maples had already lost their leaves, and warm sunlight flooded the path.

"I've told you many times about the dream your mother had before you were born. What I haven't told you is how stubborn your mother was. Because she had heard your name in the dream, she pestered your father to death to get him to pronounce it—to make sure she had heard it right. But he didn't want to. Like Grandmother, he thought you should be called Hehron, your Onondaga name. He reminded her time and again that to speak your sacred Unami name would be bad luck. But your mother wasn't convinced. So every day, she'd ask again. Finally he gave in." Sarhak lowered her voice. "'Okay, okay, Honarha. You win. You're driving me crazy.'"

Nushèmakw giggled at her aunt's silly imitation.

"'It's pronounced nushèmakw!'" Sarhak continued, exaggerating each syllable. "'Nu-SHEM-awk! Are you happy now? Finally I can have some peace!'"

They both laughed.

"I couldn't believe it" Sarhak said. "I'd never, ever heard Achimwis raise his voice. Not once. A storyteller like your father is trained early on to hold his temper, to always express himself with dignity. But he was mad that day, and it's something you don't forget. That's why I know exactly how to say your name," Sarhak said adjusting the tumpline strap across her forehead. "And I'll tell you something else. Everyone's always saying how much you're like your father. But you're more than that. You're stubborn, and that's your mother through and through." She laughed again and put her arm around Nushèmakw.

"After your mother died, that's when Grandmother agreed to let you be called Nushèmakw. 'To honor her mother's vision,' she said, 'she can use it as her nickname.'"

They came to a place where the deer path opened to a sprawling meadow, a comfortable spot to rest. Already the elders were seated under the shade of the tall pines and scarlet oaks. Up ahead where the creek narrowed, the scouts were lashing logs together, building a raft that they would use to ferry the tribe across the water. Below them, a huge beaver dam spanned the width of the creek. Beyond it, the water raced ferociously stirring up whitecaps before it plunged over the falls. On this side of the dam, the water had formed a calm pool perfect for the crossing. Nushèmakw relaxed against the trunk of a tree, glad to be relieved of her pack. Sarhak handed her a biscuit. She crunched into it, and the nuts and sour berries tasted good.

Sarhak helped herself to one too. "I know it's been hard for you, Nushèmakw," she said. "To lose your mother like that isn't easy. I'm sorry that she died when you were born. I wish you had a chance to know her. It happened so suddenly, her leaving us like that."

Nushèmakw watched the water wash over the stones, catching sparks as it tumbled over the falls. "I used to think it was my fault.

That I killed her by being born. Sometimes I still do."

"Oh, Nushèmakw," her aunt said, hugging her. "You shouldn't think that way. How can a baby be responsible for something like that? It's the Great Spirit who ushers us into this world and takes us out. Why your mother was taken so soon is not for us to know. But she's gone, and we all still miss her." Sarhak blinked away tears. "I'm glad you're old enough now to hear all of this, Nushèmakw. It helps me to talk about it."

"I'm glad I'm finally old enough, too."

"I don't know if I'll ever stop missing her. Her death was hard on all of us, and especially hard on you. But I think it was hardest of all on your father. He just couldn't bear the fact that his beloved Honarha was gone, that she'd been taken from him so fast and so soon. It was a crushing grief. It wasn't long after she died that he told us he was leaving too. That he needed to go back home to his Lenapé Unami family among the Kechemeches. We all tried to convince him to stay, but he wouldn't. He just couldn't stay, he said, because we all reminded him too much of her. We miss them both so much. Your mother and your father." She didn't hide the tears. "But we have you, and that makes us happy. No matter what happens, Nushèmakw, you'll always be your mother's daughter. You belong to us. You'll always be Onondaga."

"I wish everyone thought so," Nushèmakw said, tossing a rock in the water.

The scouts were already shuttling the elders across the creek. Nushèmakw and her aunt grabbed their packs and joined them.

They arrived at the greater Onondaga village before dark. They labored up the long incline to the entrance of the Great Council campgrounds. Nushèmakw marveled at the tall palisades that encircled the village, a double row of impenetrable log fencing barricading the entire hillside from unwanted company.

They crossed the wide yard that led to the longhouses.

"Who's Grandfather talking to?" asked Nushèmakw, pointing to Turtle Chief.

"That's the Tadodaho, the Bear Clan Chief who's assigned to be the Keeper of the Council Fire."

Nushèmakw stared. She already knew that the Tadodaho was the one responsible for calling the meetings of the Haudenosaunee Five Nations. She'd heard about him all her life. But seeing him in person was another thing altogether. He was a striking man, older than their Turtle Chief, but just as strong. And like her grandfather, the Tadodaho wore the formal headdress that bore the elk antlers signifying their station.

Nushèmakw slowed as she passed them, then she hid in the shadows so she could hear them.

The delegations from the other nations hadn't arrived, but they'd come tomorrow, Tadodaho was saying. "Where are your cousins, Dehayatgwareh?" Tadodaho asked, addressing Turtle Chief by his formal name.

"Our Beaver cousins were right behind us, and our Hawk and Eel siblings were not far behind them," Turtle Chief answered.

Tadodaho nodded. "Good. Soon all fourteen Onondaga chiefs will be ready to assemble. The Council Meeting agenda is a long one. There's talk of war in the south if the Susquahannock continue to raid our villages. Just yesterday, a Mohawk scout brought news of the appearance of white men deep in the snow country to the northeast." Tadodaho rubbed his jaw. "The alliance of Five Nations holds fast at the moment, but for how long, I can't say. The prophecies have increased. They speak of the Haudenosaunee's weakening position against the growing military power of the Susquahannock. I've been told that they're strengthening their numbers by raiding the Lenapé bands scattered along the south river. Then they intend to press further into our territory. If that's true, we haven't much time to counter their encroachment."

Sarhak pulled at Nushèmakw's sleeve. "Stop your eavesdropping, child. Come with me," she said, dragging Nushèmakw behind her. "The Clan matrons are waiting for us. There's plenty for us to do."

At dusk, Tadodaho lit the ceremonial fire. It was time for the entire Onondaga nation to gather together—the only chance they'd have before the other four nations arrived. All eight clans that comprised the Onondaga were present: the Bear Clan and Deer Clan; Beaver, Wolf, and Snipe; Eel and Hawk; and Nushèmakw's Turtle

Clan. An elder stood to give the blessing of the meal, a call-and-response prayer familiar to Nushèmakw. They ate heartily, and still the women kept passing around stew and pone and fried berry cakes. They had only until morning before the other nations arrived. In the comfort of the fire and the company of their own people, the stories began to flow.

The Chief from the Eel Clan told legends about ancient times, when the Haudenosaunee and Susquahannock were one people. "We are distant cousins," he told the children. "Long, long ago, when the frozen north country began to warm and the snow was melting, we traveled with the Susquahannock from our old home far to the south to our new Haudenosaunee home. When we arrived here at our Longhouse territory, our cousins left us and moved south again, and they have been separated from us for the countless years since. Our cousins have not been friendly. They've invaded our lands again and again for no good reason, and we've fought back. They've been our enemies for a long time."

"They've been nothing but trouble," Turtle Chief said, loud enough for everyone to hear. "There's a reason why the Great Peacemaker never chose them to be among us in the confederacy. They love nothing but war."

"Then the rumors are true?" Wolf Chief asked, turning to Tadodaho. "Are the Susquahannock's preparing for war?"

"We shall see," answered Tadodaho.

Sarhak combed Nushèmakw's hair, fastening it into a neat bun at the nape of her neck with a strap of soft deerskin adorned with colorful beads. They would look their best for the Thanksgiving Ceremony taking place later that morning at the edge of the forest. They'd slept comfortably in the large longhouse built close beside two others. The sun poured in through the eastern door, rich and golden. Like home, their platform bed was close to one of the fires burning in the center of the wide aisle that spanned the length of the house. Similar compartments ran along both sides, an amazing twenty in all. Each was covered with soft fur blankets that kept out whatever cold the fires could not.

The house was smoky but pleasant, and Nushèmakw watched

the families rise from a night's sleep to ready themselves for the special day ahead. One of the young aunts walked up to them. "Are you excited for the Thanksgiving Ceremony?"

Nushèmakw nodded energetically.

"And what's your name?"

"My name's Nushèmakw."

The woman tilted her head toward Sarhak.

"That's right," her aunt laughed. "It's an unusual nickname but Grandmother has allowed her to use it. Her real name is Hehron."

The woman smiled at Nushèmakw and turned to her aunt. "Sister, we have a little time before the ceremony begins. I see that you've brought your medicine bundle. Would you mind showing me your herbs and preparations? I'm a healer too."

"I'd love to," answered Sarhak. While the two women chatted away, spreading their dried stores across the bed, Nushèmakw slipped quietly out the western door.

A crowd was gathering around a large roaring fire pit. An entire deer carcass was strung above the flame sizzling as it roasted. Large vessels of cold water sat outside the pit, and men dipped their cups to quench their thirst.

Nushèmakw saw her cousin Guiarasi come around the corner of the longhouse, and she ducked behind the bushes before he spotted her. He was carrying a fur shawl over his arm and heading straight for Clan Mother, who was seated under the broad branch of an elm tree. "I noticed that you were cold, Grandmother, so I brought your shawl," he said, draping the fur over Clan Mother's shoulders. "Are you thirsty, Grandmother? I can bring you water."

What a fake, Nushèmakw thought, and she hoped Clan Mother could see through his charade. She'd heard his double talk before. Like the time he said just loud enough for Turtle Chief to hear: "We are so grateful to have a chief like Grandfather. He's so wise and powerful." Then when Turtle Chief walked away, he said to his brothers: "Grandfather is too old and frail to be chief much longer. Have you seen how his hands shake when he draws the bow. Soon Grandmother will choose his replacement, and we all know who she'll pick." He had spoken with his chest puffed out like a breeding loon.

Nushèmakw wanted nothing to do with him. She circled in the other direction to help the women serve breakfast. She passed around a plate stacked with warm flat cakes, dotted with seeds and dried berries. A woman was spooning porridge from a huge pot that boiled and bubbled at the edge of the pit. Nushèmakw watched her pour an amber stream of maple syrup into each bowl before she served it up.

All the preparations were finished by mid-morning. Now the Onondaga were ready to formally welcome the other four tribes, a confederacy that spread across their homelands forming the proverbial Longhouse of nations spoken of since ancient times.

The Cayuga and Oneida arrived first. They were called the Younger Brothers, and they flanked either side of the Onondaga settlements. Then the Older Brothers came, the Seneca who guarded the western door, and the Mohawk who guarded the eastern door. There were forty-nine chiefs in all, with the Mohawk ceding the fiftieth seat in memory of the great and legendary Ayonhwathah. All was done according to the sacred constitution of the confederacy, introduced ages ago by the Great Peacemaker.

Tadodaho called the people together. The Thanksgiving Ceremony would now begin. The Wolf Chief from the Oneida Nation was chosen to give the Thanksgiving Address. He was an impressive man, Nushèmakw thought, as she watched him step into the clearing where the autumn light fell on his ornate headdress and glinted on the intricate patterns of quill and shell beads that graced his leggings and breechcloth.

He began to speak. First he acknowledged his gratitude for the Creator who had brought them all together. "Our brothers and sisters, aunts and uncles, grandmothers and grandfathers, and especially our children, who will speak these words to their children and their children's children for seven generations."

He thanked the Creator, "and the Sky Dwellers who instruct us to be grateful for our health and happiness and to be content."

"Nyho," the people said.

He thanked the Creator for all the people moving about the earth.

"Nyho," the people said.

He thanked the Creator for the earth, the water, the sun, the wind, the moon and the stars, each time reciting the grand purpose of each gift the Creator had bestowed upon the people.

Each time, the people answered, "Nyoh."

The tribes were filled with reverence as the ceremony advanced from prayers to chants and to the stomp dance around the fire. Tadodaho closed the ceremony with a sacred song. The crowd thinned and people retreated into the longhouses of their clans.

A Bear Clan girl asked Nushèmakw if she wanted to play. They wandered off to the far side of the longhouses, where thick tall posts rose from an earthen barricade that encircled the village. Under its shadow stood a large pen made of sturdy poles and netting. Inside the cage were two white dogs, a female and a male—a breed Nushèmakw had never seen before.

Nushèmakw and the girl squeezed inside the fence and began to play with the dogs who licked at their faces relentlessly. These were beautiful sturdy dogs. Their thick, lustrous coats were nearly identical. The only difference Nushèmakw could see was that the male had a black patch on each of his four paws. Nushèmakw hugged this one before she and the girl slid back through the fence.

"You're so lucky to have dogs," Nushèmakw said. "I wish we had a dog at our village. I love them. What are their names?"

"They don't have names," the girl told her. "My mother said that we shouldn't name the white dogs because of what will happen to them. That way, we won't become too attached."

"What do you mean?"

"My mother said that after the Grand Council Meeting, just before the Smoke Ceremony, the dogs would be strangled and brought to the longhouse yard to be burned as a sacrifice for the Five Nations."

"What!" Nushèmakw was horrified. "That can't be true. I don't believe it."

"It is true. Ask your mother. She'll tell you. It's the white dogs that get sacrificed."

Nushèmakw slept wretchedly. *The girl has been right. It was* true; her aunt had confirmed it. She spent the night plagued with a stampede of frightful images. Toward morning, still haunted by the ghosts of her dreaming, she snuck out of the longhouse to clear her head. The air snapped with frost and it felt good. The village was dark and empty and she headed back across the yard to the palisades where she and the girl had gone the day before. She slowly approached the dogs, and they jumped and barked in their cage when they saw her.

"I can't let you go. I can't!" she told them. "I've caused enough trouble as it is. Let someone else save you."

They sat on their haunches and looked at her, wagging their tails. Nushèmakw's heart sank. She looked around to see if she was alone.

The annual games of the Haudenosaunee were to begin that morning, and Nushèmakw made her way up the to the top of a rocky embankment to watch. She found a place where she could see the whole valley, the ancient basin hollowed long ago by the movement of ice and snow. High atop her perch on that northern ridge of bald rock, the river sparkled blue and white giving way to the fields and grasses that stretched westward to the edge of the forest.

It wasn't long before the players appeared. The Hawk Clan ran out first with their netted sticks held high, and they positioned themselves on the far side of the field. Then came the Wolf Clan, lining up opposite them. The other clans clustered at the sidelines, waiting for their opportunity to challenge whichever team emerged the victors.

The sun rose quickly, chasing away the shadows that had darkened the field. Its warmth saturated the chilly air. A cool breeze burst over the grasses and up the bluff. Soft billows rolled to the top of the ridge and blew through her, the scent oddly salty and sweet and cool in her lungs. When the sun's rays reached the river that snaked through the forest, the water ignited, a mirror of the sky.

Below her, the light had changed. Even though the sun was bright, the field looked dark, like a veil had fallen behind it. A strange mist was rolling in from the river, but the men didn't seem to notice. She shook her head to keep the dream from coming upon her. The mist thickened, and the players began to wade through it to take their places, each a hundred strides from the next across the field's wide perimeter. They held their netted sticks and waited. The scene became both distant and magnified, the colors pronounced. The only sound was that of the wind over Nushèmakw's ears.

The first man began to run, the ball cradled carefully in the stick. With one smooth and powerful swing, the ball sailed upward, rising endlessly in its slow arc. She could see it clearly now in the sharp light of the sky. *Oh!* she thought, *It's not a ball after all.* It was a turtle shell, and it soared through the warm breeze. With great skill and infinite care, the next man caught the shell in his stick and pitched it down the field. Round and round the turtle shell flew, slow and steady, etching a circle that bound the teams together. Suddenly the players froze where they stood. Nushèmakw rubbed her eyes trying to stop the dream.

The mist grew thicker and the colors brighter and the sun played on her eyes making ghosts of the men. Their stiff empty forms faced east, and she turned to see what they were looking at.

The river, shining through the trees, began to swell. The wind blew in from the east, kicking up whitecaps that crashed and tumbled. The river rose, leaping over its banks and flooding the forest. Water rushed everywhere, pushing through the woods and into the field.

"Run!" she yelled. The men didn't move. She shouted again, but her voice was lost to the roaring tide. It had become an enormous body of water, larger than anything she had ever seen. She looked across the expanse. The smell of salt was strong in her nose and throat. The water rose and the men stood in it waist deep. Something began to move in the water, and the men came alive. She could almost see it—something huge and terrifying. The men pushed against the tide to the edge of the forest and positioned themselves for battle. The man in front swung his stick, and the turtle shell, glowing as if on fire, sailed into the air and over the trees. A dark and monstrous mass rose up from the forest, engulfed the turtle shell in its gaping maw, and retreated back into the water.

A crow cawed from a branch above her, and Nushèmakw woke up. She shook the dream from her eyes and looked around. She was still on the cliff with the taste of salt in her mouth. The field was cold and empty. The air was still. She jumped up, brushed off her skirt, and ran down the bluff toward the village.

Plumes from a large fire licked the air near the edge of the forest not far from the village's huge and ancient sacred pine. It was midday, and the Condolence Ceremony was about to begin. The men were seated around the fire and the women were behind them. The Mohawks, Onondagas, and Senecas were on one side; the Oneidas and Cayugas on the other. It was the Mohawk nation who had lost their chief since the last Council meeting, and a new chief would be raised up during the ceremony. Everything took on an air of deep solemnity when Tadodaho stood to give the eulogy for the deceased.

Sudden shouts tore through the quiet of the gathering. Heads turned toward the skirmish at the edge of the woods.

"Let go of me!" cried Nushèmakw. Guiarasi was dragging her by the arm. The women gasped. "Let me go!" she shouted again.

Turtle Chief jumped from his seat. "Silence, both of you!" he demanded. "The ceremony has begun. You disgrace us with this outburst."

"The white dogs are gone, Grandfather!" Guiarasi said.

"What?"

"She let them go," her cousin snarled. "Again she shames us. Again she shows that she's not one of us. She never will be. Look how she behaves," he said pointing an accusing finger at her. "Without the dogs to sacrifice, what will happen to us, Grandfather? She's a danger to us all!"

Nushèmakw flushed with anger and shame. Unable to speak, she looked at the ground.

Turtle Chief whispered to Tadodaho who nodded his consent. The Council would wait until the matter was settled. Turtle Chief walked over to Nushèmakw and lifted her chin. "What have you done, little one?" he asked. "Did you release the dogs?"

She looked away and began to cry, "Yes, Grandfather. I let them go. I had to. It was important for me to save them."

"But why?"

Before she could answer a man stepped out from of the shadows. The young warriors leaped up, grabbing their blades. Nushèmakw turned to Turtle Chief who looked like he'd seen a ghost.

"Can it be true?" said Turtle Chief, stepping closer. "Is it really you?"

The man nodded. He approached the Chief and bowed his head in respect. Turtle Chief dropped his knife and embraced him.

Clan Mother came running from the other side of the fire and nearly knocked down the much taller man. Her eyes welled with tears, and her words caught in her throat. "I can't believe it. How we've missed you!"

Nushèmakw tried to move closer, but Guiarasi only clutched her more tightly.

The man turned to Guiarasi. "Release her," he said quietly.

"Why should I obey a stranger? Especially one who barges in on our Condolence Ceremony?" He spat on the ground.

"Hold your tongue," Turtle Chief warned him. "He asked you to let her go. So let her go."

Guiarasi reluctantly obeyed.

"Do you know who this is, Nushèmakw?" Clan Mother asked.

She shook her head. "No, Grandmother, I'm sorry. I've never seen him before."

Clan Mother bent down and gently rested her hands on Nushèmakw's shoulders. "Little one, he's your father."

Murmurs rose from the crowd, and a scout whistled. The younger people were only babes when Achimwis, the Unami Story-teller, left Onondaga, and rumors of him abounded, but they thought he was a legend, not a real man. The older chiefs began to move forward to greet their old friend.

"But Grandfather, what about the dogs?" Guiarasi dared to ask, sending Nushèmakw a scathing look.

Achimwis answered instead.

"I must ask the great Council Chiefs to forgive my daughter for her unruly behavior and to pardon me for disrupting this most solemn event." He bowed to show respect. "As the elders know, before the days of my long absence, when I lived among you, I did my best to help my adopted Onondaga brothers and sisters in any way I could. And whenever possible, I offered my services to the other esteemed Haudenosaunee nations present here today." He spoke in perfect Mohawk, the traditional language of the Grand Council.

"Now I'm meeting my daughter for the first time. I look at her and see her mother." He paused to collect himself, and Nushèmakw squirmed nervously where she stood. "But you can see as well as I," he continued, "that she's Lenapé, too. And if she's anything like I am, then she has succumbed to my people's belief in the Great Spirit's purpose for dogs."

Nushèmakw's eyes widened.

"You see," Achimwis went on. "The Unami hold dear the legend of the dog and its sacred mission to be a friend to man. We believe that upon our death, it is our dogs who guide us to the gates of the Star Path, and so it's in our blood to protect them as they protect us. I believe that's why my daughter freed the dogs. Even though she is largely ignorant of our ways, still Lenapé Unami courses through her."

He turned to Tadodaho. "I fully understand the seriousness of her error, and I ask that you forgive her. Her fate is in your hands." A chill ran up Nushèmakw's spine. "And while I cannot replace the dogs, I have brought something else as restitution." He unfastened a bag that hung at his side. "I have a gift that I hope you will find acceptable. I understand that in recent times marauding thieves have plundered your village, stealing your treasures. Have they been recovered?" The oldest of the chiefs shook his head. "That's troubling news, my brothers. But don't lose heart." He reached into the bag and drew from it the most beautiful and ornate fifteen-strand wampum belt Nushèmakw had ever seen.

"News of the theft of the sacred wampum belt has traveled to my Unami people—the Kechemeches. To honor our brothers, we offer the Five Nations of the Haudenosaunee Longhouse this new belt made in the Onondaga design of the Peacemaker, crafted from the whelk and quahog shells so rare in your land. It is our hope that this belt, while only a replica, will be acceptable to carry out the Requickening Address in the traditional way. I ask you to accept the belt and forgive my daughter and myself of our transgressions."

By now all of the clans had gathered in a tight knot around them. Nushèmakw could hear nothing but the crackling fire as they held their collective breath.

Achimwis held out the belt, and its purple and white beads glinted in the sun. "My dear Tadodaho, my brother, my friend. Please accept my gift—a gift from my People Down the River."

Tadodaho turned to the other chiefs, "Is there anyone among us who would accuse our brother Achimwis or his daughter of malicious or irreparable harm? Speak now, and I will not accept our brother's gift."

Sweat broke out on Nushèmakw's brow, and she scanned the crowd. She'd never heard such a grave silence. Even Guiarasi was reduced to awe.

"Very well then," Tadodaho said holding out his hand. "On behalf of the Haudenosaunee, I, Tadodaho, accept your gift."

The crowd cheered, and the clan mothers raced forward.

"And now," said Tadodaho, holding up the wampum belt, "let us begin the Condolence Ceremony, as prescribed by the Great Law of the League."

The ceremony proceeded without further disruption. Various chiefs gave the eulogy and presented the Laws of the Confederacy. Tadodaho held the wampum belt and recited the fifteen matters of the Requickening Address—one for each strand of beads—to dispel the grief of all who were bereaved. Finally, they chanted the condoling song signaling the end of the ceremony.

The crowd dispersed, and Nushèmakw went searching for her aunt. She found her talking with her father. Seeing him confused her. For so long, no one knew if he was alive or dead, so she had resigned herself to the fact that she'd never meet him. Now that he was standing right in front of her, rather than feel excited, she felt awkward and shy. What did she really know about this stranger who looked like her? Her father saw her staring and smiled.

Tadodaho walk up and tapped her father on the shoulder.

"You must stay for the Grand Council Meeting, my brother," said Tadodaho. "I'm sure you saw for yourself how short we are on interpreters. Not everyone here is fluent in Mohawk and it is crucial that we all understand each other. These are difficult times, and so the proceedings will be especially arduous. I'm thankful that the Great Spirit has allowed your return, Achimwis. There's so much at stake. You come upon us in a dark season."

"I'm honored that you would ask me to stay," her father said. "I'll do whatever I can to help."

Tadodaho smiled. "I know life has been hard for you, Achimwis, and hardship can change a man. I'm glad to see that your generous spirit is one thing that hasn't changed." He turned and disappeared into the thinning crowd.

Clouds moved in and it looked like rain, but the weather held long enough for the women to prepare the meal. It took three large fires and all the cooking stones and pots they could find, but by nightfall, they were close to serving up the feast.

"We need to thin the stew," Sarhak told Nushèmakw. "Go and fetch some water."

Nushèmakw grabbed the water pot and headed down to the creek. Halfway there she heard a noise, and she snuck through the forest to see what it was. It was a dark night, without moon or stars, and although she couldn't see, she recognized their voices.

Turtle Chief and her father were deep in conversation.

"You'd been gone so long," she heard the Chief saying.

"I know," her father admitted. "After Honarha died, I managed to make my way back to my village. I am still a shattered man, but my people helped me find room in my heart for the grief. I'm glad I came back, Uncle. But I'm sorry for the hurt I've caused. It's been twelve years, and only now am I meeting my daughter. How will I ever repay Nushèmakw?"

Turtle Chief allowed the silence to linger.

"*Nushèmakw,*" Achimwis continued. "So you named her that after all. It suits her."

"We shall see," said the Chief, shaking his head. "We shall see."

"What is it, Uncle? Has she been a burden to you?"

After a long sigh, the Chief added, "Yes and no, Achimwis. We love her deeply. You can see that for yourself. The truth is that she's a handful for Sarhak and Clan Mother, but they adore her nonetheless. The child is bright and kind and wise beyond her years."

"But?"

"But she is also a troubled child."

Nushèmakw began to sweat. *What would her father think of her now?*

"She is a child of visions. Visions and power. And she's so young, not yet in her moontime." Nushèmakw could hear the sadness in his voice. "It's becoming dangerous for her to stay here. Some of the children, and even their mothers, are afraid of her. Not because she is bad or mean, but because she's different."

"Because she's like me," Achimwis finished.

"These are hard times, Achimwis. Peace is eroding to the south of us, where the Susquehannocks are terrorizing our villages. And your Algonquin cousins to the north are not much better. All around us, the air smells of war. Our people have become mistrustful of anything that isn't Haudenosaunee. I'm thankful that she isn't entirely Lenapé. She is her mother, too, and her aunts and uncles are comforted by this. Unfortunately, she carries her mother's most troublesome traits. The child is stubborn and headstrong, with a temper like a thunderstorm. Over time, she's made matters worse for herself."

"How so?"

"Sit down, my friend, and I'll tell you." Their voices carried through the damp and dark forest. Turtle Chief told her father about the mother bear and how Nushèmakw thwarted Guiarasi's brutality. "Her actions were justified. A true warrior is never cruel without cause. But there was no convincing Guiarasi. Now she's become the object of his loathing."

"If only I'd been there. Maybe I could have stopped it."

"No, there's nothing you could have done that we hadn't tried already. Even if we were able to prevent it, something else would have come along."

"Like the dogs."

"Yes, like the dogs. We both know that Nushèmakw meant no harm. Still, it was a bold and impulsive act. She should've known better. Now she's given Guiarasi another reason to shame her. The boy has revenge in his heart, and he'll stop at nothing until he breaks her. I'm sure of it. He may become a warrior one day, but he's a hothead, too. Such a bad combination."

She heard her father's long sigh. He struck a flint, and a spark caught the end of a dried reed he held in his hand. He lit his pipe, illuminating the face of a Lenapé forest keeper that was carved on the bowl. He passed the stick to Turtle Chief, careful to protect the tiny flame. Turtle Chief touched his bowl with it, and the scowling face of a sacred hawk came to life. The men sat in silence and smoked their pipes. In the soft glow that surrounded them, Nushèmakw could see the worry in their faces.

Her father spoke first. "What can I do to help, Uncle?"

"You must take her with you. To your own people. Honarha had been right after all. She *is* like you. She is Unami at heart. You must teach her to control her temper and to use her visions for good. She will need guidance with this. Your Kechemeches people allow such a ritual for women more than we do, and it will help her. She's twelve. Soon she'll be in her moontime. Her rite of passage needs to happen with her People Down the River not here among the Onondaga. Am I making sense, Achimwis?"

Nushèmakw nearly fell over, and she clutched the ground to keep from being heard.

"When should we leave?" her father asked.

"Tomorrow. After the Grand Council Meeting is finished but before the Thanksgiving Address. I don't trust Guiarasi, but he's a proud boy who will do nothing to fall out of favor with the chiefs. He'll be so absorbed with impressing Tadodaho that it's not likely he'll notice that you and Nushèmakw have gone. At least not until you've traveled a safe distance. Be careful, Achimwis. The boy is dangerous."

Nushèmakw felt a chill run up her spine.

After the sun had set and the sacred songs and ritual dances had been performed, the people began to reassemble. Nushèmakw sat with her aunt and all the other women. She counted the chiefs, all forty-nine of them, and admired their ornately feathered and beaded headdresses, each an insignia for their own nation, and each adorned with the sacred elk antlers denoting their status.

The Grand Council Meeting began with the Tree Ceremony. Tadodaho stepped out from under the high branches of the Sacred Pine of Peace and into the ring of firelight that fell across the camp.

"I open this meeting of the Longhouse of Nations by reciting the story of the Great Peacemaker, the one whose vision formed our confederacy." He paused and faced the children. "The story is told at every Grand Council Meeting so that you—the younger generation present today—will hear it and remember it and tell it to your children."

The Chief spoke slowly. Nushèmakw knew the story of the Great Peacemaker, a story told often around the fires at home, but this was different. Here was Tadodaho, a man respected by all, a man full of wisdom and honor.

"It was a time when war was the normal state of things," Tadodaho began. "North of Ontario Lake there was a young Huron woman who lived apart from her mother. Although still a virgin, the young woman became pregnant. Her mother dreamed that the child was destined to do great things. In due course, the child, a boy, was born."

The campfire flickered across his face illuminating his headdress of feathers and bone. A sense of awe fell upon the crowd.

"The boy grew quickly into a handsome young man. He had a gift for speaking, and he preached to the children of his clan." Tadodaho continued, reciting the legend as it had come to him, and his father before him, passed down in this way generation to generation for as long as anyone could remember. He told of the message brought by the Peacemaker, which was rejected by his own people. About how he left his country and traveled in a stone canoe to the land of the Five Nations. It was a time filled with violence and vengeance and war. The Peacemaker traveled to Mohawk territory and convinced the Mohawks of his power and the truth of his message of peace. "Our brothers the Mohawks, therefore," recited Tadodaho, "were the first of the nations to join the League. When the Peacemaker passed through Onondaga territory," the Chief continued, "he met Ayonhwathah who was soon converted to his way of peace."

The children began to squirm impatiently. They knew their favorite part of the story was coming. The Chief smiled at them as he spoke about the mission that the Peacemaker gave to Ayonhwathah— to convert the evil Onondaga Tadodaho to the ways of peace.

"Ayonhwathah was to do this," the Chief said, grabbing a fistful of his hair, "by combing out the snakes that were in evil Tadodaho's hair!"

The children squealed and their mothers shushed them. Chief went on with the story. He recounted how the evil Tadodaho of old shunned Ayonhwathah and killed all three of Ayonhwathah's daughters. Ayonhwathah fled the village and wandered about stricken with grief. Along the way, he came upon a lakebed covered in shell beads, and he made three strings with them as symbols of his grief. Then he came upon the Peacemaker, who took the strings of beads and added his own.

"Laying the strings out one at a time," said the Chief, "the Peacemaker uttered the words of the Requickening Address for the first time. With fifteen strings, the Peacemaker recited the fifteen matters that wiped away Ayonhwathah's grief. Then together they sang the Song of Peace, the Hai Hai." Tadodaho crossed the yard so those on the other side could hear. "In time, the Peacemaker and Ayonhwathah convinced all the tribes to take up the message of peace. That's when the Mohawk, Oneida, Cayuga, Onondaga, and Seneca became the League of Nations.

"But there was still one man who would not join. Do you know who he was?" the Chief asked the children.

"The evil Tadodaho of old!" they yelled in unison.

"Yes! Now with the power of the Five Nations behind them, the Peacemaker and Ayonhwathah returned to the evil Tadodaho, and with great difficulty, they made his mind straight, and Ayonhwathah combed the snakes from his hair. Thus the Peacemaker made Tadodaho first among equals in the role of Haudenosaunee Chief. The Peacemaker placed elk antlers on the Tadodaho's head, as well as on the heads of all the other chiefs as a sign of authority. Then he taught them the words of the Great Law."

Tadodaho's recitation came to a close, and he took his seat before the fire.

A reverent pause was allowed between speakers before a Mohawk Chief came forward to present the first issue on the Council's agenda. "With respect for all of my brothers who are gathered here, I ask this," he said with a voice that carried through the night. "How should the League respond to news of the appearance of the white men?" There had been reports from the Algonquin to the east along the Great Salt Lake of men with pale skin coming ashore on their giant canoes bringing exceptional knives and beads, and also other gifts that they had little use for. Now the Algonquin were saying that the white men were coming more frequently, continually asking for furs and making other demands. "These white men have not yet traveled to the sacred lands of Haudenosaunee Longhouse territory," the Mohawk Chief concluded, "but it will only be a matter of time before they do. And when that day comes, my brothers, how will the Five Nations respond?" The Chief sat down.

Now it was time for the Seneca Chief to speak. Rebuttals came from the Cayuga and Oneida, each chief debating the issues until a decision was presented to the Onondaga Firekeepers who had power to veto the decision. The night wore on in this way, with the proceedings droning endlessly in Nushèmakw's ears. Finally she fell asleep.

She dreamed she was on the cliff again watching the men throw the turtle shell down the field with their netted sticks. Again it lit up like the sun. From across the field, where the dark salt lake spread out as far as the eye could see, the water began to roil and race. One by one, the men began to fall. The two left standing held the turtle shell high in the air, where the sun's rays gathered on its thirteen plates. Suddenly, something broke the water's surface. It was a monster snake with rainbows of fiery light flashing off its scales. It raised its broad neck and horned head, searching for the men. It found them. Ready to strike, its flashing green eyes turned to red. The men shouted and tossed the turtle shell high in the sky. Up and up it went gaining brilliance that filled the sky. It was Father Sun, who cast his mighty rays upon the beast. The monster snake thrashed and screeched and shook the earth before it retreated back into the watery depths.

"Wake up, little one, wake up!" It was Aunt Sarhak. "You're having a nightmare. The ceremony has finally ended. It's morning, and there's so much we need to do."

Nushèmakw shook off her dream. She was sure it was a vision, but the more she thought about it, the less it made sense. She'd keep it to herself, for now anyway. She didn't want to frighten her aunt. "Where are we going?"

"Back home," she said, collecting their things from around the

Council fire. "We must pack and do so quietly. No one is to know. You and I must leave for our village right after the Council Meeting ends later this morning. Your father will follow later. You are to tell no one about this. Do you understand, Nushèmakw?"

"But why?" she began. Then she remembered what her father and the Chief had decided.

Sarhak held a finger to Nushèmakw's lips. "Shhhh, not now. Your father will explain everything later. Not a word, promise?"

"I promise."

Nushèmakw and Sarhak left for home early that morning, avoiding the crowds that were preparing for the final Thanksgiving Celebration. They headed south taking the deer path that ran along the edge of the woods next to the river. All went well until they approached the headwaters, where they were stopped by a Mohawk scout.

"Where are you going?" he demanded.

Without blinking, Sarhak said, "Some of our sisters are having problems with their monthly cleansing, my cousin. We're searching for remedies to help them." Even though the scout could see the medicine bundle around her neck, he still eyed her suspiciously.

"You're pretty far from the Council fire to be picking herbs." Yet, like most young men, he didn't pry too hard into the details of a female's moontime, and he let them pass. "Make it quick and return to the Council. The woods aren't safe for women traveling alone."

They pressed on toward the river and boarded the raft left ashore by the scouts. The water was calm, and it was an easy paddle across. When the sun was high in the sky, they stopped to rest under the shade of beechnut and oak. Sarhak went foraging for food while Nushèmakw sat by the river tossing stones.

She heard something in the woods behind her. It was the sound of animals, and they were coming straight for her. They pounded over the rise and bounded down the hill, a blur of motion rippling through the underbrush. She tried to hide but it was too late. The largest of the beasts caught her by the shoulders and knocked her down.

This is my end, she decided, and she closed her eyes.

The beast stood on top of her, pressing his large paws into her shoulders. She could smell his hot, moist breath. Then the dog yipped cheerfully and proceeded to lick her face.

"Stop it!" she yelled, but the dog was persistent. She pushed him away. He pressed his muzzle into her hand demanding to be petted.

A whistle sounded from the woods, and the dog retreated. Her father appeared from the top of the hill, laughing. "I was going to surprise you, but these tricksters had other plans." He gave Blackpaw a good scratch behind the ear.

Blackpaw and Snow dove into the water and fought over the remains of a fish that floated along the current. Achimwis sat down next to his daughter. He tossed a few stones into the creek and told her what he'd decided. They would continue on to Nushèmakw's Onondaga village as soon as they were refreshed. Hopefully, they would arrive before dark.

"How'd you find us?" Nushèmakw asked.

"Atsi, the Mohawk scout who stopped you, came back and told me when you'd left the Council and where I'd find you. Plus the dogs had your scent." He handed her the small leather bundle she had forgotten to take with her.

They arrived back home at her Onondaga village just as the stars pierced the sky. Sarhak, though exhausted, immediately began packing the things Nushèmakw would need for the long journey south to the lands of the Lenapé.

"Will you be coming with me?" Nushèmakw asked.

Her aunt stopped what she was doing.

"I am afraid not, little one." She said. She turned to Nushèmakw and took her in her arms while she cried. "Oh Nushèmakw, how I'll miss you. But don't worry. I know you'll do well among your father's people." She held her at arm's length. "You're nearly a woman now, and look how beautiful you are. When you settle in your new home, seek out the best of the medicine women. They will teach you everything you need to know. And one day, maybe you'll come back to Onondaga and show me everything you've learned."

That night, Nushèmakw slept in her aunt's tight embrace,

wondering if she would ever see her again.

She left with her father before dawn. First, they would travel to the Lenapé Munsee settlements southeast of Onondaga, where a large band of Minisink lived. Nushèmakw and Achimwis would stay with their Minisink cousins until they were renewed. If all went well, they would push further south down the Lenapéwâk River to her father's Unami homeland among the Kechmeches.

Nushèmakw's heart raced at the prospects of such an adventure. She took a really good look at her father. So handsome, tall, and strong. And she really did look like him. It was a comfort to know that there were other people in the world that looked like she did. "Thank you, Father," she said.

"What, no Papa for me?" he smiled and took her in his strong arms. "Nushèmakw, I wish I had been with you over these last twelve years. I'll make up for that now." She was surprised when her tight shoulders began to relax. What surprised her even more was that she found she was crying.

OWEN

1520 AD

JUNE

Owen sat as quietly as he could in a dark corner of the cottage. "You shouldn't go, Madoc," pleaded Owen's mother. "This is a voyage for fools. Anyone can see that. The old man is grasping for miracles, anything to fill his coffers that already bulge to bursting. His greed has blinded him. Tell him he should look for riches elsewhere or find another captain!"

Owen saw in his father's face a passing fear, as if Master Blazer might hear his mother's impetuous rant from their thatched home across the meadow. "But I *must* go, my sweet Elen," he said switching to their native Welsh. "You know I must. The ship is old but solid, and I know her ways better than anyone. I need to remain indispensable to our Master."

"Indispensable! That devil thinks nothing of anyone in our lowly station. You are not indispensable, Madoc. He sends you because your life means nothing to him. It's his own hide that he cares about most. He throws his gold into this dangerous enterprise because he thinks he can impress the King. He's nothing but a madman!"

Owen had heard the same story down at the docks. Master Blazer had told the crew that they would sail from Bristol tomorrow to beat "that bastard Cabot" to the prize.

"He's sending our husbands off to die," his mother wailed.

"And for what?"

"But Elen," his father consoled. "It's not just the wealth and riches of new lands that we're after, it's Hy-Brasil! Not some worldly place, but a magnificent piece of heaven. Think of it," he said with the stars in his eyes that always brought scorn across his mother's face. "Eden reborn! An island aglow by the light of our Savior. What if we are the ones chosen by God to find her once again? We can do this, Elen. I know we can. If Saint Barrind and Saint Brendan could find it those eons ago, then so can we. And when we do, just imagine our good fortune and the happy days that will come. Now is the time to rediscover this holy of all places, this place where the glory of God shines like the sun, where gold and silver and gemstones line her shores. This place, once found again, will surely usher in our good Savior's Second Coming. Think of it, Elen. The Second Coming of Christ!"

"Hy-Brasil? You would risk your life in pursuit of this folly? There is no Hy-Brasil, Madoc. The Voyage of Saint Brendan is just another Irish myth they've been telling for a thousand years. Wake up. This isn't faith. It's a child's dream. Men have been wasting their lives in search of this fairy tale island for centuries. And what's their reward? Death. That's what they receive, and that's how they will find their Savior. Have you forgotten? No one has ever returned from Hy-Brasil. No one!" Her voice began to shake as her fury gained strength. "Don't you care about us, Madoc?"

Owen's father took his mother in his arms. He rocked her slowly side to side to calm her down, and they spoke no more about it.

❦

1526 AD

MARCH

Despite his mother's pleas, Owen's father left their hamlet the very next morning and boarded *The Mary Margaret* for the high sea. That was six years ago, and no one had heard from him since.

Owen looked up into the endless sky and wondered if his father had found his magical island. Maybe he had and decided never to leave a place so grand. Or maybe they had shipwrecked, and the bodies of his father and his crew lay on the bottom of the ocean for eternity.

Owen had no desire to follow in his father's footsteps. He felt fortunate to have been spared a life at sea. Other boys weren't so lucky, having been conscripted to serve as cabin boys before their fourteenth birthday. It was his mother's determination that kept him at home. Shortly after his father left them, she gained the ear of Lady Bentley and convinced her of the benefits of having another shepherd on the manor. After all, she had delicately proposed, having her boy learn the trade from the best of all breeders could only mean profits for the good Lord and Lady well into the future. The fact that "the best of all breeders" happened to be Owen's grandfather was an added convenience.

And so began Owen's apprenticeship. Day after day and week after week, for the past six years, no matter the weather, he strode out onto the rolling pastures of Bentley Manor with his grandfather, Hywel ap Rhys. Together they tended the flocks and cared for the lambs. In time, under his grandfather's watchful eye, he became skilled at breeding the sheep and sheering their downy wool. He learned to save a ewe in troubled labor, to coerce a lamb reluctant to nurse. The work was interesting and brought with it the vast open stretches of field and fen that were a constant source of solace to Owen's agitated mind.

It was late afternoon. Owen and his grandfather sat together on the hillside watching the sheep and enjoying the sunset. "Makes the world look slight, doesn't it, *mab?*" his grandfather said.

"It does indeed."

His grandfather took a short blade to a square of wood he carried in his pocket and worked the edges. "You've not had much to say these last few days, Owen. May I ask what troubles you?"

Owen pulled at a clump of grass. "Nothing, I suppose. I don't know, exactly."

His grandfather, eyes trained on the distance, waited patiently.

"I overheard Peter in the kitchen the other day," Owen said finally. "He was saying that *The Mary Margaret* may never return."

"Did he now?"

"I can't help but wonder what caused my father to go in the first place. Maybe the Master pressed him to it, but I don't think so. He wanted to go. Seems like he was always chasing after something, never happy to be home. Gone six years now and we've still heard nothing. Do you see what it's doing to Mam? It wears on her, his absence does."

"Yes, I know it does. And what about you?"

"How can you miss someone you don't even know?"

His grandfather nodded. "Yet something's bothering you."

Owen threw a stone, scattering a flock of sparrows. "It's just that I can't imagine leaving my home for anything, much less a fabled island."

"I see. Well, not everyone believes Hy-Brasil is a fable, you know. If old Saint Barrind could find this island of glory, why not an ordinary man in our own time? It could happened, I suppose."

"But why couldn't my father be satisfied to find the glory of God right here just like we do, Grancha? Right here among the trees and marshes, at the fireside, under the stars." The words started to catch in his throat.

"I can't tell you what drives another man's heart. Maybe he's not the poet you are," he said, smiling at Owen. "Maybe he seeks for the riches of God in all the wrong places."

"What do you mean?"

"I mean that you're only fourteen and yet you speak with the knowledge of a man twice your age." He worked the pine with his knife, and Owen watched a long curl fall to the ground. "'The kingdom of God is within you.' Do you recognize that, Owen?"

"Friar Andrew has told that story nearly every Sabbath since I was a babe."

"The Greyfriars do a service by sharing the scriptures. Especially when so many among us can't read them for themselves."

"But I already know the stories. I know them all by heart. *Neque dicent ecce hic aut ecce illic ecce enim regnum Dei intra vos es.*"

"Auk! Now you're just showing off. It's a gift to have memorized the scriptures, Owen, and you should be especially grateful that you can read them too. It was my grancha who taught me to read the Latin, but I have to say, I liked it better when he told the stories to me in our mother tongue. That was the old way. It was beautiful to hear the old Welsh spoken. I taught you the Latin to nourish your mind, but the Welsh is for your soul. English you learn to make your way in this life. Be thankful for this, Owen. Not many boys hold three worlds inside their heads. Be glad languages come so easily to you. It's a rare gift for a shepherd."

"But what about Friar Andrew? Every Sabbath, he enters the chapel and offers the prayers. He sings *Gloria in excelsis Deo*, he recites the gospels, and gives communion. He blesses us and then we go. Peter says that he does this every day, not just on Sundays. How can he do the same thing over and over and not go mad?"

"Maybe he does tire of it. Who's to say? But he does it because he's been told to do it. Not every man loves what he's doing. Monks and friars are no different. That's probably true of Brother Andrew."

Owen nodded. "But he doesn't have to stay there, does he? He's not so old. Why does he lock himself inside Greyfriar when he could do something else? Be something else. Surely Master Blazer could find him some other trade."

His grandfather laughed. "Serving God is not a trade, son. I know it appears that way more than it should. I expect Brother Andrew wouldn't change his ways even if it were delivered to him on a platter. Besides, just like most of his parishioners, he can't read or write either. Did you know that? He delivers the liturgy from memory. He was sent to Greyfriar at a young age and hasn't been trained to do much else. Plus he has a fairly easy life there. He eats well from their gardens and has a place to rest his head each night. And it's no secret that he takes the bread and the wine more than he ought."

Owen's eyes widened. "Really! It's hard to believe Master Blazer would allow something like that. He keeps a tight rein on everything else that belongs to him."

"Yes, he does. All the Blazers from time immemorial have held a close watch on their purses. I guess it's why they're so wealthy still. They've clung to their landholdings and have been shrewd about acquiring more whenever they could. By the time our Lord reached marrying age, his father had died leaving him his fortunes, including Greyfriar, which continued to turn a tidy profit, a fact that was not lost on the Bentleys when our Master Blazer came courting. He won them over instantly with his charm and his wealth. With no sons of their own to claim as heirs, it was Lady Margaret Bentley, the oldest daughter, whom he would wed. In doing so, he doubled his landholdings overnight. I was here when Master Blazer took over as the Lord of Bentley. You should've seen the ruffled feathers as he went about, proud as a cock, poking into everybody's business, telling all the hands and maids and servants that they'd have to answer to him from now on. "

Hywel ap Rhys blew the shavings from his knife and tucked it into his pocket. "So the answer to your question, Owen, is yes. With Greyfriar just a few miles away, Master Blazer keeps a keen watch over her. But he only cares about the property, and its ability to increase production and yield. It's revenue he tends to, not the particulars of how devoted the brothers are to their sacred oaths. So I don't think it's the kingdom of God that our Master has his sights on with Greyfriar. He leaves that to Friar Elis."

"I don't know Friar Elis. It's always Father Andrew in the pulpit when I go to Mass." Owen said.

"Well, I hope you have a chance to meet him one day. Now there's a man with a pure heart. If you ask me, he puts up with Friar Andrew's excesses because he's a kind man who knows how to pick his battles. Besides in the scheme of things, Friar Andrew and his idle ways do little harm."

Owen wondered if Grancha knew everything. "Still I can't imagine settling for a life like that."

"Then be glad that Master Blazer allows us to be out here on the pasture rather than in the pew," he chuckled. "Even *he* has read enough scripture to know that the sheep need tending on the Sabbath."

He looked at his grandfather. "What do you think about the scriptures? Are they true?"

"Ah, I should play Pontius Pilate now and ask, '*Quid est veritas;* What is truth?'"

"I'm serious, Grancha."

"So this isn't so much about your father after all, eh?"

"Sometimes it is. If it's true that God lives in us, then why go anywhere? But what if it's not true? Then maybe my father is right to do what he did." He lay on his back and watched the clouds. "Grancha, I am nearly a man now, and I need to know. Is the kingdom of God really within me? Do you believe it is?"

"In the end, Owen, it's what you believe that's important. You *are* nearly a man now, and as a man you need to find this out for yourself."

"How do I do that?"

"When the time is right, you'll know what to do. Remember the promise. *Seek and ye shall find.* If in fact the spirit of the living God abides in the hearts of those who ask, then ask. The moment you take a look at the world around you, a hard and honest look," he said sweeping his hand across the hamlet unfolding before them. "When you do that and yet see nothing but cruelty and violence and suffering, and in your heart you find nothing but pain and sorrow, then that is the moment to ask."

Owen's time of asking came on that horrible day when all he

knew about love and reason and trust fell from his life like so much sand. The next morning, when they left to take the sheep to pasture, Hywel ap Rhys had trouble scaling the hill.

"Are you okay, Grancha?"

"I'm fine, Owen. Don't worry about me. Just a little croup, that's all."

His grandfather held his chest and began to cough. Owen helped him sit down.

"I'll get you some water," Owen said, but before he could, Grancha was racked by a spasm of coughs that wouldn't let up. Owen offered him the rag from his pocket. His grandfather held it to his mouth, and Owen saw that there was blood in his spittle.

"I'll take you home, Grancha. You shouldn't be out here when you feel like this."

His grandfather, unable to speak, waved him away.

"Let's go." Owen took his grandfather's arm and helped him up. His skin was burning hot. "Don't worry, Grancha. I've got you. Here, lean on me. I'll take you home."

They worked their way back down the hill one slow step after another. Grancha slumped, and Owen caught him around the waist. He could feel his grandfather's bony ribs pounding against each labored breath. How had he gotten so thin? When they finally reached the long drive that led to the manor house, Grancha fell to his knees.

"I'll go for help," Owen said, but then thought better of leaving his grandfather alone. "Help!" he shouted. "Help!" but they were too far from the manor house for anyone to hear.

Grancha collapsed and lay motionless on the cold ground. His face was gray, his lips blue, and the rasp of his breathing sounded like sawing wood.

Every nerve Owen possessed tensed, and his heart pounded. He lifted Grancha up in his arms, holding him close to his chest. Then he made his way down the drive as best he could holding tight to Grancha's fevered body.

"Hang on, Grancha," he said. "We're almost there."

He reached the manor house yard so out of breath he thought his lungs would burst. "Help! Someone, help! We need help!" he shouted.

Peter came running out the kitchen door. "What's happened, man?"

"Grancha's sick, Peter. Where's my mam?"

Peter took one look at Hywel ap Rhys. "Dear God!" he gasped. "Let's go."

Peter helped Owen carry Grancha's limp body across the yard and through the meadow.

Owen's mother came racing out the door before they reached the cottage.

"Grancha's in bad shape," is all Owen could manage.

His mother blanched. "Bring him inside."

Owen laid him down on the cot. His mother felt Grancha's forehead and pressed her ear to his chest.

"He's full of croup. Get me some water and clean towels. Where's Peter?"

"Right here, Elen."

"I need onions, lots of them."

Peter ran out the door.

Owen handed his mother the bucket. She dipped the towels, wrung them out, then placed them on Grancha's forehead and neck.

"Stoke the fire and set the pot over it."

Owen did as he was told.

Peter returned with a sack of onions and set it by the fire.

"Owen, sit here and change these towels every few minutes. We've got to get his fever down. Cover his arms and legs, too."

She raced to the hearth and grabbed a knife. Instantly, peels of onionskins went flying everywhere as she pared and sliced them furiously and threw them into the pot. They sizzled and popped and the room filled with their pungent odor. Owen's eyes burned in the acrid steam.

His mother dumped the poultice into a pail and stirred it until it cooled.

"Help me take off his shirt," she said.

Owen lifted his torso, and his mother carefully slipped the worn shirt over Grancha's head. She dipped her hands into the steaming onions, squeezed out the juice, and pressed the poultice onto Grancha's chest. She kept at it, handful after handful, until the pail was empty and her hands were blistered.

Grancha began to stir, and then he coughed. A good sign, his mother said. He coughed again and again until he was seized by a bout of retching. The sound rattled the walls.

"There, there, *Tad*," she whispered, placing another cold towel across his forehead. "The devil's got you good this time." He opened his eyes and tried to speak. "Save your strength. I'm right here. So is Owen," she said, patting his limp hand.

She turned to Owen. "Go find Aunt Beatrice. I'm going to need her help."

Hywel ap Rhys remained confined to his bed as one day after another slipped away. Owen stayed by his bedside day and night, only leaving to bring in the flocks.

At first, there were moments when his grandfather seemed to improve, when the poultice and other remedies his mother and Aunt Beatrice applied seemed to gain ground. But it didn't last. Now, Grancha wheezed through thickened airways, and his chest pumped up and down irregularly. It went on like this for more than a week.

"It's late, Owen. You need to sleep, my son," his mother advised. "I'll watch him tonight."

Owen shook his head. "I can't."

Little by little, Grancha lost strength. His face was haggard and white, his cheeks sunken. His breathing shallow, his body spent with fever.

Owen leaned back on the stool and closed his eyes. How can this be happening?

Two days later at Grancha's bedside, Owen woke to silence. No wheezing, no rasping, no breath. He looked down at his grandfather in the middle of that dark night and knew he was dead. His mother walked up beside him.

"He's gone," Owen said.

"Yes," his mother said.

On that miserable moonless night, when in one passing moment this man he loved so dearly died, Owen felt himself die, too. Grancha was gone. Gone from this world. Thrown into the cold unknown.

Owen took a last look at his grandfather's lifeless body and walked out the door. He leaned against a brooding oak unable to breathe, the world spinning in circles around him.

"Owen?" his mother called from the cottage. He turned and ran the other way. He dashed across the manor yard, into the terraced orchards, and through the winding pasture, crushing the meadow grass under his feet. He didn't stop until he reached the marshes. He stood there in the silence of the lowlands, then fell on the ground, and cried.

Under the wheeling stars of midnight, beneath the infinite dome that once filled him with awe and wonder, he looked heavenward and felt nothing at all. He stared into that black void, its meaningless expanse, its cruel joke. The loneliness crushed him like a fierce beast devouring his world and casting him into a dark and impenetrable abyss. His crying turned to great gasping sobs, and he felt ashamed. "My grandfather wouldn't weep like a baby," he told himself. "He'd be strong and know what to do." He wiped his nose on his sleeve. "What am I supposed to do now, Grancha?" he said to the winking sky.

Then he remembered the last words his grandfather had spoken to him.

When you see nothing but cruelty and violence and suffering, and in your heart you find nothing but pain and sorrow, that is the moment to ask.

Owen got on his knees. He opened his arms toward the dark spinning heavens and poured out his heart. Rent with abandonment and grief, he asked. The words shook as they passed through his throat, a frightened and sorry sound escaping into the black and consuming night.

When he finally opened his eyes, something had changed. He was still the same Owen ap Madoc who sat on the cold earth looking out over the night. Yet there was something else. He looked up. Was this the same sky and the same stars that he'd witnessed not moments before? Now, that marvelous expanse held within its infinite reach an ancient sensibility. Why couldn't he see this before? It was as if the universe had only just become aware of its own magnitude. It wasn't the largeness of space unoccupied after all, but an endless abiding, an infinite comfort that poured forth in and among everything.

We are one and the same, he thought. He knew now that he wasn't alone and that he never would be. He sat under the stars that began to fade along the edges of the world, mystified by the kindness they held. Like a column of light bathing him head to toe, invisible to the eye but real and solid and knowable, the abiding and sacred promise was born within him. Then he realized that his grandfather had known this all along.

❧

1527 AD

MARCH

Owen sat on the hillside watching the clouds sail across the end-less sky and thought about the day his father left him. It had been seven years since he, a boy of only eight, waved goodbye to *The Mary Margaret.* His mother had stayed home. "I'll not give my blessing to this God-forsaken voyage," she had said, and refused to go. So he stood on the dock that cold morning, holding his grandfather's hand, watching the ship shrink in the distance until it disappeared over the edge of the earth.

He picked up a stone and hurled it toward a feral cat that had crept too close to one of the lambs. "Scat!" he shouted. Seven years and still no word from his father or his crew. So much had happened since he left. It felt like a lifetime ago.

The flock chewed mindlessly at the grass. The wind died down when dusk approached, causing a bank of clouds to gather at the horizon ready to receive the sun.

He rubbed his eyes and grabbed his shepherd's crook. Like every other evening since his grandfather died, he gathered the sheep and carefully led them into their pens, securing them against the wolves and foxes that would be on the prowl when the moon rose. As he latched the gate, he heard the hammering of horse hooves at the end of the drive that led to the manor house. A crowd was gath-ering along the portico.

Rumors had come weeks ago that the return of *The Mary Margaret* was imminent. Since that ominous pronouncement, Owen saw little of his mother who, upon hearing the news, fled to the lighthouse that overlooked the marshy coastline. There she stationed herself day and night straining toward the horizon for any hint of the ship that carried his father.

Bentley Manor grew more brilliant with the lighting of torches and lanterns. News of the voyage must have finally reached them. Owen skirted the crowd, careful to stay in the shadows. He went around the tool shed to the back of the house.

He entered through the kitchen door where Peter stood weeping. "She's in there," he said. "Your mam, she's in there with the Lord and Lady." He pointed up the steps to the grand room. "They're waiting for you." Peter patted him on the back and then pushed him up the staircase.

Owen took the steps one by one, their familiar creaks ringing in his ears. The light coming from under the door cast a beam across his chest. He was nearly to the top, and he knew that when he opened the door, once again, his life would change forever.

He entered and the room fell silent, a thick carpet of stillness descending on the clamor he had heard just moments before. The Blazers' little girl, Mistress Lizzie, spoke first. "There he is, Mum!" she yelled pointing a finger. Lady Bentley stood in a cone of light that bled through the door and placed her thin pale hand on Owen's shoulder. "I'm so sorry," she whispered. She took her daughter's hand, and they left the room.

The gaunt and shadowed faces of the sailors are what he saw next. They stood pressed against the far wall wringing their caps and choking on the room's stale air. "My God!" said one of them, raising a bony hand to his mouth. "It's Madoc come to life again!"

"Shut up, old man," hissed Owen's Uncle Seamus from the corner. "Any fool can see it's his son."

The servants were shoulder to shoulder, vying for a better view. The bakers and cooks, scullery maids and gardeners, even the stable boys had rushed in to see what was going on.

Then Owen heard the wailing, a strange animal sound that filled the room. He turned and saw it coming from his mother's distorted mouth, her face mangled with a flood of tears. She ran across the room and stood before him with her head hanging. Her weeping slowly succumbed to soft sobs.

Owen took her in his arms. His mother felt so small, smaller than the lambs he had carried home from the bogs, as small as a sparrow with its hollow bones. He lifted his gaze, and it landed on the face of Master Blazer. Had he been crying too? Owen closed his eyes against this impossibility, shutting out this room filled with people whose sorrowful stares told him all he needed to know.

"He's gone, my son, he's gone," his mother moaned. "Overboard, they told me. Out like a lamp, thrown into the dark and endless waste of death! Owen, tell me it isn't true. Tell me he'll come back!" He felt his mother's legs give out, and he carried her to the only face he could recognize through his blurred vision. Aunt Beatrice took his mother into her fleshy arms, muffling her sorrow against her ample breast.

"Come with me, boy," announced Master Blazer from the corner of the room. Owen followed him into this master's quarters.

A fire had been laid, and a splendid meal was spread across the sideboard. "Sit down, my boy," said Master Blazer, nodding toward the chair next to the hearth.

"If you don't mind, my Lord, I prefer to stand."

The old man nodded and sat behind his desk. "Unaccustomed to the indoors, is that it? Or is it me?"

"Both," answered Owen.

The imposing man blinked twice, and a faint curl tugged at his mouth. "Something to eat then?" he offered, indicating the laden table.

"No thank you, Master. I'm not hungry."

"I suppose not. Bad news will do that. Steals away the appetite," he said, picking up a slice of bread. "So like your father, you are, Owen."

"In looks only, my Lord. I favor my grandfather in every other way."

"We shall see. You've taken the news like a man, Owen. Two losses in less than a year. I'm sorry."

Owen only nodded.

"Your grandfather's death was a hard blow, too. A year's gone by and still it's felt among us." Owen looked away. "Let's not forget, though, that ol' Hywel ap Rhys lived a good long life. He was wise, Owen, honest and wise. You'll never again meet a Welshman who clung to the old ways more than Hywel. I wish the Crown were as honest. They've all but abandoned their Welsh roots. Instead, they knock about Windsor pretending to be a pack of bloody Englishmen."

"I learned a lot from him."

The Master sighed, his face sagging against the outlay of air. "I'm sure you did, Owen. But I didn't bring you here to talk about Hywel. It's the loss of your father that weighs on us now." He rubbed a fat hand across his bearded chin. "The world is changing, lad. We must change with her or she will eat us alive. There are new lands to be found. Those who claim them and their riches will be the ones to hold power. Your father knew this as well as anyone, but his eyes were always on heaven. Always the glory of God for him. That was his weakness, Owen, but it's not mine."

He eyed Owen carefully. "There are those who say that England and her Church have become nothing but harlots who handily sell themselves to the highest bidder. Who's to say it isn't true? Bristol is brimming with trade. You've seen it yourself. Ships clot her harbors and jockey for space to dump their loads. It's the merchant whose wealth is rising, Owen. At last we may see a day when we merchants surpass even the Church and the Crown in wealth and power!" He barked with such abandon that Owen wondered if he forgot he was there.

"Mark my word. The time is coming—and coming soon—when kings and princes will bow to the merchant. And I intend to be among that worthy class when they do!" He crossed the room to where a cloak of fine silver fur hung from a hook on the wall. "Have a look at this, son. Have you ever seen a pelt so full of luster?" The Master ran his fingers gently through it. "Last week, my worn but faithful *Hopewell*, that loyal sister ship to *The Mary Margaret*, entered port at Bristol. She'd come from a land old man Cabot dubbed New Found Land only a few years ago. They'd been out for seven long years searching for treasure, the *Hopewell* and *The Mary Margaret*. Word came back telling of people they'd discovered who were already living along the coast. Beastly men who live like animals and throw harpoons. Look here," he said lifting a large flat stone from the mantel. "What do you make of this?"

Owen ran a finger along the chiseled blade, and the facets of black flint caught the light from the fire.

"It's one of their spearheads. A beauty, too." The Master tenderly placed it back on the mantel. "*The Mary Margaret*," he continued, "was anchored along the icy shores for those seven years, camping among the natives just as I had ordered them to do. Those primitive creatures knew nothing of us or our mother tongue. In time, though, your father and his crew were able to make them understand that I intended to bring them goods far better than their own. But I had my price, and they paid in pelts. Thousands of them. So I sent the *Hopewell* to and from those shores where *The Mary Margaret* was stationed. Each time, she went laden with metal knives and other weapons superior to anything the natives had ever seen. We gave them netting, linen, and wool, items of little value to us but cherished by them. In return, the natives filled my hull to overflowing with furs such as these, beautiful things, some from animals we never knew existed. Do you know what that means, my boy?"

Was this the way Master Blazer talked to his father? Diatribes that went round and round before landing on the point. Owen shifted uncomfortably while the man raved on. "Bounties of animals in that New Found Land, pelts that could clothe a nation for centuries!" he said banging the desk. "Owen, the Dutch may have stuck the first finger in that pie, but I will not stop until my whole fist is in it, too."

Master Blazer wiped away the rivulet of sweat that ran down the side of his face. He poured himself a drink and then another. When he held the empty decanter up to the light and swirled the traces of amber around and around in the cut crystal, he appeared to come to his senses. "Not to worry, my boy, not to worry. There's plenty more where that came from," he snickered. "See that portrait?"

Owen looked at the life-size painting of Lady Bentley hanging on the wall. "I do, Master. It's a very good likeness, too."

"It'd better be for what I paid for it. I bribed the artist away from Chelsea where he was working on a portrait of Sir Thomas More. He had his price, and I paid it. He dashed off this beauty before Sir Thomas even realized he was gone. Now my fine wife is happy, and so am I," he said, tucking his hand behind the frame and springing a lock.

The painting covered a secret door that revealed a large room covered floor to ceiling with shelves groaning with whiskey, rum, and wine. "Don't look so astonished, son. Never seen a buttery before? The other end of the room leads to the kitchen, where there's plenty more. I've got secrets all over this place," roared the Master in a way that made Owen realize he was drunk.

He shut the door and straightened the painting. Lady Bentley's somber eyes stared down at Owen. "I didn't force your father to go, you know. Do you believe me, Owen?" When Owen didn't answer, he shrugged. "Why would you?" He crossed the room and slumped at his desk. "Madoc asked to go. That's God's truth. Your father and all those other Celts down at the docks convinced me to take on that voyage. They saw it as an amazing stroke of luck if I'd let them go. And why, you ask?" Owen wasn't asking. "Because if they could talk me into pursuing the riches at New Found Land, then they'd have their chance at finding Hy-Brasil. It's Hy-Brasil that captivates them. It always has. Hy-Brasil, the isle of endless mystery. The island that shows herself only once every seven years. Once in seven years, Owen, and they meant to be there when she rose again. There was talk that old John Cabot, or his bloody son, would try again, too, so I decided that I would beat those bastards to it. We would be the ones to take both New Found Land *and* Hy-Brasil!"

The Master looked surprised when Owen spoke. "My mother didn't believe in it."

"In Hy-Brasil? A woman like your mother would never be lured by such legends. It was your father who gave it credence and threw his faith in its direction. He asked to go, and I didn't stop him. After all, useful servants and capable captains are hard to find."

Master Blazer looked at Owen. "Whether you believe me or not matters little," he said with a sniff. "Nevertheless, I leave you with this. Your father was a good man who served me well. He lost his life under my lordship. You may go now, Owen ap Madoc. Go and tell your mother that she shouldn't worry. I will see to it that all your needs are met. You and she shall have a place at Bentley for as long as you live. I owe that much to your father."

Owen bowed slightly. "Thank you, my Lord," he said as he opened the door.

"And Owen?"

"Yes, Master?"

"You should ask your Uncle Seamus what really happened to your father on that voyage."

※

1527 AD

APRIL

It was out on the vast stretches of salt and mead where Owen missed his grandfather most. With each passing day there was so much he wished he could share. He wanted to tell him about his mother, about how fragile she seemed, as if at any moment she would shatter into a million pieces. He wanted to tell him that *The Mary Margaret* had returned to port after all but without his father, and about the mystery surrounding his death, about the secret that Uncle Seamus was keeping. And Owen wanted to tell Grancha that he was a man now, if becoming a man meant knowing that life would be hard.

It had been so easy to sit with Grancha at times like these, eyes on the horizon, their breath mingled in the fragrant air swept clean by the steady wind pressing inland from the sea. No man knew him as well. No man ever would.

It was the lingering grief that caused Owen to spend long hours thinking about their days together. Looking back over his short and simple life, he could see more clearly how fortunate he was to be a shepherd and not a sailor like his father. He was bound to the earth through and through, not made for the sea as some boys were, their skin already leathery from life on the ship's scorching deck.

"Madoc, I can't believe you'd even consider turning Owen into a sailor." he remembered his mother saying not long before his father left. "Haven't I sacrificed enough to that bloodthirsty ocean? It's nearly taken you from me completely, with the time you're gone on one voyage or another. Now you stand there and expect me to let the sea have you *and* my son? I'll not hear of it! Go tell Master Blazer that my father will apprentice Owen instead. Tell him that he will teach Owen all that there is to know about lambing and breeding. There's more money to be had right here on the Master's own green meadows than at sea, and there's no better shepherd in all of England than Hywel ap Rhys to make it so."

It was true. With precision Hywel ap Rhys had bred the Cotswold with the Lincoln longwools to excellent effect, as his father had before him. Through a century of careful selection, putting the finest rams to ewes, they had kept Bentley Manor on the map of the royal mind from as far back as the 1300s, when the House of Lancaster reigned. Even before Master Blazer had married into the Bentley family, Hywel ap Rhys's fleeces were famous, fetching a fine price at the Bristol markets to the delight of his Master-to-be.

Now that Grandcha was gone, Master Blazer would expect no less from him. At fifteen, he was no longer an apprentice. He hoped that he had learned everything he needed to know to carry the weight of his grandfather's legacy.

A squat and spirited dog came bounding up the hill, and the sight of it made Owen laugh. *Such an unlikely animal to set to the task of herding,* Owen thought. *Her legs are much too short to be good for anything, much less for chasing sheep.* Yet Grancha would consider nothing else but the old and dependable corgis for corralling the animals. His grandfather loved them, and so did Owen. "*Bore da,* Teg!" he said. "Good morning!" After she received what she came for, a hearty scratch behind her brindled ears, Teg set off again, down the way she had come to the pastured expanse on the other side of Bentley where the cattle grazed.

How small Bentley Manor looked from where Owen stood, the sheep merely dots along the lush landscape. The spring sunshine poured over them, drawing steam off their damp wool. As the morning wore on, he moved the flock hillock by hillock to a stretch of pasture that skirted the moor where they could graze on the scrubby wind-worn grasses. He found a perch on a fallen log, where he had a commanding view of the entire lowlands. He leaned back and let the day slip away.

It was here along the mead that Owen's mind would settle and his heart would soar. And it was here along these marshy inlets where he first came to know his God in a way he would never be able to explain.

From a distance, Owen heard a short piercing cry. Only one cry and then it was gone. Maybe it was the ewe he left at the foothill, unable to navigate the bog due to the enormous swell of her belly. Had she begun to birth? He jumped up and ran over the spongy ground only to find her gnawing peacefully on a tuft of sea oats, her expression fixed on nothing.

The sun sat low on the western edges of the marsh, lighting up the patches of brine that pooled around the reeds. He heard it again—another short cry that vanished as quickly as it came. His heart leaped, and he turned around. Then he saw it; the one small pool among them all that rippled and bubbled, a faint echo of a splash. He threw off his shirt and climbed down to the pool careful not to land in the mud, which could suck a man down its throat before he knew what had happened. Gaining purchase from one slimy rock to another was difficult, but soon he reached it. On hands and knees, he peered into the watery depth. The black pool was full of shadow, and he strained to see into it. His eyes, fresh off the bright landscape of the open moor, adjusted slowly to this dark place. He tried to make sense of it, as if he were squinting into a conjuror's mirror waiting for a vision. Then the horror seized him. A face, he saw a face. So white, so white. A ghost, a devil. No, this was no devil. It was a little girl! Her mouth contorted, thin blue lips opened in a scream. Her eyes stared skyward, her flaxen hair fanned out around her head. "My God!" he cried. It was little Mistress Lizzie, Master Blazer's daughter.

Thrusting his arms into the frigid slough, he grabbed the elfin child and pulled her out. He drew a long breath before he realized Lizzie wasn't breathing. How long had it been? He pressed his fist under her breastbone and began to pump the way he did with the lambs that came to him stillborn. Nothing. "Come on, Mistress Lizzie, breathe. Dear God, make her breathe!" Still there was nothing. Again and again, he pumped her chest. How long before her ribs cracked under his weight?

A gasp. Not even a gasp, but a puff, like a child blowing bubbles; a sound so soft he almost missed it. He laid his ear on her chest. From deep in her throat, he heard a gurgle, a gurgle then a cough. "C'mon, Lizzie, you can do it." And she did. He sat her up and she began to spew, hurling vomit across the bog. She shook violently then gulped for air. She breathed. *Thank God!*

He braced her firmly in his arms and headed for safety, one cautious step at a time. He picked his way through the tangled maze keeping a keen eye on the shoreline not twenty feet away. An old root jutted across his path, and he tripped over it. He tried desperately to regain his balance, but it was no use. He was going over. He held tightly to the girl, and they both plunged into the sludge. Immediately, the sucking mud began its work. Slowly and methodically, Owen's legs were pulled down until his knees disappeared. Then his thighs were swallowed. He shouted for help, but he knew there was no one out this far on the moors to hear him.

With time at a standstill and every second an eternity, he looked skyward. "Dear God, do you take us now?" He leaned back into their murky tomb and lifted Lizzie up and across his chest.

He lay there and stared at the sky, succumbing to their fate. It was at that moment of his resignation when he felt it. Ever so slightly, his legs begin to loosen. His heart pounded. He leaned back even further into the mud, and slowly his legs responded in kind. It was Lizzie's body that had weighted his torso enough to lever him up. "Come on, keep going," he said. Finally, he saw his knees poke through the surface.

Darkness fell upon the lowlands while Owen and Lizzie floated in the cold bog. He held his breath afraid to move a muscle. His body was numb and frozen, so he didn't feel it when, with a loud thwack, the back of his legs broke free. He was buoyant at last, light as a feather on top of the thick mud, stretched across the pool like a raft with Lizzie curled on top of his chest. Gently, he flexed one leg and then the other, and they started to move. He paddled carefully, steady and slow, skimming over that dank pool until they reached the dry shore.

He heaved Lizzie onto the bank and crawled out, both thankful and bewildered to be on dry ground. He laid her on a soft bed of fern and stripped her of her wet and icy clothes. She was so fair and tiny and close to death even still. His shirt! He grabbed it from the shore where he had left it and wrapped her tight, rubbing her chest and limbs to spread warmth throughout her small body. Her cheeks were pale, but the blue of her lips was fading. She was coming around. He scooped her up and ran through the night as fast as his frozen legs would allow.

Owen's head hurt and his eyes burned. All he wanted to do was go back to sleep, but the noise and clamor coming from outside their cottage prevented it. The door opened. Even with his eyes closed, he recognized the raspy growl of Peter Maddock. "Our Lady Margaret Bentley to see you," he announced.

"Lady Bentley? To see me?" It was his mother who answered. He remembered now. He was safely at home and in his own warm bed.

"Yes, Elen. It is I," answered Lady Bentley. "I've come to see your boy. Is he awake?"

"Not yet, my Lady. He's slept straight through these last three days. But I think he's out of danger now."

"And the fever?"

His mother laid a hand on Owen's forehead. "It's gone."

"I'm awake, Mam," Owen said, having just recalled what had happened in the bog. He tried to sit. "Mistress Lizzie, my Lady. Is she..."

Lady Bentley sat on the edge of his bed. "Lie back down, Owen ap Madoc. Our Lizzie is ailing yet but gaining strength. She lives, my dear boy, because of you." She took his hand and squeezed it. "I've come to say thank you. To let you know how grateful we are."

"So she lives?"

"Yes." Lady Bentley smiled. "We owe you a debt, Owen."

"My Lady, why was she so far from home? So small to be wandering down by the marshes alone." He lay back down.

"You can be sure, dear lad, that I will find out how and why she ventured out. But that's no worry of yours. Right now, you must rest.

We will talk when you're better." To Owen's amazement, she bent over and kissed him on the cheek. He blushed profusely and forgot to thank her.

His mother laughed. "Poor boy," she said. "Hasn't fully regained his senses yet. Thank you for coming, my good Lady. We are filled with appreciation."

Lady Bentley waved her hand, "I will hear none of that, Elen. When the boy is well, Master Blazer will call for him." She gathered up her skirts and nodded to Peter who led her through the door.

❦

1527 AD

MAY

The morning dew was thick on the grass and damp underfoot as Owen made his way to the paddock. Peter came running out from the kitchen and onto the lawn waving his arms. "Owen, wait up a minute. I just got word from Aunt Beatrice. She was clearing away the Lord's breakfast this morning when he asked her to find you. Master Blazer wants words with you."

"Right now?"

"Right now."

They raced through the galley and into the kitchen. When Owen started up the stairs, his aunt barred the way. "Wait just one minute, young man. What in heaven's name do you think you're doing barging up the stairs to the Master's quarters like you've come to clean the barn? I think not! Besides, I'll not have you tromping through these halls knocking mud all across my clean floors. Get over here."

From a lifetime of such encounters with Aunt Beatrice, it was futile to resist. Peter left in a hurry, slipping through the back door.

"A ragamuffin is what you are, Owen," she said throwing a hot soapy towel at him. "Clean your hands and face whilst I brush off those boots." He kicked them off, sat next to the sink, and began to scrub. "You'll need to make a good impression today, Owen," she said, scratching the dirt from his soles into the wide fireplace. "The Lord and Lady think mighty highly of you lately. They're not ones to forget." She blew the last bits of dust off the old leather. "It's time your mam got you some new laces. Here you go," she said, and he slipped them back on.

"Now turn around so I can tame that mop of yours." This was the worst part. She would always go at it like a rake through bramble, leaving the comb filled with clots of hair when she was through. "Why is it that the boys always get the curls? And look how yours have gone to red with sun bleach. There! Even Lady Bentley herself would be proud to carry a mane like that. Go now, and do your best to stay in their good graces!" she admonished, and Owen flew up the stairs.

He took a deep breath before knocking on the door.

"Who is it?" bellowed the Master.

"It's Owen ap Madoc, my Lord," he said as bravely as he could.

"Come in, Owen ap Madoc."

Owen opened the door, and it squeaked on heavy hinges. He was surprised to see that the Master wasn't alone.

"Don't look so stunned, my boy. Haven't you ever seen a holy man?"

"Yes, my Lord, I have," he said, removing his cap, which he immediately began to wring in his hands. "I'm surprised, Master, not by the friar, but because I didn't expect you to have company. I can come back later if it suits you." Owen bowed and began to back out the door.

"Nonsense, my boy!" William Blazer strode over and grabbed him round the shoulders. "You are the very reason Friar Elis has come."

"*Bore da*, Owen." Friar Elis greeted him in his native Welsh. "*Mae'n dda gen i gwrdd â chi Mae'n braf cwrdd â chi!*" The man smiled with eyes deeply lined from long years of kindness and concern.

"*Diolch*," Owen replied, "Thank you. I'm pleased to meet you, too." The friar's bald dome shined above a short fringe of hair, and he wore the coarse gray robe common among the brothers.

"You've made quite an impression on your Master, Owen."

Unable to muster a response, Owen said nothing.

"Look at him, Friar," said Master Blazer. "Have you ever seen a creature so suited to the outdoors? Bursting as he is with good health and vigor, he's become like those young strapping rams he tends. Soon he'll have all my pretty maids sniffing and chasing him like ewes in heat."

It was Friar Elis who saved Owen from further mortification. "Must I point out, William, that you could use a little more time outdoors yourself," he said slapping the Master on his bulging belly. "Wasn't so long ago that you were a trim and hearty lad like Owen and happy to captain your father's ships. Now look at you!" The friar tipped back his head and laughed.

Owen, frozen in disbelief, held his breath against what might come next. He studied Master Blazer's face, which to his surprise became so filled with mirth that soon he began to roar. Owen, forgetting his shyness, watched the spectacle of these two powerful men acting like little boys.

"You've always been able to get me going, Elis," he said, drawing a kerchief from his vest and wiping the tears that squeezed from his eyes. "And that's the best medicine in all the kingdom. But we divert from the task at hand." He turned to Owen. "Have a seat, my boy."

"Owen ap Madoc," the Master continued, "I'm a man who doesn't like to hold debts very long. You saved my daughter. By doing so you interrupted the cruel course of the devil's grip. Had we lost her, there would be no end to the heartbreak this family would have suffered. It was you, my boy, who altered the course of our lives—an angel on the marshes, striking down the demons that come. Now it's time to return the favor." He dropped into his chair with a thud, threw his arms across his desk, interlaced his fingers, and leaned in toward Owen.

"You will be leaving Bentley, my boy, to become an novitiate of the Order of the Friars Minor at Greyfriars. There you will be under the tutelage of none other than Father Elis," he said, indicating the Friar smiling in the corner. "He will oversee your training as a scribe. Those who advance in their learning move to the colleges at Oxford and Cambridge. Friar Elis has lost three such men to the demands of the colleges and now to the offices of law as well. As the Father will tell you, he is spending more time translating the ancient texts for the King's advisors than he is serving the Pope. Father Elis knows your disposition, and he assures me that you will receive the balanced life of the scribe and the shepherd. As you know, the flocks at Greyfriar, while no match for our own stock, are good enough. You will strengthen your mind through hard study and your body on the pasture. Your soul I leave to the good friar." He leaned back with a satisfied smiled. "What do you have to say to that, Owen ap Madoc?"

Owen stared a moment, blinking as if trying to wake from a dream. "I'm not sure what to say, my Lord." Then he remembered his aunt's admonition. "I mean, thank you. Yes, I'm grateful, my Lord, very grateful." The men chuckled at this rough attempt at etiquette. "But I'm not prepared to leave just yet. Don't forget, my Lord. The lambing season has only just ended. Who will take care of them if I'm gone? We could lose some of the ewes and their lambs if I'm not there to help them."

"My dear boy," Friar Elis interrupted. "It's good to hear your concern for the sheep. Our Lord and Savior would have you care no less for your flock, be they men or lambs. But we have a plan, Owen. At Greyfriar, we have a yeoman from Bristol who has been tending our flocks. He's a good and honest man. I'm sending him to Bentley to work with you until the lambs are strong. Come summer, he will take over your post, and you will move to Greyfriar. At that time, I'll send Brother Michael to help you pack. Although, since you will be required to adhere to the friars' sacred call to poverty, you'll have very little packing to do."

"Any more questions, Owen?" William Blazer asked.

"Yes, Master. May I bring my dog?"

❧

1527 AD

JUNE

"Come in."

Owen entered the dark windowless room. A peat fire smoldered on the grate, and the smoke escaped through a hole in the thatched ceiling.

"I wondered when you'd come." Uncle Seamus stoked the fire until the blaze rekindled. "Sit awhile."

Owen took the stool next to the Irishman he considered an uncle, although he and his father were brothers only through the bond of long friendship.

"How has life treated you, Owen?"

"Fair enough, I guess. How about you?"

"Same. Could be worse."

How he's aged, Owen thought, looking at the gray that crept along his thinning blond hair. His face was puckered with time and weather, and a scruff of beard bothered his jaw.

"I'll be leaving Bentley soon, Uncle Seamus. To take up as a scribe at Greyfriar."

"So I've heard. I hope it goes well for you there among the brothers. So you've come to say goodbye? Is that it?"

"I suppose. That and to ask about my father."

"I thought as much. It's been lonesome around here without him."

"For you maybe. To tell you the truth, I haven't missed him as much as you might think. It's like he's just on another voyage."

Seamus nodded. "He was away from home a lot. I know how it can be hard on a boy to grow into manhood without his father to show the way."

"I had my grandfather."

"Ol' Hywel," Seamus said with a smile. "I'm sure that's true. How old are you now, Owen?"

"Almost sixteen."

He ladled a bowl of stew from the pot simmering on the coals and handed it to Owen. "He was proud of you, you know. We spent many nights on the watch, passing time on the deck. He told a lot of stories about you. How smart you were. Running before you walked. Learning your letters and numbers while other boys were still in diapers. You have ol' Hywel ap Rhys to thank for that. He had you speaking both Welsh and English before you were knee high."

"I'm surprised my father knew anything about me."

Seamus dipped the ladle and served himself. "So what did you come here to learn, Owen?"

"Tell me how he died."

"You've had words with Master Blazer?"

"He had a few words with me. That day the ship came in. He said you would know what really happened."

Seamus looked up at the ceiling, blackened with soot, and sighed. "Did he, now? That mongrel." He sat down his bowl and leaned in toward Owen. "You really want to know this, son?"

Owen nodded.

"Well then," he said, rubbing his hands near the fire even though it wasn't cold. "Owen, I can hardly look at you. You favor him so much it frightens me. If the good Lord hadn't tempered your red hair with a bit of your mother's brown, you'd be Madoc incarnate." Finally he managed to look Owen in the face. "Such eyes he had. Blue as an autumn sky. You got those, Owen, and in the face of a man now. That's why you're bound to upset folks here for a time. You look so much like him." He patted Owen on the knee. "But you've come here for answers. You have a right to know what happened to your father. But that comes with a price. Your father was given a sacred trust and was duty bound to keep it."

"And you?"

He waved his hand. "This sacred trust must stay with only a few. If I tell you what happened to your father, you must swear that it will go no farther than these walls."

"Grandcha taught me not to swear, Uncle. He said my word should be enough for any man."

Seamus closed his eyes and sighed. "Do I have your word, then?"

"Yes."

"Your father may still be alive."

"Impossible!"

His uncle shook his head. "No, Owen, it's very possible. Keeping this secret won't be easy for you. Your mam has been told that he was lost at sea, that he died. She should never know anything different. If she believes there's a chance that he lives, she'll perish longing for his return. If we find him—and I'll never give up trying—then thanks be to God for keeping him alive. That would surely be a happy day for your mam, and the rest of us. But if we discover that he's dead, we'll have caused her the pain of losing him twice. So she must not know about this, Owen. Can you abide by that?"

"I can."

His uncle leaned back into his chair. "Then I'll tell you the whole story."

NUSHÈMAKW

✄

1530 CE

HUNTING MOON

Nushèmakw and her father, Achimwis, embarked at dawn, leaving her Onondaga village behind. The two dogs, Snow and Blackpaw, ran ahead. They followed the deer path south, hiking all day. They arrived at Kanata Creek before nightfall, and made simple work of setting up camp.

"Is it safe to spend the night here, Papa?" Nushèmakw asked.

"As safe as anywhere else. Atsi should be here soon and he's well equipped to guide us through his territory. If all goes well, we'll arrive at the Mohawk River by tomorrow evening."

The sun dipped quickly behind the wall of thick trees, gleaming brilliantly over the murmuring creek. A lone figure was paddling upstream, and his canoe cut a dark ribbon through the bright water.

"It's Atsi," her father said. "*Kwehkwe!*" he called to him in Mohawk. Then he switched to Onondaga so Nushèmakw could understand. "So good to see you, my friend. The Great Spirit has blessed you with safe passage," he said embracing his friend. "Many thanks for bringing my canoe all this way. That was no easy task against the current. I'm grateful."

Atsi laughed. "I'll be glad to get back into the woods, Achimwis," the Mohawk said in broken Onondaga.

The men dragged the canoe onto the bank. It was laden with provisions for their trip, and they covered it with a deerskin tarp

— 69 —

to keep out marauding raccoons that would be on the prowl before long.

"Is it safe to build a fire?" asked Achimwis.

Atsi nodded. "My brothers know I'm here and will keep watch. And a small fire will keep away the bears. Besides we need to cook this," he said, holding up a speared brook trout, its rose-colored belly shiny and wet.

The roasted fish tasted delicious, an opinion weighted by Nushèmakw's ravenous appetite. She leaned back and watched the stars light up the sky. Soon the Star Path appeared in full spangle. By the warmth of the fire, under the blanketing night, where the voices of her father and his friend ebbed and flowed like the songs rising from the passing creek, she fell fast asleep.

Morning came on suddenly. It was Blackpaw who woke her, licking the lingering bits of fish that clung to her face. It took her a moment to remember where she was. Her father had let her sleep while he and Atsi prepared for departure.

She saw him down by the creek.

"Nushèmakw!" he called to her. "Grab your things, sleepyhead. It's time to go."

She boarded the canoe and her father shoved off, pushing them from the shore with his long paddle. They headed downstream hugging the coast along the shallows. The watchful Atsi ran ahead, ensuring their safety, and the dogs chased after him.

The day passed without event. They were entertained by the robins and wrens calling from bushes, their songs riding on the autumn breeze. Squirrels chattered frantically from the naked branches above them. "Rit, rit, rit," they warned, guarding their leafy nests. They scurried down to the forest floor, digging through the dried litter in their endless search for acorns to fill their winter stores.

It was a warm day for so late in the year, and the ride was smooth and soothing. Nushèmakw caught sight of Atsi in the distance before he plunged back into the woods.

"How did you and Atsi meet, Papa?"

"It was a long time ago," her father said, dropping a fishing line over the side. "I was a young man then and traveling far from my

Unami village for the first time. I left with my older Kechemeches uncles just about this time of year, under the hunting moon, and they took me up the Lenapéwâk River in search of deer and bear. I was in charge of hauling the pack of whelk and quahog shells prized by the Haudenosaunee that we hoped to trade when we arrived at the Lenapé territory of our cousins, the Minisink."

"Isn't that where we're going now?"

"That's right. Their northwest border lies alongside Mohawk territory. The Mohawks have traded with many of the Munsee bands for a long time. That's when I met Atsi. He was younger than I was, and too small yet to hunt with his uncles. Instead, he came to the river's headwaters with his mother to help her trade their furs in exchange for the whelk and other goods hard to find in your Long-house territory along the lakes."

Her father pulled up the line, baited the bone barb, and dropped it back in the creek. "When my uncles finished the hunt, we stayed with the Minisink to rest and to trade with the other bands and tribes. Atsi and I became good friends. We didn't leave until the cold moon was upon us. By that time, Atsi had taught me quite a lot of Mohawk."

They had drifted toward the center of the creek. Her father dipped his oar and steered them closer to the water's edge. "That's a gift saved for the young, Nushèmakw. It's much easier to learn other tongues when your mind is new and fresh and empty of the troubles of this world. Remember that." He dropped another line over the side. "Atsi and I have been friends ever since. He's been my companion all the years I've traveled from Unami territory to Onondaga and back again."

"Why do you do it?"

"Travel?" He was surprised by her question. "So much like your mother!" he said shaking his head. "She'd always ask me the same thing."

"It's a good question."

"I know. And I don't have a good answer. Except that I am Achimwis, the Unami Storyteller. I was born to journey far and wide. Born to gather the stories of not only my people, but of all the people who walk the earth."

Sarhak had told Nushèmakw about her father's endless quest many times.

"We are a people who live and breath by our stories," he continued. "Without them, we would cease to exist. Through storytelling the Great Spirit passes through us, carrying our great purpose from generation to generation. We are nothing without our stories!"

They came to the wide mouth of Kanata Creek and paddled to where it emptied into the Mohawk River. Atsi stood on the bank with Snow and Blackpaw and waved them over. Her father drew up the lines heaving with silver-backed fish. Atsi helped him haul the canoe up the bank. Nushèmakw unloaded it, while the dogs leapt and nipped at her skirt. They hiked a short ways to a small Mohawk village where they were welcomed and fed. Nushèmakw was given a place in the Turtle Clan longhouse to sleep the night. No wonder they called the Mohawks cousins. Everything about this place felt familiar, except for the language, but even that was beginning to fall on her ears in patterns that made sense.

The next leg of their journey would take a week, maybe more. The Mohawks gave them enough corn biscuits and dried deer meat to sustain them along the way. They would replenish their provisions when they reached the west branch of the Lënapei Sipu.

They were four days into their journey when, at dawn, Atsi turned to leave. "I'll be heading home now, my brother," he said. "We are now too close to the Susquehannocks. They loathe anything that looks or breathes like a Mohawk. If you're seen with me, it will be a death sentence."

"I know. Still I'm sorry to see you go."

"Be well, my friend."

"Ó:nen," her father said, "Farewell." Atsi waved and disappeared into the forest.

The hairs on Nushèmakw's neck stood on end as she imagined what the next few days would be like with just she and her father finding their way.

"Don't worry, Nushèmakw," he reassured as if reading her mind. "We'll be fine. Besides, we have the dogs." He whistled and they came running.

She pulled her pack onto her back, tightened the strap across her forehead, and followed her father into the chilly woods.

They had come a hundred miles since they left her Onondaga village. As they traveled, she noticed subtle changes in the landscape: the hills, while ample, where not so high as hers at home, and here the maples still held on to a few of their golden leaves. The nights felt a little warmer too, but not much. Winter would soon be upon them.

"How much farther do we have to go, Papa?"

"Far enough," is all he said.

As the day wore on, they looked for a good spot to spend the night. They found it in a quiet hollow that overlooked the Susquehanna, an elbow in the river that would take them further south. Too tired to eat, she lay down under the bows of a pine in a bed of fragrant needles and fell asleep.

The deep and heavy quiet woke her the next morning. Her father and the dogs were gone, hunting for the trip ahead. She stretched her limbs. Hunger pains settled in her noisy stomach, and she walked along the riverbank searching for food. Luckily, she found plenty of ripe nuts strewn generously under the tall beech trees.

Munching away in mindless satisfaction, she was startled by the sound of a branch snapping behind her. She whirled around. Planted on the ground were two of the largest feet she had ever seen. She looked up. Before her stood the tallest, thickest, most ferocious man in the entire world. Bear teeth hung in great strands across his expansive chest. The hard jawline, the painted face, the head shaved clean but for a crest of coarse hair standing on his crown. Most dreadful of all was the bear claw than hung from the end of his nose! He was so tall she could barely see the top of him. She stumbled backwards, tripped over a stone, and landed in the river.

All at once the giant and imposing Susquehannock lost his guard. His face contorted and strained until he finally gave into roaring laughter.

The dogs came running, barking and snapping, showing teeth and ready to protect and defend. A sharp whistle pierced the forest, and the dogs stopped in their tracks. Her father came bounding through the brush, confused and then relieved at what he saw.

"Sarangararo!" he cried. "It's you!" The formidable Susquehannock, choking now on his own laughter, could only point. Achimwis looked at Nushèmakw, and he was kind enough not to smile or cause her any further embarrassment.

"What happened, Nushèmakw?" he asked as he graciously helped her out of the water.

"She's your daughter?" Sarangararo asked finally. She was surprised to hear him speak something that sounded a little like Onondaga. "She has your face, my brother. And she's brave," he added, finally suppressing his mirth.

Nushèmakw soon learned that her father and Sarangararo had prearranged this rendezvous. Achimwis was cashing in a debt owed when he saved Sarangararo's life years ago. Sarangararo would guide them through Susquehannock territory to where the river widened and a canoe awaited for their passage south.

They hiked along the banks of the Susquehanna River for most of the day, then boarded Sarangararo's canoe to journey the next few hours by water. They made good time with Sarangararo as their guide, and found a suitable place to camp before nightfall.

The next morning they headed east, floating down creeks when they were passable, taking portage across stretches of field and forest when they were not. By the end of the day, they reached another milestone: the western banks of the Lënapei Sipu. The river was wide and full, with trees rising high on either side. Her father stared at the water. "It's starting to look like home," she heard him say.

They canoed down the welcoming river for the next several days without incident. At the upper reaches of the land of the Munsees, the river turned sharply and entered a huge gorge with towering rock walls. Sarangararo would go no further. "I'm not welcome here," he said to her father. He steered them into a sandy inlet carved in the face of the gorge, and they disembarked. The men embraced. "We will meet again," Sarangararo said. He stepped back into the canoe and shoved off, paddling upstream the way they'd come.

Nushèmakw followed her father across the inlet to a path that wound up a stony embankment to the top of the gorge. They took the path further south where the cliffs tapered to gently rolling hills that hugged the river. From there, the hike was easy. It wasn't long before they reached the northern reaches of the Lenapé settlements. The sun cast long shadows by the time they approached the village. The dogs led the way, following the scents of the people up ahead.

The village was huge. Almost as big as the greater Onondaga village where the Grand Council had gathered. Her father told her that this was the territory of the Munsee-speaking people and a gateway for commerce among many tribes, not just the Lenapé. A man met them at the edge of the river and ferried them to Minisink Island. He spoke to her father in a language she didn't understand as they crossed over. The island was one giant field edged in forest. Scores of pathways cut between blankets spread over the ground as far as Nushèmakw could see, each laden with the wares of the various tribes. They walked across the field, and Nushèmakw was impressed by the piles of beads and furs and pottery that lay everywhere. Arrowheads, hatchets, and knives were proudly displayed on colorful woven mats. And the food! She had never smelled so many wonderful things all at once. She was suddenly starving.

Achimwis stopped to talk with a Sankikan woman who stirred a simmering pot. He pointed to Nushèmakw, asking the woman for something to eat. Her father waved her over, and they sat with the woman, who handed Nushèmakw a bowl of hot porridge with beans and generous chunks of roasted duck floating on top.

Nushèmakw watched the crowds while she ate. This was an active port, her father told her— a hub where trading and passage was vibrant between the Unami speaking bands from the south, the friendlier Algonquian tribes from the northeast, and the Mohawk traders and runners who took the safer eastern route to avoid the Susquehannock. Nushèmakw strained her eyes on the moving mouths of the Minisink, trying to understand their dialect. Her head was spinning. Finally, a Mohawk father and son stopped by, and she was able to parse out a few words she had learned from Atsi. They told her that they were getting ready to head back home with the goods and wampum they had traded for their thick, rich pelts.

She loved everything about this wonderful place: the unfamiliar scent of their herbs and strange blends of tobacco they called *kwsháhteew*, the Manteses and Atsayonck women in their beaded skirts and headbands, and the colorful shell necklaces that hung around their necks. Unlike the Onondaga, only a few women had tattoos. Mostly it was the men who wore them, with their intricate patterns of the wolf, turkey, and turtle.

They left the market and walked to the other end of the island, where a village stood on rocky terrain—the home of a large band of Minisink. They crossed into the commons where clusters of domed wikwams lined each side. Nushèmakw was surprised at how enthusiastically they were welcomed. She learned that her father, the Storyteller, was well known here, especially among the children. It was not yet winter, the season for storytelling, but her father stopped to tell them a few silly tales.

Signs of the wolf were everywhere. It was punched into their leather clothing, tattooed on their arms and legs, and carved into the wooden poles that stood close to the fire pit where slabs of deer and bear meat hung to smoke and dry.

Their neatly built wikwams looked so small to Nushèmakw. Her father explained that unlike her Onondaga longhouses, only the immediate family lived in these homes; mother, father, children. They had a few longhouses, where multiple families dwelled, but nothing the size of the Haudenosaunee. He pointed to a wikwam under construction on the other side of the commons. A young couple was almost finished lashing elm bark to the sapling poles that sloped inward to the chimney hole at the top. Family members worked on the opposite side, coating the bark with gray river clay, which would provide additional insulation during the winter months. Nushèmakw thought the whole thing looked like a giant beehive.

An elder mother led them to the home of their chief, Kíhkay. He rushed out to greet her father. "Achimwis! *Kwíinaweew. Wiítapóomeew.*" the Chief said.

Nushèmakw tugged on her father's arm.

"He said, 'Glad to see you.' He's invited us to stay with them."

"*Anúshiik.* Thank you," her father said. "*Ngíiskaweew ndáanus.* I'd like you to meet my daughter."

The Chief turned to her. "*Awéen éet há ná kwáy?*" he asked.

"He wants to know your name," her father said.

She pointed to herself. "Nushèmakw."

"Nushèmakw!" repeated the Chief with outstretched arms.

They walked across the village and were greeted warmly. Everywhere they went, they were offered irresistible food and drink. Nushèmakw devoured a bowl of bean soup and acorn bread. The cold water was every bit as tasty and refreshing as her water back home. By the time they ate their way across the village, they were too full to move. Her father courteously excused them, and he and Nushèmakw hiked up the narrow path that led to a small plateau overlooking the southern tip of the island. They needed to rest, and more then that, they needed to be alone for a while. Under a leaf-less copse of sugar maple, they could see the Lënapei Sipu sparkling in the late afternoon sun making its lazy journey to the land of the Unami, the People Down the River. Her father's people. Her people now too.

As the sun disappeared over the blue mountain ridge, Nushè-makw asked her father if they could sleep there under the stars. "No, Nushèmakw. That would offend our hosts. I'm sure they've already prepared a wikwam for us." They went back to the village and joined the Minisink around the fire.

⚜

1530 CE

GREEN BEAN MOON

Their Lenapé cousins treated them well. Chief Kíhkay invited Nushèmakw and her father to stay with them through the winter and into the growing season. They could use another hunter, he told her father, and the dogs would be a great help, too.

"I told Grandfather that if we could be of some help, we'd be honored to," her father said.

So they stayed on. Soon the autumn days turned cold. Frost coated the grass, and flurries of snow blew in off the river. The nights grew longer. Nushèmakw spent her time with the other children learning their songs and dances. It didn't take her long to make a new friend. Her name was Njó—an outgoing and talkative girl, who seemed to be a constant annoyance to her older sisters. Every time they shooed her away, which was most of the time, Njó would seek out Nushèmakw. There was no disputing that she talked a lot, but Nushèmakw was glad for her company anyway.

Winter settled in, and it was the time for storytelling. Every evening, Chief Kíhkay would call the people together, and her father would tell his stories. She loved the sound and cadence of her father's voice, and over time, she began to understand the Munsee language. By the midwinter moon, it was beginning to feel like home.

Nushèmakw spent many snowy afternoons with Njó in her wikwam trimming the deer hides in patterns her older sisters would later stitch into new leggings, skirts, and loincloths. On cloudless days, they'd head outside to grind corn in the wide basin of a log mortar, taking turns pounding the kernels with the heavy stone pestle. Other days, they'd help Njó's aunts gut and clean the game the men brought home, hanging strips of flesh to dry by the fire. No matter the task, Njó would talk as they went along, describing each and every step in detail, hardly taking a breath.

"Be quiet!" reprimanded one of her sisters. "You're driving us crazy."

Njó would become sullen for only a few short minutes. Then she'd turn to Nushèmakw and begin again, this time in whispers. Nushèmakw had to keep from laughing. She must have been the only one who liked this about Njó. Because of her friend, she was able now to speak a little Munsee herself, something she wouldn't have been able to do without her.

The end of winter brought the men back to the village. After they had rested and recuperated from their long hunting excursion, they turned their attention to clearing the land for planting. Early each morning, while the women were tending to the children, Nushèmakw could hear the men and boys out in the fields felling the trees they had girdled the year before. Soon Njó, Nushèmakw, and the other girls would join them, doing their part by dragging the dry boughs and branches back to the village to use for firewood.

By the time they had finished clearing the field, the ground had grown soft under the warmth of longer days. Now Nushèmakw and Njó spent their time preparing the ground for planting. It was hard work. In most places, the soil was shallow, riddled throughout with large rocks. Still, with the sharp edges of their stone hoes, she and the other girls were able to scrape the earth into the large mounds that would soon receive their seeds. Working next to Njó and her aunts, the feel of fresh loamy soil, and the smell of spring flooded Nushèmakw with thoughts of Sarhak. She would be in the fields now, too.

"I miss you, Aunt Sarhak," she whispered, holding back tears.

The heat of summer came early, bathing the Lënapei Sipu

with sunshine and rain. It was a bountiful season with bumper crops for the tribe. Nushèmakw and Njó spent endless days picking beans and squash and new corn until their fingers were sore.

The striped bass were running upriver. Her father left before dawn with the rest of the men to haul in their catch. The dogs went, too. They would be useful in helping to scare the fish into their large nets.

By afternoon the overcast sky had burned off, and the day grew hot. Njó helped Nushèmakw slather her skin with bear grease to keep her skin from burning and the bugs from biting.

Across the commons, the grandmothers were busy hanging the orange flesh of pumpkin and squash across lines strung in the sunshine. The first of the blue corn was spread out on large woven hammocks to dry. Younger children laced together bursting pods of shell beans that would later be cooked into stews or saved for the leaner winter months. By the time the summer solstice arrived, their stores were nearly overflowing. Nushèmakw smiled when she heard a grandmother say that her arrival at their village had been a good omen.

She woke the next morning to the sound of rain on her wik-wam. She watched the drops gather on the edge of the roof hole and fall to the floor. She stood and stretched and scratched her head. She missed the attention of her Onondaga aunts and sisters, who every day would patiently comb the knots and burrs from her long black hair. Now she simply patted it down in places, and did the best she could tying it back. When it became hopelessly tangled, she went outside to see if Njó would help her. She spotted Njó's mother stirring porridge in a large pot on the coals.

"Hello, Aunt Nŭmíis," she said. "Where's Njó?"

"I'm surprised she didn't tell you," she said, passing Nushèmakw a steaming bowl. "She left this morning with her aunt for the wiktut."

"Maybe she did tell me. It could be that I didn't understand her," she said in her broken Munsee.

The woman looked at Nushèmakw sympathetically. She sat down on a long flat stone and patted the place next to her. "Sit with me," she said in Onondaga.

Nushèmakw nearly spilled her soup. "You speak Onondaga!"

"Some, although I'm better at Mohawk. I'm one of the traders at the Minisink gateway post," she said, pointing northward toward the port where Nushèmakw and her father had first landed. "It's profitable for me to know Haudenosaunee. Some Algonquin doesn't hurt either. Fortunately for me, the season of trading is over. The men are all finally going home to fish and help with the harvest. I'm glad for a little rest."

"When will Njó be back?"

"Nushèmakw, the word 'wiktut' is Lenapé for 'menstrual lodge.' She and the other women in their moontime have gone there to stay for the duration of their cycle. You have the wiktut at home, no?"

"Yes, my sisters have a separate *hononchia*, too," she said, happy for once to be able to answer a question, "and because my aunt is a healer, I've seen it too. It's also where the babies are born. It's where I was born," she said.

"Well then, it looks like we have the morning to ourselves. The fields will need to dry a little before we can do any picking, and Njó won't be back for a few more days. This is a perfect time for bathing." She took Nushèmakw's empty bowl. "Go get your moccasins. You'll need them on the stony path to the pool."

By the time they arrived, more than a dozen other women and girls were already in the water. The deep pool looked black under the long hanging branches flush with leaves. A rocky bluff rose high on one side offering a number of excellent perches where the girls were hurdled themselves off a ledge, laughing and hollering, as they plummeted into the cold spring. Nŭmíis and Nushèmakw undressed and carefully stacked their cloths next to the others at the water's edge. Nŭmíis slipped into the pool with a satisfying sigh and closed her eyes.

"Nushèmakw!" shouted one of the girls, waving for her to come and join them. Growing up next to a creek at home, Nushèmakw was as comfortable in water as on land. She dove in and swam across. "Up here! Up here!" they yelled. She scaled the cliff's smooth gray face until she reached the highest ledge. One of the girls took her hand. They looked at each other and laughed, then flung themselves off the cliff, arcing through the sky and plunging into the startling cold depths. Nushèmakw could not remember ever being so happy.

They arrived back at the village hungry. The grandmothers wasted no time doling out deer stew from pots bubbling on the fire. The boys had already returned with their grandfathers, wet and exhausted from a similar outing.

Nushèmakw was about to sit down to eat when she jumped.

"What is it?" asked Nŭmíis.

"The rain's coming," Nushèmakw whispered. "Don't you feel the wind?"

The air hung heavy and motionless. Nŭmíis looked at Nushèmakw curiously. "No, Nushèmakw, there is no wind."

"I can smell it too." She looked past the village to the northern horizon where, not clouds, but a strange flickering light was gathering.

"What is it, Nushèmakw? What's bothering you?"

Nushèmakw was reluctant to speak with the other girls sitting so close by.

"Tell me in Onondaga. That way, the others won't understand you."

"I had a dream last night. I have a lot of dreams. Did you know that?"

"Yes, your father told me about your dreams. He too is a keeper of visions. But I can see that this one scares you."

"It does. It's a dream I have over and over," she said, drawing in the dirt with a piece of straw. "It still scares me." She searched Nŭmíis's face, which was an open bloom, inviting and caring. "I have an enemy. A boy in my Onondaga Turtle Clan. He's almost a man now, and he's growing meaner. He hates me because of what I did to him. Even though I was right to do it, still he hates me. He enters my dreams sometimes. He's looking for me." She was stabbing the ground now. "Last night, I dreamed that he found me. That he followed the thunder and then the rain and that was how he found me. I'm afraid of him, really afraid. What should I do?"

Nŭmíis put her arm around Nushèmakw. Thunder indeed rumbled in the distance now, with the smell of rain blowing in on its heels. "Do your people know about *Pethakowe*, our Grandfather Thunder?"

Nushèmakw shook her head. "No, not by that name."

"The Lenapé's believe that Pethakowe was father to the first people, and that the moon was our first mother. In the old days, Grandfather Thunder was the one who kept evil away from the earth so our people could live in peace. After a while, our people forgot about Grandfather Thunder, and he became insulted by this great disrespect. That's when the dangerous thunder and lightening came, burning villages and killing people. Since then though, we've come to love Grandfather Thunder again, and honor him with our rituals. In the spring, when we first hear the thunder, we know it's time to burn *kwsháhteew* and greet our Grandfather with respect. Now once again, he brings the rains and water to help our crops grow."

Dark clouds rolled in and the wind whipped up the dust. Nŭmíis hugged Nushèmakw a little closer. "So this is what I think," she continued. "Since this enemy of yours has not heard the story of Pethakowe, he must be living in an older time, stuck in his anger and resentment. He may follow Grandfather Thunder thinking he'll find you. But remember, Pethakowe is our friend now, our protector grandfather. I'm sure he will lead this enemy of yours in another direction, or he will calm his hateful heart."

Nushèmakw was not convinced, but with a full stomach and the warm arms of Nŭmíis around her, she felt safe enough.

1530 CE

BLUEBERRY MOON

Nushèmakw heard Snow and Black Paw before she saw them, first their barking, then the hammer of their stride as they galloped through the forest and into the Minisink village. Nushèmakw ran to greet the dogs, and they were overjoyed to see her. The men, back from their expedition, came next, hauling an impressive load of fish and mussels.

"Mama!" cried Njó. "Papa's home. Come on. Let's go!" She found her mother in their wikwam, and they both ran down the path to meet him.

Nushèmakw searched for her father. Finally she saw him at the end of the line talking with Chief Kíhkay. She didn't run to greet him as the other children did. Instead, she sat and waited, petting Snow. Unlike Njó, she wasn't sure if her father would be glad to see her.

He was taking his time. He and Chief Kíhkay were deep in conversation, and she could see that her father was troubled. When he spotted her, his face softened into a wide smile. "Come, my Nush-èmakw. Come and greet your father," he said with opened arms. She hugged him, and his skin smelled of sun and soil and dead fish. Black Paw wedged his way in between them and started licking her hand.

"I think he's jealous of me," her father said. She blushed, but felt a rush of pride, too, for being the daughter of Achimwis.

"So you'll talk with her?" the Chief said, more of a statement than a question.

"Yes," he answered, and the Chief walked away.

"What is it, Papa?"

He looked at her and knitted his brow. "I need to rest, Nushè-makw. Will you see if Nŭmíis will bring us some water and soup. Let's eat and rest. Then we'll talk."

They made a small fire up on their perch overlooking the river. The quiet was comforting. Her father held a twig in the flame and lit his pipe. She watched the smoke rise in blue furls through the branches and disappear in the sky beyond.

Finally he spoke. "Nushèmakw, you are a good and loyal daughter, and I know that soon, very soon, you'll grow into a fine woman." He paused and leaned back against the tree. "But because you're both Lenapé and Onondaga, you are different."

This came as no surprise to Nushèmakw. She'd felt different all her life.

"Because of this," her father continued, "some will say you belong to both tribes. But there are as many who would say you belong to neither."

"What do you say, Papa?"

He looked at the sky. "I say that the Great Spirit has a plan. You've been born with an extraordinary gift, Nushèmakw. It's your obligation to use it to help others. The world is changing rapidly. We must do all we can to see that the good outweighs the bad, no matter what lies ahead."

He paused again to smoke.

"I saw Atsi when we were fishing. We were pretty far north on the river, but still I was surprised to see him so close to Susquehan-nock territory. He'd been searching for me. He had bad news."

Nushèmakw listened.

"Atsi tells me that your cousin Guiarasi has finished his rites and is now a man. He has chosen to follow the path of an Onondaga warrior. Since the last Grand Council Meeting, he's lost favor with the Turtle Chief. No longer is Clan Mother considering him to succeed as the next Chief. She's told him that the new Chief will be a man of peace and reconciliation, not a man of violence. 'We have too many warriors already,' she told him. 'What we need now is a chief like the Great Peacemaker.'" He took a long draw off his pipe. "Clan Mother's right, of course."

Nushèmakw could feel it coming.

"The decision has poisoned Guiarasi. His mind is clouded, and he doesn't see straight. Now all he wants is violence and revenge. He blames you. Atsi told me that he has made a pact to find you and make you pay."

Nushèmakw's heart pounded and fear crept into her limbs.

"Don't worry, Nushèmakw. I'll make sure he doesn't find you. I have friends in unlikely places. I belong to everyone and no one, just like you, and it has served me well."

He smoked his pipe until the embers were cold.

"We leave tomorrow for our home among the Kechemeches."

She hadn't noticed that a storm had gathered upriver, but now she could hear the rolling thunder.

OWEN

❧

1529 AD

FEBRUARY

He sat at a desk in the library. It was a narrow space above the refectory with high vaulted ceilings and thick stone walls. Heavy wooden shelves overflowed with moldering manuscripts organized in a way Owen didn't understand. The top shelf held a single row of newly published books. Most of them had been printed abroad in Belgium or Paris, but there were some that carried the King's imprint from the publishing house in London. These were precious items secured with a lock and chain across their bindings.

His desk was stationed under a tall mullioned window that opened to a sprawling cloister on the backside of the friary grounds. Beyond this were the fields cultivated by the friars and their hired ploughmen, and further still lay the pastures where the flocks and cattle grazed.

The effort of the sun on the frozen earth was slight. Even in late afternoon, frost clung to the sage and holly bushes that grew along the wall. Two years had passed since that hot summer day when Owen first stepped onto the grounds at Greyfriar. How different his life was now. He'd hoped to spend his summers with the flocks, but instead the vicar only released him from the scriptorium to help in the fields. There he and the brothers would brandish scythe and sickle to make hay during the summer, and harvest wheat and barley in the fall, drying and threshing the sheaves heavy with grain. After planting the winter wheat, it was time to cull the flocks, and just like at home, his heart would ache as he loaded the oldest sheep onto the wagon for the trip to the slaughterhouse. By All Hallows Day, the heavy work was finished, the crops safely stored for winter use, and the excess meat and grain sent to the markets in Bristol to fetch a good price. This year had been particularly bountiful. Master Blazer would be pleased.

Owen rubbed his hands together to stave off the cold that seeped through the window's leaky muntins. Unlike the lowlands at Bentley, the wind here blew over the River Avon and up the hill with stubborn constancy. It was especially harsh on the pastures, where the flocks grazed contentedly, protected by their extraordinarily thick fleece.

A gust fingered its way through the window and caught the edge of his manuscript, sending it to the floor.

"Better get that before it gets soiled," Brother Michael warned as he bent over his work. "The last thing you want is for Father Elis to come and see you've had to start over."

Owen picked up the sheet and shook it gently. "No harm done, brother. It's dry." He placed it inside a similar page folded on his desk and arranged them neatly on top of the others. He anchored a fresh quire along the desk's grid, dipped his quill, and began.

Quid enim in hoc iudicio.

He leaned back eyeing his work making sure the baseline wasn't pitching upward as it tended to do.

What justice is there in this,...

He continued, nib to paper, shaping each character with resolve, careful to mimic the new Roman font so popular now among the presses in Europe. Once in awhile, they'd still be asked to write an official pronouncement or royal invitation in the traditional script, with all its flourish and embellishment, but Owen was glad those were few and far between. It was so much easier to write the letters in the blocky style of this modern typeface. Owen continued the Latin verse.

...that a nobleman, a goldsmith, a banker, or any other man, that either does nothing at all, or at best is employed in things that are of no

*use to the public, should live in luxury and splendor, upon what is so ill
acquired;...*

He paused and considered this. He had heard of this book
well before it was assigned to him, when the brothers were discuss-
ing it over supper one evening. It had begun easily enough, with the
friendly banter common among the friars. But then, their voices
gained volume and their passions rose up in defense of some particular or other. They eventually became so heated that the vicar had to
break it up and send them to their cells. Now Owen was beginning
to understand why.

*...and a mean man, a carter, a smith, or a ploughman, that works
harder even than the beasts themselves, and is employed in labours so
necessary, that no commonwealth could hold out a year without them,
can only earn so poor a livelihood, and must lead so miserable a life,
that the condition of the beasts is much better than theirs?*

The book had first been put to paper only ten years ago, a new
piece compared to the works of antiquity they were used to copying. This was unlike anything he had read before, and the words
came alive as his hand moved across the page. Who was this man,
Sir Thomas More, to speak in such a way, heralding his blasphemous
ideas from the highest tower rather than from the safety of dark
and hidden shelter? Who can speak so boldly and not pay for it?
Certainly not a shepherd, Owen was sure of that. *What would Master
Blazer think of this?* he thought, imagining his master going red in the
face with veins popping from his neck, tearing up the vile pages and
throwing them in the fire.

"You daydream too much, Brother Owen. Better get on with
it," Michael warned. "Another hour and it will be dark as pitch in
here."

The friar was right. While the light was perfect now, pouring
through the tall windows in diffuse golden rays, the sun was falling fast. He ran the pumice stone over the pages and powdered the
sheets, then added the quire to the bottom of the pile. One more and
he would be done. He bent over his work again.

But after the public has reaped all the advantage of their service, and they come to be oppressed with age, sickness, and want, all their labours and the good they have done is forgotten; and all the recompense given them is that they are left to die in great misery.

Owen stopped. Visions of his grandfather flew into his head. Why had he not realized this before? Now he saw that life could have been different for Grancha Hywel. All those years of service; all his knowledge and skill. How much had Grancha been responsible for Master Blazer's wealth? How little was he remembered? He thought about Grancha's last days in that dark room unable to breathe. Owen found he was having trouble breathing, too.

"Is something wrong, brother?" Michael asked.

"No, no. I'm sorry. Just a little something caught in my throat. I'm almost finished here." Owen blew on the wet ink. He wondered how Sir Thomas could create a story so fantastic—this fanciful island where all men lived together like brothers. In these times, even the friars found it difficult to live together without rivalry or deceit. It was an incredible notion. Owen allowed himself the pleasure to imagine what it might be like to live in such a world.

He dusted the last of the sixteen-page quire and added it to the others, tamping down the whole on the table until it aligned. The stack was sizable. Together they amounted to nearly three hundred pages, seventy sheets of folded vellum, the largest work he'd done so far. The language was simple enough, yet so beautiful in the author's Latin. Almost a decade old, and according to Brother Michael, the book was still a sensation everywhere but in Sir Thomas More's own England.

Father Elis opened the door. "How's it coming along, my sons?"

"Well enough," answered Michael. "I'm nearly done."

"Very well. And Owen?"

"I've finished."

Father Elis nodded, pleased with his apprentice.

"May I ask you a question, Father?"

"Always."

"I'm very interested in this work of Sir Thomas's. Brother Michael tells me it's popular all over Europe and sells well at the publishing houses there. So why do you need a manuscript when so many books have already been printed?"

"It's a good question, Owen. It's our King Henry who is critical of Sir Thomas and his book, and he doesn't care to see this kind of thing circulating throughout his kingdom. In fact, he forbids it being translated into English," Father Elis told him. "That's why I've asked you to copy them in Latin. We must please the King when it's possible.

"If the King doesn't like it, then why copy it at all?" Owen was stepping lightly. He didn't want to offend Father Elis, but he was afraid to disobey the King. He had seen what happened to men accused of less.

"Because some of the old manuscripts are being moved from Oxford to the library of Erasmus of Rotterdam where they'll be better cared for. Sir Thomas wants to help Erasmus preserve the original parchments. I told him I would help."

"You know Sir Thomas More?" Owen asked, amazed.

The friar smiled. "Yes, Owen, I know him well. We met years ago at a time when he was considering a career among the friars. But God had other plans, and so did his father. He left Oxford to go to London, where he studied law instead. Yet he has never abandoned the faith and God's call to service. You'll not find another advisor to nobility who argues a case with such consideration for the weak and the poor. In any event, he's a good friend who has asked me a favor. You have made this copy for our library in Oxford and I will send the original to Erasmus. After all, there is no harm in creating a replacement."

Owen wasn't so sure.

"Brother Michael," Father Elis said. "When you're finished, bring your manuscript and Owen's down to me."

"Yes, Father. I will."

"And Owen, you are free to spend the rest of the evening tending the flock. You've done well."

"Thank you, Father."

The light was fading from the room when he slipped the old

parchment on top of his own finished copy, securing it tightly with string and wax.

The air was cold out on the pasture that evening, scoured by the bitter wind off the river. The dark sky was endless, an infinite stage for the stars that danced across it. It was late, yet Owen lingered. The sheep were cold and ready to bed down, but the chill was not so severe that they'd feel the bite of frost. He stayed longer, gazing at the black River Avon as it drifted past Greyfriar on its faithful pilgrimage west to the bay at Môr Hafren. Out there, where the river met the sea, the moon broke free of the horizon, her magnificent orb rising gently in the night. He wondered if his father saw her too.

Although his assignment was finished, the words lingered, gnawing at his heart like biting midges. Over and over in his mind, he laid that fabled island of Sir Thomas More's against Hy-Brasil. There was no way to avoid thinking they might be one and the same. Both talked of a mysterious hidden island west of the continent, difficult to find among the dangerous barrier reefs that hugged its shoreline. Both had rivers running straight through them. A place where people had dwelled for thousands of years in the contentment of God's grace and glory.

He thought of his father and wondered if he had survived, like his Uncle Seamus claimed was possible. It had been more than two years since he asked his uncle for the truth. At first, Owen had refused to believe it. Now, with all he had learned and all he had seen, he began to wonder. He remembered his uncle that night, the story he told, and the way the light from the fire showed the sadness that wrecked his creased and weary face. How he told Owen that the ship had lost her way. Drifting haplessly, they stayed trapped in unending doldrums with a listless ceiling of clouds blotting out the stars that guided them.

And so it began, his uncle had said. "The night was thick and dark and heavy. We were desperate men. We'd gone through our stores and were near crazy with hunger and thirst. That's when it happened."

Through that dark impenetrable night came a soft illumination on the water, then a gathering mist. With the ocean still as glass, the vision appeared before the startled men, rising from the blinding fog in brilliant splendor. "We all stood gaping at it, unable to move," his uncle said. "All but your father. He knew at once that it was Hy-Brasil. He called the crew together. Right there on the deck, with the men as witnesses, he turned the ship over to me. But he had one more command before he gave her up. He commanded the men to drop the cockboat that was tethered portside. He boarded it just as the island loomed over us shining like the heavens. He was a madman now, rowing feverishly toward the island until he vanished into the glare of the rolling mist."

His uncle had stood then and faced the smoky fire, lost in the memory.

"The storm blew in fast after that, with unrelenting gales battering the ship's lateen sails before the crew could lower them. Huge swells came at us pitching us to and fro, and nearly washing us off the deck. The hail began to fall like daggers and tore the square sails. The wind hit again, harder this time, and before we knew it, we were swept further out to sea. As fast as the squall came, it left us. In just minutes the sky opened up to the shine of morning, the blue sky falling on an empty ocean. The island was gone. So was your father."

It seemed like a lifetime ago since he sat in his uncle's cabin that night. Uncle Seamus had told Owen that he believed his father had made it to the island and was living there still. He intended to find out, his uncle said, even if it took him the rest of his life.

Owen pulled the hood of his robe over his shaved head to stave off the cold, thankful for the extra layers he thought to wear under his cassock before he went out. "Teg!" he called with a whistle. The corgi came trotting up the hill toward him. "Let's gather the sheep. It's time to go home."

The next morning was bright and blue, with a cloudless sky that washed the courtyard with pale winter light. Owen ran through the gate and called to the friar who was harnessing a couple of old mules to a cart.

"Brother Jonathan! Hold up a moment," Owen called. "Can you take me to town with you?"

"Sure I can, brother, if the vicar doesn't mind you being gone most of the day. I've got a pile of stuff for the smithy to mend, and that's bound to take awhile."

"Father Elis is still in London. Until he returns, I've got nothing much to do."

"Climb aboard then." Jonathan snapped the reins, and Owen fell into the seat. "What business do you have in Bristol?" Jonathan asked.

"I'm hoping to visit my Uncle Seamus. It's been a long time since I've seen him, He was due back on *The Mary Margaret* a few days ago. Have you any word of her making it to port?"

"No I haven't heard, but I don't hear much of anything that goes on outside the walls of Greyfriar. The boatman will know."

They rolled down the rutted path and through the gate. The load was light, and the mules made good time crossing the field to the wide lane that led to the river.

"What are you and Brother Michael working on up there?" Jonathan asked. "Seems like you've been holed up in the scriptorium forever. Look at you. Your face has gone all pasty from lack of sunshine. What've you done wrong to earn a sentence like that?"

Owen smiled. "Brother Michael and I are helping Father Elis transcribe old letters and church texts for the library at Oxford. It takes a long time."

"Transcribe? What do you mean by that?"

"It means taking something written down and either copying it in its own language or writing it down in another language."

"You can write in other languages?"

"Yes."

"How'd you manage that, Owen ap Madoc? A simple boy born in the same village as me?"

"My grandfather taught me."

The boatman had just docked the punt when they arrived, and they waited while he tied it off.

"Jenkyn, have you heard if *The Mary Margaret* has come in?" Jonathan asked, while the boatman opened the gate to let the passengers off.

"Yes she has," he said. "Got in last eve. Had a helluva load too. Took most of the night for the crew to empty her, so many furs there

were. Don't know, but it seems this New Found Land they keep
sailing to has more animals than any place in kingdom come. Those
poor creatures must march right onto the boat to be slaughtered and
skinned."

"Was Seamus Llewellyn on deck?" Owen asked.

"He was indeed."

It was low tide, and the docks smelled like rotting fish. He
passed *The Mary Margaret*, which was moored fast to the slip, her stern
groaning against the tension of the lines. Even though the passage
of time and her many long voyages had left her worn and tarnished,
she was still a regal vessel. He followed the docks along the wharf
to a footpath that veered inland. Up ahead, a number of small huts
were clustered beside a large open shed with ropes, nets, tackle, and
other gear strewn all around it. He walked up to his uncle's hut and
knocked.

"Who in bloody hell is it this time in the morning!"

"It's Owen, Uncle Seamus."

Owen heard the pad of stocking feet rush to the door. It flew
open, and before he knew it, his uncle's arms were around him so
tightly, he nearly cracked a rib.

"My God! It's really you," Seamus said, holding Owen at arm's
length. Owen could see him struggle with tears. "What have they
done to you, boy? Just look at you. A priest now among a family of
sailors and shepherds?"

Owen laughed. "Good to see you too, uncle. But I am not a
priest, I'm a friar."

"Ah, they've made you a father then?" he said, showing Owen
through the door.

"No, not a father. A brother. Not even a brother, really. Not
officially. I've not taken all the vows."

"Good boy. Keep 'em guessing. That's what I say. Why didn't
you take the vows?"

"Of the three, there was one that I wouldn't accept. For me,
the vows of poverty and obedience were easy. What shepherd hasn't
already learned these things? But chastity?" Owen shook his head
while his uncle roared. "I know, I know," he said, "but I'm not as cor-

rupt as you think. There are brothers who have fallen to it, and some are so brazen that they don't even try to hide it. But I've not been tempted that way. Besides, I've promised Father Elis that while I'm at Greyfriar, I'd be chaste. He knows I hope to leave there soon, find a wife, and raise a family. Even so, he said as long as I'm living among the friars, I need to look like one." Owen tossed off his hood, and his bald head shined through a fringe of chestnut locks.

Seamus stared at him and smiled. "You look ridiculous."

His uncle rekindled the fire and hung a pot of water over it. "Try a bit of this," he said pulling a small, netted pouch from his pocket that he dropped into the kettle. "Traded for it at the dockyard yesterday. Came from a merchant round ship from Venice. All the way from Porta Magna, they said. Well, this vessel had a troubled time coming to port. Must have been her first time through Môr Hafren because she was crazy enough to catch the riptide hard on her starboard. Sent her bobbing and listing something awful. Looked to me like a bucking stallion out there. We watched while she dropped her sails and sculled her way into the bay, which was hopeless. Then my men and I took the cutter and went out to get her. The crew was grateful. The captain took me aboard and insisted on compensating our generosity. Down in his cabin, he showed me a stash of precious powders he'd collected from the Turks, who he said control the waterways along the Red Sea. He took the time to tell me what each and every spice was, and in English that was better than mine," Seamus said slapping his knee. "He asked me to choose one, a gift from his country to mine. So I took this," he pointed to the kettle steaming over the coals. "They call it coffee. You're supposed to brew it."

Owen held his nose.

"I know. I think it stinks too. It smells better once it has steeped for a while. And it's best to shore it up with honey."

Seamus poured some into Owen's cup. Owen held the mug between his hands and took a sip. "Ew," he said. "It's bitter stuff."

Seamus handed him the honey pot. "Here, sweeten it up a bit more."

Even sweet it was awful stuff. Owen choked it down anyway to spare his uncle's feelings.

Seamus poured himself another cup. "So before I left, this Venetian captain unlocked a drawer that was built into the side of his cot and pulled out a scroll. He unrolled it onto a table anchoring its corners with what appeared to be precious stones. It was a beautiful thing no bigger than the maps I carry onboard, but this was nothing like I'd ever seen before. It was gilded and painted, bold and precise. The compass rose alone was a work of art, with fine lines and amazing detail. A master had created this, I was sure of it. I peered down to get a closer look and could see that it charted the continent in a peculiar way. 'Who did this?' I asked the man. He said it is a new map by the Turkish master Piri Reis. 'I want you to have it, Captain Llewellyn,' the man said, 'for saving our ship and for the debt I owe Madoc ap Morcant.'"

Uncle Seamus was talking so fast, Owen was having trouble keeping up.

"Those were his exact words: 'for the debt I owe Madoc ap Morcant.' That means he knew your father! Come over here." He led Owen to the other side of the room. He pulled the scroll from a low rafter. "I want to show it to you." Opening it with the greatest care, he weighted it to the table. "What do you see?"

"I see a beautiful map, crisp and clean as you described." Owen leaned in. "The continent is well defined. So is your Ireland. Scotland too. Here's old Wales and England. But what's this?" he said pointing across the parchment.

"That's the new world, my boy, look at it. Think of it. That's New Found Land up this way, and this is said to be the course Columbus tracked not long ago." He ran his finger along the strange and endless coastline. "Look here," he said pointing to the middle of the ocean. "Do you see that? That's Hy-Brasil, clear as day."

Owen gasped. "What? Hy-Brasil so far west?"

"According to the Venetian captain, she can be and she is. The other maps are wrong. This man knew all about Hy-Brasil, and he knew that your father was looking for her. So he brought this map to me." He rolled it up. "Hold your tongue about it, Owen. I mean it, not a word. But in the spring of 1534, when she's appointed to appear again, we will sail. And this time we shall find her!"

Owen and Brother Jonathan returned to Greyfriar barely in time for vespers. They stabled the mules and flew across the cloister with their robes flapping behind them, slowing only when they arrived at the chapel steps.

The villagers were still filing in, old women, most of them, with their white bonnets and starched aprons tied across thick woolen skirts. Owen took his place with the other friars in the front pews. As the brothers began to chant, low rays filtered through the stained glass, casting blue and red patterns on the floor.

Deus, in adiutorium meum intende. Domine, ad adiuvandum me festina. Gloria Patri, et Fílio, et Spirítui Sancto.

He listened as they sang, the echoes full and resounding in his ears.

Sicut erat in princípio, et nunc et semper, et in saecula saeculorum. Amen. Alleluia.

From the pulpit, Father Andrew announced the evening hymn and psalmody, and the parishioners dutifully launched into song. Owen held back, closed his eyes and felt the sound rise to the clerestory and fall upon him in waves. Father Andrew began the Bible reading, droning on in his familiar way. Then came the *Magníficat*, the Canticle of Mary, Owen's favorite part of the evening.

Magníficat anima mea Dominum, et exsultavit spiritus meus in Deo salvatore meo, quia respexit humílitatem ancíllae suae.

He had heard it so many times, this beautiful piece. The Blessed Virgin's praise to the Lord God, and it always settled him. The sun hugged the horizon and shined through the stained glass window. It was the Madonna, the light catching on the leaded glass. The singing continued while he stared at her, the blues and golds and greens blending one into the other, and falling across him in splendid repose. Mary's face grew dark against the backlit window, her hair a black mane tumbling from her halo, down her neck, and across her breast. Then the incense came, floating billows of smoke, a sacred screen across the dimming light. What was this scent? Not the sage or rosemary he was accustomed to. Maybe it clung to the parishioners who were taking the Holy Sacrament or maybe it leaked in from the open doors, but the incense that swirled and tumbled through the light, gathering in a cloud above the Virgin, this incense was unlike anything he'd ever encountered before; its fragrance sweet and smoky, pungent and peppery all at the same time. He pondered this in the wondrous calm of the chapel. The parishioners departed, dusk gave way to dark, and Owen ap Madoc watched the Virgin fade slowly into the endless night.

NUSHÈMAKW

※

1532 CE

GREEN CORN MOON

They baked in the stifling sun as they made their way downriver. Nushèmakw dipped her arms in the water and splashed her face.

"Don't tip the canoe," admonished Uma, her Kechemeches grandmother. It was nearing Nushèmakw's first moontime cycle, and they were on their way down the sluggish Atsayunk River to the wiktut.

"But I'm hot," Nushèmakw said.

"I know. So am I. We're almost there. It'll be cooler under the trees."

The river wound and coiled endlessly. Even in the oppressive heat, Nushèmakw was enthralled by the new sights and sounds opening up before her. Cicadas, hiding in the protection of the woods, screamed their shrill vibrato, and the impossibly yellow finches swooped and dove through the bushes, busy building their summer nests. Oddly, the further they traveled down the river, the shorter and shorter the trees became, until Nushèmakw felt like a giant among them.

"Why are these trees stunted, Grandmother?"

"These are special trees. A gift from Earth Mother Kahèsëna Hàki," Uma said. "The pines may be small, but they're sturdy. Their bark is so thick it can withstand anything."

Uma told her that these trees were full of pitch, and that every few decades, they'd catch fire from a lightening strike and burn to the ground. "It's the heat from the fire that opens the pinecones so the seeds will fall and regrow. It takes a fire to keep them going. It takes very little time for them to sprout again and for Kahèsëna Hàki to grow a whole new forest."

Nushèmakw looked across the river and over the flat plains where the squat pines stretched as far as she could see.

"But Grandmother, these don't look like seedlings. Their trunks are too thick."

"I know. We haven't had a fire in a long time."

They pulled the canoe ashore and hiked a short distance to the edge of a cranberry bog, where the wiktut stood along a pool of water under the shady boughs of a red oak. To Nushèmakw's relief, the sun had finally fallen behind the tree line and the glare off the water had retreated. She and Uma bathed in the pool's cool dark water and watched the white light of summer fade to gold.

"It won't be long now, Nushèmakw, before you start your ritual," reminded Uma.

"I know. It makes me nervous to think about it."

"You'll do fine. You're not the only one who will go through it."

"But I'm the only one among my sisters who will."

"That's true, but there are years when other women in our family have done so. It doesn't happen often, but it does happen. Especially for the *nëntpíkes* medicine women."

"Did you go through the ritual?"

Uma looked across the river with a gaze that held deep memories. "Yes, Nushèmakw, I did. It was a long time ago. I was about your age when I undertook it, but my naming ceremony was much earlier, when I was only four years old. But since you are Onondaga, it's only now that you've been able to be named. When you receive your real name, you'll be officially adopted into our Kechemeches family."

Nushèmakw felt reassured knowing that Uma had gone where she was now asked to go. Unburdened by worry, if only for a while, she floated in the pool and stared at the sky until the sun went down.

Nushèmakw left the wiktut cleansed and purified. She and Uma canoed across the river to the sacred mound where her father and Chief Kitakima were waiting in their ceremonial dress. They climbed the rise to where a small fire was laid.

"Are you prepared?" her father asked.

"As much as I'll ever be, I suppose."

He hugged Nushèmakw and led her over to the fire ring where Chief Kitakima was transferring hot coals to a large ceramic pot. Uma took some kelekenikàn from her medicine bundle and sprinkled it into the coals as a gift to Grandfather Fire before she offered her prayer.

"Grandfather Fire," she said, "with this kelekenikàn, I am seeking your kinship and help. Clean our hearts and our minds. Help us in this ancient custom of name-giving. Befriend and help our daughter as she becomes known to the Spirit World by her real name."

Uma handed the medicine bundle to the Chief. He filled the ceremonial pipe, touched a firestick to the coals, and lit the pipe. He handed the pipe to Uma, and facing east, she puffed on the pipe four times. Then she looked upward at the Creator and prayed.

"Our Father, Creator of us all, from this day hence, please recognize our daughter who is being named *Nushèmakw*. Take care of *Nushèmakw* all of her days on this earth. Give her good health and happiness. Let her be known throughout the Spirit World as *Nushèmakw*. She is now and forevermore will be known as *Nushèmakw*—The Mother Tree."

Uma handed the pipe to Nushèmakw. She faced east and took four puffs, then handed it to Chief Kitakima, who did the same. Uma sprinkled red cedar in the pot of coals sending up wafts of aromatic smoke. She took her eagle feather fan and guided the smoke over Nushèmakw's outstretched palms, then handed the fan to her father, who did the same.

Uma faced Nushèmakw. "Granddaughter, you have smoked the pipe, and thereby have accepted your real name. You are forevermore *The Mother Tree*, and forevermore an adopted daughter of the Kechemeches Turkey Clan," she announced. She handed Nushèmakw a beautifully beaded medicine bundle containing all she would need to begin her ritual journey.

Nushèmakw carefully placed the bundle's leather cord around her neck. "Thank you, Grandmother. I will cherish it always. And I have a gift for you," she said.

She handed Uma a small bag she had prepared for this occasion. "Grandmother," she said, "please accept my gift of tobacco and a string of Wampum. I am humbled and grateful."

Her father stepped forward and smiled. "You're one of us now, my daughter. It's time to celebrate with a feast.

And they did feast, well into the evening. Nushèmakw felt both gratitude and satisfaction at becoming a part of something so much bigger than herself. She slept soundly that night and woke ready to start the fast that would begin her ritual journey.

Uma was up early to start a new fire and prepare the smudge pot with fresh coals. After once again purifying Nushèmakw with the cedar smoke, she painted Nushèmakw's eyelids and cheeks in intricate red patterns. At the fire ring, Chief Kitakima was ready to begin. He shook the turtle shell rattle while her father beat the drum. The invocation started with a call and response—a prayer sent up first by Kitakima and repeated by Achimwis. Over and over again, the prayers were released skyward until the air was filled with the sounds and vibrations of the sacred song. Then the men performed the ritual dance circling the fire counterclockwise. When Kitakima was satisfied that all was done according to tradition, he approached Nushèmakw.

"My daughter," he said softly, "your initiation begins now with *linkwehëlan*, the ritual fast. Go forth with all the blessings that Earth Mother and the Great Spirit have bestowed upon you. You have three days to return."

She received an embrace first from Chief Kitakima, then from Uma. And when her father hugged her, she cried.

"You can do this, Nushèmakw. Remember that there are good spirits in this world and beyond who will be looking out for you," he whispered. "And so will I."

Nushèmakw nodded. "I know, Papa." The sun was dim in the western sky when she grabbed her small pack and medicine bundle and headed down the hill. She took one last glance over her shoulder. It seemed a long time before the sounds of the rattles and chanting had disappeared in the distance between them. She continued east through the pine forest, following the white sand that cut a clean trail along the narrowing Atsayunk River. With the sun warm on her back, she dipped her hands into the tea-colored water, quenched her thirst, then retreated to a protected moss-laden hollow to camp the night. The duff was especially thick here and very dry. It crunched underfoot as she made her way to a soft springy nest between two large rocks. She lay down and watched the Star Path emerge from the cloudless sky, glad to have made it even this far in her ritual journey.

Dappled light greeted her the next morning. The air was un-usually cool, and a soft breeze had kept the dew from settling on the ground. She sat with nothing much to do except listen to the chatter of waking blue jays and robins. Without a meal to prepare for herself and her brothers and sisters, she felt a void. Across the river she saw a thick haze rising along the edge of the water. "It's the *Wemahtekēnisàk*, and they've already lit their pipes!" She grabbed her medicine bag and flew down to the river to join the small Earth Spirits before they disappeared.

By the time she got there, only one remained. A little man half her size sat lost in thought with his back toward her and his head shrouded in smoke. She approached carefully so not to disturb him.

"Come, Nushèmakw. I know you're there. You can't fool me. Smoke some kelekenikàn with me so that our thoughts will be as one."

"How do you know my name, dear Wemahtekënis?" she asked. She found a place next to him on the soft needle-laden ground. "Have we met before?"

Wemahtekënis chuckled, "Of course not. Very few humans have met me. I'm the Keeper of the Forest, and as such I know about everyone who passes through these woods. Now light your pipe and we'll begin. I'll not wait forever."

Nushèmakw did as she was instructed, removing the small pipe and pouch she had tucked away in her medicine bag. When she had filled and tamped the bowl, the little man lit the kelekenikàn and then fell into silence. As quietly as she could, she drew on the pipe stem, coaxing a small ember. Soon a fragile plume of smoke curled upward and drifted overhead.

A long time passed before he spoke again. "Very few women

smoke the pipe. Your smoke is much different from your brothers. And so go your thoughts."

"Really?"

"Of course. Otherwise I wouldn't have said it."

She looked up. Through the canopy of pine, she could see the sky slowly changing. Where only a short time ago, it had been blue and clear, thin wisps had moved in, then clouds so thick they obscured the sun. When her pipe had gone out and Wemahtekënis made no effort to relight it, she stood to go.

"Wait!" he shouted loud enough to echo off the water. "Sit down. I'm not through with you. Do you see those clouds? Before long they will darken as the night, and Grandfather Thunder will send his lightening. It will strike the ground exactly where you're sitting. You're afraid of thunder, no?"

"Yes, I am, and I'm tired of being afraid. What should I do, Wemahtekënis?"

The little man tapped the ashes from his pipe and returned it to the pouch around his neck. "I know your story, Nushèmakw. We've been waiting for you. The mother of many lands. The one who has traveled from our forest realms in the north through our stony cliffs in the east, and now you've come south to live among us. The girl afraid of thunder. The girl who runs from her enemy."

"You know about Guiarasi?"

"I do." He stood, and the top of his head barely cleared her waist. "Remember this, Nushèmakw. The Great Spirit uses your Onondaga cousin, Guiarasi, to test you. These tests aren't easy. And there are harder tests to come. Hard times are upon us all. These woods and the beings within, this domain of the Keepers of the Forest will be with the Lenapé for only a short time longer. Soon there will be such a disturbance that Earth Mother Kahèsëna Hàki will come for the Keepers and carry us home to realms impossible for you to breach. There is no more time for your fear, dear Nushèmakw. You must face your fear, and in that way it will let go of you."

"Do you mean I must face Guiarasi?"

He shook his head. "Guiarasi is merely a man who has allowed himself to be consumed by dangerous forces. You must move quickly now. Time is running out. Continue east until you can go no further.

Then swim across the river where it narrows at the marsh bay. There you'll find a small island known to the Wemahtekënisàk as Little Turtle Island. The island will protect you from what's coming. When fear arrives, stand and face it. It will come from the northwest as a raging wind. Then a great and terrible fire will consume all the land. Little Turtle Island will be immune to the fire, and it is there that you will stand and face what's coming. When the wind and flames retreat, the animals, my animals, will come to you seeking shelter and guidance. Then you will return to your village, and a new peace will come upon you, but only for a short time. When the new moon passes over twice as many times as the fingers on your hand, then a darkness will return once again. When it does, return to your island and face it. This time, it will blow in from the east. In time, it will reveal your destiny."

Before the last words left his mouth, a giant crack of lightening charred the sky and shook the ground. "We are out of time. Go! In the realms of all that is sacred, you are a girl no longer. You are Nushèmakw. You are The Mother Tree. Now Go!"

The lightening fell all around her. She got up to run, and a blinding bolt struck the rock where she'd been sitting. The shock passed straight through her. The crashing thunder tore the ground from under her feet. She moved as fast as she could, stumbling over the tangled mounds of brush and bramble that covered the forest floor. Again and again the lightning crashed, and she could hardly see through its blinding light.

Then it started. In the path in front of her, the underbrush began to smoke. In an instant, it burst into flame. Out of nowhere, a powerful gale rolled in behind her, whipping over the dry brush, and igniting a thousand small fires in its wake. Flames sprouted under her feet. She leaped away as they jumped into the trees above her. Behind her, the pine forest was covered in monstrous tongues of licking fire. Feasting on the infinite expanse of pitch and debris, the fire grew higher and higher while the thunder roared. She covered her ears against the deafening peals and ran as fast as she could down the path to the river.

The flames followed close behind. She could feel the scorching heat on her back. She ran and ran until the woods opened to a bend in the river that spilled into the marsh bay. She dove into the brackish water that was already venting steam from the firestorm. She swam, pumping her arms furiously and staying under as long as she could to keep the hot air from burning her. When her feet touched down on the sandy bank on the other side of the river, and with her lungs bursting with smoke and exhaustion, she turned and beheld the sight.

The spectacle that lay before her was horrifying. All of Lenapehokink was ablaze. As far as she could see, sweeping billows of white smoke choked the sky. Angry flames tore through the forest fueled by the western wind blowing relentlessly through the trees. A colossal wall of fire rose up and charged across the land consuming everything in sight. It was heading right toward her.

Then suddenly, like a caged beast, the blaze stopped in its tracks and hovered over the shoreline. The stubborn Atsayunk was not to be thwarted. The river had cut a deep line of demarcation in the fire's path. The inferno towered over it spewing sparks and blackening sand, leaving nothing but splintered char across the boiling water that lapped the shore. Farther out, the fire still raged over the mainland that buckled and fell before its unforgiving advance. The deafening roar of the wind carried the blistering heat across the water. Nushèmakw scrambled up the beach to the protection of Little Turtle Island.

She found a place to lie down under the cover of a gigantic white pine. She stared up into its spiraling branches dancing in the cool breeze, grateful for the protection against the terror taking place only a short distance away. The ancient tree, with its trunk spanning the reach of twenty men, was planted firmly along the wide bowl of an odd rock formation that circled the island. It was this ridge of rock that for centuries had protected this magnificent tree and everything else the basin contained. No amount of fire could climb it, no amount of water could crest it. Wemahtekënis had told her the truth. Little Turtle Island would protect her. This tree—so like the sacred pine at her Onondaga home—would protect her. Overcome with fatigue, she relaxed into the pine's soft and welcoming bed and fell asleep.

"Is it she?" said the first one, so softly Nushèmakw could barely understand. "Is it The Mother Tree?"

"Yes," said the second one.

"It's a good name, The Mother Tree. When I'm a mother tree I love to let my nimble branches dance in the breeze."

"And when the wind blows hard, The Mother Tree will bend. She will not break."

"Who's there?" Nushèmakw called out.

"Earth Mother Kahèsëna Hàki is here. And so am I," said the second one.

"Who are you?"

"I am who I am. Who are you?"

"I'm Nushèmakw." She sat up. "I must go. My home is on fire!"

"Don't worry, Nushèmakw. It's not burning anymore," said Kahèsëna Hàki. "There's no more thunder left in Grandfather. Now he only sends rains. The fire's gone. Come with us."

Nushèmakw floated out from under the formidable boughs of the white pine and followed them through the tall grasses that swayed rhythmically in the moonlight. Cascades of tiny white flowers bloomed across the fertile ground shining like a million stars along the top of the ridge.

"Sit here between us, Nushèmakw," Kahèsëna Hàki said. "Tell us what you see."

The ridge sloped gradually down to the lowlands below it, a patchwork of sand and marsh and bog that cut through with channels where it met the river. The moonlight on the water reflected the grandeur of all the heavens. She felt like she was flying.

"Look!" Nushèmakw said.

Rising up from the mud and sand were untold numbers of fireflies winking their secret message. As they pushed out and over the charred remains of the forest, the river began to rumble and splash, churning and roiling.

"What's that?"

Kahèsëna Hàki laughed. "It's the animals. I've told them to come to the island. Their homes are in ruins, and so they've fled. They're coming here, Nushèmakw. I've told them that The Mother

Tree will shelter them until they can go home again."

"You need to help them, Nushèmakw. They'll be safe here," said the other one.

"But who *are* you?"

A stillness fell upon her unlike anything she had felt before.

"I am the sky and the stars, the sun and the moon, the earth and the rivers and the rain. I am each passing day. I am time itself."

"But where do you live?"

"I live in the hearts of my people."

"Which people? I'm the daughter of many people. Do you live in me?"

"I live in everyone and in everything, everywhere. Yes, I live in you, The Mother Tree, the mother of many lands."

"Wemahtekënis called me that. I remember. He called me 'the mother of many lands' too."

"I am Wemahtekënis. I am all things."

"Then who am I?"

"You are Nushèmakw and The Mother Tree and the mother of many lands. Be at peace, my little one. Who you are is a gift. You travel many lands because you are many lands. You are the daughter of many and you are the mother of many. Because you willingly walk the path I have chosen for you, and because you heed my words without fear or malice, from this day forward, it is I who you will see in everyone and everything you encounter. Go forth, The Mother Tree. The animals are waiting for you."

Nushèmakw woke slumped against the giant pine. The sun had risen over the ridge, filling the whole basin with golden light. The dream was still with her, but like the stars fading from the sky, it was beginning to disappear. From where she sat under the tree, she could see the entire bowl of the basin lush with long grass and meadow flowers. A wide creek flowed through its center, and chokeberry and sassafras and cedars flourished along its sandy banks. She was curious to learn what else was growing down there. When she stood to go, it was as if the island itself had come alive. Suddenly, every kind of creature that ever walked the forest began to show itself. Scores of rabbits, chipmunks, squirrels, and turkeys were flushed from the grasses, startled by the larger animals wedging past. Redwing black-birds, robins, jays, and cardinals burst from the ground and charged the sky, their wings a rush of color against the brightening horizon. Now the otters came, the beavers, and the snakes, all scurrying as fast as they could, out of the flowing creek, finding a way back to their watery homes across the bay.

It's happening just as Wemahtekënis promised, she thought. *I must offer up the prayers to help them!* She reached for her pouch but it was sopping wet. There would be no smudge or pipe to light today. So instead she sang her favorite song. The one she sang to the fawn that lost its mother. The one she sang to the bog swans before they left for the north country. And it was the one she sang to the little bear cubs she saved from her cousin Guiarasi. With each passing verse, she sang a little louder until she could hear her voice echo through the basin. Go now, my little ones, she sang. Go now to your home in the bay, your dam along the river, your den beneath the ground. Go. Kahèsë-na Hàki is waiting for you. Go now, GO!"

She sang it over and over, and all the animals—swallows and warblers, beetles and moths, deer and heron—found their way up the sloping hollow and over the ridge back to their pineland home.

A dark shadow passed over her and she looked up to see if a cloud had covered the sun. The sky was clear. Suddenly, from behind the huge trunk of the sacred pine, came the largest black bear she had ever seen. He moved toward her slowly, casting his giant skull this way and that. Then he stood on his haunches and roared.

"I won't budge, Maxkwe," she said. "I'm not afraid of you." His great bulk quivered with each step. He circled her several times and then sat down.

"It's time to go, Maxkwe," she told him. "Look at the others. They're leaving now. It's time to go home."

The bear looked away.

She cocked her head. "Maxkwe, are you protecting me?"

The bear moved a little closer.

"Oh Maxkwe! Has Kahèsëna Hàki sent you to be my Guardian Spirit? Has she?"

He looked up at her.

She stretched out an arm and extended her hand. He bowed

his head, and she scratched the fur between his thick brows. She gently took the beast's massive head between her hands and pressed her forehead against his. She closed her eyes.

"My dear friend," she whispered to him. "Now I understand that you watched over me while I slept, and you kept me from any harm. I will always be grateful. But it's time now for you to go back to your forest home, and I must return to mine. The fire is gone. I'll be all right now, Maxkwe. And so will you."

The bear growled softly.

"Oh, my dear Maxkwe. Please, you mustn't worry. I promise you, we'll meet again. I'll know how to find you when the time is right. I'm sure of it."

The bear licked Nushèmakw's hand, then lumbered across the grassy field, up the side of the ridge, and disappeared into the forest.

1534 CE

SUGAR MOON

It had been almost two years since Nushèmakw had returned to the village from Little Turtle Island, and still her purpose felt unfinished, even more so in her father's absence. It was nearing the end of hunting season, and he had left with the men on one last expedition. He was the one who kept her grounded, and reassured her that she walked a true path. Whenever he left to hunt or fish or travel to other lands to tell his stories, doubt began to seep in. She had to remind herself that Wemahtekënis had been right about everything. As he predicted, her family was spared the destruction of the fire, which had surrendered to the torrential rain before it reached their village upriver. The storms and fire left her unscathed but for a few burns and scars. The animals had returned to the forest, too, just as Wemahtekënis said they would. And so she waited and waited for the last of his predictions to come to pass. The darkness that he said would return to her had never arrived. In fact, the opposite was true. Ever since her rite of passage, she lived her life in relative peace.

The restoration of the pinelands was astonishing. Uma was right. Kahèsëna Hàki took no time setting to work replenishing her forests. The oaks came back first racing ahead of the pine sprouts that soon poked out of the charred trunks. The cranberry vines emerged next, their roots well harbored beneath the bog away from the heat of flame. Then the blueberries sprung up everywhere covering the land with their plush undergrowth. The blaze had opened up new fields, too, with soil fertile and ready for planting their corn, beans, and squash.

Among the birds, *papaxès* the woodpecker was the first to return feasting on the beetles and grubs that quickly burrowed new homes in the dead wood. With so much canopy gone, a flood of light poured onto the forest floor, and thousands of pine seedlings sprouted from the warming black ground. The white tailed deer were back, as were the otter, skunk, and squirrel. The creeks were diverted all along the bogs where the beavers had built fresh dams. Everyone had finally come back home.

All except for one. Maxkwe hadn't yet returned. She hoped she might find him further inland deep in the remote and ancient forests.

She was up before dawn rekindling the fire in the center of the village. When the coals were ready, she set the cooking pot on them and filled it with water. Soon her sisters would be up to make the cornpone that they would eat later in the morning. She headed down to the river for more water and to gather what greens she could find along the way.

It was a wonderland in this forest that had virtually sprung out of the ashes. When she was out in the quiet of the lowlands, it was like Earth Mother had dropped her into another world. She never tired of exploring this place so wildly different from her mountain home in Onondaga and the rocky cliffs of the Munsee territory. She was sixteen now, a grown woman, yet out here along the beach and bog and river she felt like a child again. It still amazed her that the ground thawed so early along the Atsayunk. Red root was already popping up through the sandy soil where the sun touched the forest floor drawn out by the longer days of the encroaching spring. It was especially thick along the banks of the sleeping *pakim* cranberry bog, where the buds of the alder had emerged with their soft yellow catkins hanging from bare branches. *Kahèsëna Hàki is waking up*, she thought and was grateful the cold winter was behind them.

The bog swans were nearly gone now, summoned by the coming thaw to begin their migration north. One particular bird remained, however. She spotted Nushèmakw, and glided over the smooth water to greet her.

"I brought something for you, Mother Ice," Nushèmakw said, extending a handful of ground corn. The swan stretched its long white neck and gently nipped the grain from her palm. Soon this last magnificent bird would fly away, too, and head for the cold tundra of the north country she preferred. "Mother Ice," she whispered, "I know you must go home soon. When you do, please stop by my Onondaga home and let my Aunt Sarhak know that I love her and miss her, and that I'm doing well."

With her basket filled with redroot, she went back to the village where her sisters were busy with their morning chores. She joined Uma at the cooking fire. When the water pot began to steam and bubble, she dropped spoonfuls of the *pàkawĕníkàna* dumplings into it.

The children emerged sleepily from their wikwams hungry for breakfast. Nushèmakw ladled the dumplings into a huge wooden bowl. Before she could pour maple syrup overtop the rush of small hands descended. "There's enough for everyone, *mímĕnsàk*," she teased. They gobbled up their meal, licked their sticky fingers, and ran off to play in the woods.

"Look at them, Grandmother, look how happy they are," she said, admiring their sparkling dark eyes, shining hair, and smooth brown skin. She would light kelekenikàn for Grandfather Winter before he moved north for the season. He had been so kind to them all.

The rest of the clan ate next and when they had their fill, Nushèmakw and her sisters began preparing the deer stew for later in the day. It was hard to know how much to make. They hadn't yet heard from the men who were due back from their hunting trip. When they arrived, they'd be ravenous.

She missed her father and couldn't wait to see him. It had been more than a month since he had left with Snow and Black Paw, and she had so many questions for him. There were still so many things she didn't understand, and only he could help her navigate the turns her life was taking.

"They're coming, they're coming!" Uma shouted. "They've sent up the signal. They'll be here soon. Start preparing the feast!"

Nushèmakw's heart soared with the news. She ran in circles

trying to decide what to do first. She stoked the fire and added wood. She set a large cooking pot on top of the coals and spooned some bear grease into it. She dumped in the ash-soaked corn, backing away as the hominy spit and smoked like popcorn. Uma greased the hot cook stone and began pouring dough for corncakes. She stirred the bubbling vat of deer stew and added tubers and squash.

Nushèmakw felt it before she heard it. It was a shock wave that went clear through her chest. "What wrong?" cried Uma.

"Listen," Nushèmakw said.

A horrible wail tore through the sky. Another wail, then another. The hunting party had arrived, and news was traveling fast. By the time the men had entered the village, there was no doubt that something terrible had happened. Now Nushèmakw heard Black Paw, who began howling like a wolf.

They dropped everything and ran as fast as they could toward the gathering crowd. The mournful cries of the women were frightening. They were clustered three deep around the men, blocking Nushèmakw's view. When they saw her approach, all fell silent. It was then that she knew.

"Let me see him," was all she said, and they parted to let her pass.

It felt like the world had stopped. Her legs became so heavy, she wondered if she could ever move them. The faces of the women on either side of her looked like masks, dark eyes starring as she passed. A knot of men flanked the place where her father lay to protect her from the sight of it. Chief Kitakima stepped forward.

"Take my hand, Nushèmakw," he said, his face laden with sorrow. He led her through the crowd to the edge of the forest. There on an emerald bed of new spring moss lay her father. His ashen face was slack and no longer carried the weight of worry. His eyes were closed, and he still wore the roach and feathered headdress that identified him as a Kechemeches warrior. Beneath the pendant of bone and shell, the one she had made for him, a wide red stain bloomed across his chest. In his right hand he held the arrow that killed him, the bloodied point of flint at one end and Guiarasi's black feathers on the other.

She dropped to her knees. A loud and fevered wail broke

from the depths of her being, releasing its unearthly sound into the empty space between them. She closed her eyes, numb and broken. Above the mournful sound of her own wailing, she heard a deep and resonant howl. Blackpaw had found his way beside her, his own grief opened wide. She grabbed him around the neck and wept into his coarse fur. She hung onto Blackpaw until no more tears would come, and still she could not let go of the dog. It was as if Blackpaw's muscled stance and her grip around him were all that was holding together the heavens and the earth.

"What will we do, Blackpaw?"

Ever so gently, the dog nuzzled her face and began to lick away her salty tears. She pressed her forehead against his. "I'm undone," she told him, and she knew he understood.

She felt like she was underwater. Everything was blurred and cold and slow. Blackpaw whined softly, and she stroked him behind his ear. There was a white mound at her father's feet. She clutched the loose skin between Blackpaw's shoulders, and he helped her up. Together they walked over to where Snow lay still as stone. "She's gone, too."

She laid her hand over Snow's closed eyes and spoke as soft as the wind. "My dear sweet friend. My guide and my protector. Well done, good and faithful Snow. Guide my father through the Star Path to where Keeper Grandmother guards the Path of Souls. With you beside him, I know that the wise and valiant Achimwis will find his way to the seventh heaven."

Nushèmakw stood and turned away. She and Blackpaw walked straight through the staring crowd, past their village, and into the woods. They would not stop until they reached Little Turtle Island.

OWEN

❈

1534 AD

APRIL

Owen ap Madoc studied hard and most of the time he enjoyed
it. He had an endless fascination with words. It was true what his
Grandfather had said. Each language indeed carried its own strange
world. Translation came easy to him. Another reason to be grateful
for all the time Grancha spent teaching him. He translated Latin into
English, then Greek into Latin, word by word, page by page, until
his fingers blackened with ink and the waste bucket filled with worn
nibs. With time, he could think as easily in those languages as he
could in his own Welsh.

Father Elis noticed it, too, for as soon as Owen completed the
exams for his last form, his guardian took him to the library at Oxford along High Street where he began his employment as scribe for
the colleges. One week he graduated, and the next he was on a carriage to that formidable city. Once he had settled in, he was surprised
to see how similar it was to Greyfriar. Here, too, he strained over his
desk in Father Elis's cramped and stuffy quarters. But he didn't com-
plain. He owed that much to Master Blazer. If it meant toiling day
and night over piles of missives, then he would do it. Yet he could
not help but miss his sheep and his time on the pasture. Most of all,
he missed little Teg.

He started with simple translations of the Latin apologies,
letters and pamphlets defending the scriptures and justifying the vir-

tues of man's free will over faith alone. As his reed scratched relentlessly across the page, he struggled to find meaning to this endless
puzzle. What was it about these men of high learning and their need
to defend God? How could they possibly believe that the God of all
things needed any defense at all? Yet they continued to toil and spin
and wring their hands. For what? It didn't put food on the table or a
roof overhead. It didn't heal the sick. The longer a man lived in this
city, the more he forgot all about these things.

Screaming and shouting came from the street outside. Owen
ran to the window. Down the road a crowd was gathering. He leaned
into the sill to get a better look. People were raving, shoving one another, and pressing forward. He could see a man with his hands tied
behind him standing silent at the bottom of steps that led to a make-
shift stage across from the College's tower. Then two of the King's
guards began to drag the man up the stairs, while other soldiers kept
the mob at bay. A hooded figure, dressed in black, waited on the platform. A torch was burning in a sconce nailed to a railing. The prisoner stumbled onto the platform. The executioner caught him and
tied him to a tall stake. Another man, in royal dress with the Tudor
rose emblazoned on his back, stepped forward. It was King Henry's
Chief Minister Thomas Cromwell. Owen watched him unroll a long
parchment that he pompously held high so all could see. After reading the proclamation aloud, he looked up at the prisoner who said
nothing. Cromwell raised his hand. The verdict was pronounced. He
turned on his finely tooled boots and left the stage. The executioner
grabbed the torch from its sconce and set fire to the stake. Owen fell
from the window and ran from the room in time to vomit in the hall.

Evening fell by the time Father Elis came back to their quarters. Dust and the sweat of horses still clung to his clothes.

"You don't look well, Owen. What's wrong?"

"There was an execution this afternoon. Down there, across
from the tower."

Father Elis peered out the window at the empty scaffolding.
"Tell me what you saw."

Owen told him everything. The pitiful prisoner, the executioner who burned him alive, and man who ordered it—Thomas
Cromwell.

Father Elis buried his face in his hands. "So it's come to this."

"Why was he killed?" Owen asked.

"He was martyred, my son. Killed because he was unwilling to betray his Savior to the Crown."

The next morning was dank as a cave. He walked the mile through the cold rain from his cell at the friary to Father Elis's quarters at the library. He left his muddy shoes at the door and sidled up to his desk in stocking feet, removing his reeds and quills from the pouch he carried over his shoulder.

"More letters today, Father?"

"Yes, son."

"Why so many?"

Owen saw the color creep up his guardian's neck. "We're building a case against those men, if you can call them men, who dare to throw the sacred appointment of the Holy See to the swine!" he said with rising passion. "You've seen what Cromwell will do. Luther's just as wicked. Now there's Tynsdale taking his abomination to the streets, feeding our own kinsman his deceitful rot in our own language! Keep writing, my son. So much depends on our ability to tell the sacred truth in English. Our meek and humble brethren, these very souls who are the very Bride of Christ, need us." With a snort, he turned, bent over his desk again, and said nothing more.

They worked until the dark prevented it, then Father Elis gathered Owen's manuscripts and left. Owen knew his guardian was heading to London to give the letters to the Archbishop, who would have them typeset and printed, where they would have the true and sacred word of the living God dispersed throughout the kingdom before the new day dawned.

On the day of the Feast of the Annunciation, Father Elis and Owen set out to deliver the finished quires. The spring rains had set in with vigor, and Owen was grateful that his guardian had secured a covered carriage for their journey to Chelsea. As they rode through the gloom, he found it hard to keep still. He couldn't believe that he of all people was finally going to meet the revered author, poet, and man of letters, Sir Thomas More! For so long, he had wondered what the man looked like, a speculation left largely to his imagination since Father Elis spoke so rarely about appearances of any kind. He pictured a large, towering man, steady in his ways and full of confidence, with a booming voice that echoed through the halls of court, laying waste the feeble arguments of his opponents.

"Father, what's he like?" asked Owen. "Sir Thomas, I mean. His was the first work I ever read that made me realize that maybe the world could be different than it is. And now I'm going to meet him!"

Father Elis looked at Owen and smiled. "If you must know, Sir Thomas is curious about you too."

"About me?"

"'Who is this shepherd who writes so eloquently?' he said to me. 'Bring him here when you come next. I would like to meet him.'"

"He spoke about me that way?"

"He did. I brought you with me because I'm not sure when there will be another opportunity. Sir Thomas is rarely at home these days. But first we must make another stop. The library at the London Friary is holding a document of particular interest to Thomas." He leaned out the window and shouted to the driver. "Newgate Street, north side."

Soon they were approaching the streets of London, and the closer they got the more impassable the road became. The horses clipped along dodging an increasing stream of coaches that hurried past them on their way out of the city.

"That's odd," said Father Elis looking out the window.

At the center of town along the Inns of Court, bonfires raged along the sides of the street. Effigies of Pope Leo were set afire, while both clergy and laymen alike fed the flame with books. They stiffened at the sight of it.

Owen blanched. "Father, those are Bibles!"

A man ran up to the carriage.

"Whoa!" The coachman shouted and the horses jerked to a stop.

"Who do you carry in there!" the man hollered. "No one but the King's loyal subjects will get through."

"We mean you no harm, my friend," said the coachman. "Will

you tell me what's happening?"

"His Majesty's Act of Succession has passed. Those who refuse to swear allegiance to the supremacy of the Crown will be tried for treason. I demand to know who's in your carriage!" he shouted, beating on the door.

"We have no business in London, good man. I assure you, my Master is simply en route to pay respects to his ailing aunty."

"Then I advise you to turn round while you can." The man disappeared back into the raging horde.

"So now it begins," Father Elis whispered.

As soon as they were able to clear town center, Father Elis called out to the coachman. "To Chelsea! We must reach Beaufort House as soon as possible. Godspeed, man!" The carriage lurched out from under them as the horses quickened their gait.

They swept along the jutted road with the River Thames barely visible through the rain that pelted the water. Owen could smell the sweat off the horses. They didn't let up until they reached the stately manor. The coachman slowed only enough to signal the sentry, who opened the iron gates to let them pass up the wide muddy lane that led to the house. Before he could stop the carriage, Father Elis and Owen jumped out and ran through the driving rain.

Father Elis pounded on the massive oak door.

"I'm coming, I'm coming," they heard finally. The door opened slowly revealing a small, stout woman, in a crisp white apron and bonnet. "Father Elis, you look like you've seen a ghost!" She stepped aside to let them pass. "My Lord has a good fire going, which is sure to warm you in no time." She took their cloaks and led them down the entryway, through a chamber, to a large room on the east wing of the house where Sir Thomas More sat reading by the fire.

"I'm sorry to interrupt you, my Lord," said the house matron, "but Father Elis comes with urgent news."

Sir Thomas rose. Owen was astonished that he stood no taller than he was. His corpse-like complexion and black lawyer's cap exaggerated the pale hollow of his cheeks. At first he looked fragile, but when Owen considered his brow, he changed his mind. Though serious and stern, Sir Thomas More's eyes carried the weight of compassion.

"What's happened, dear friend?" he said, embracing Father Elis.

"The Act of Succession has passed. Cromwell's men are like ants crawling all over London, dragging away every soul who refuses to swear allegiance. You'll be next, I'm sure of it."

Sir Thomas sighed. "That may well be true, Elis, but I won't run," he said, smiling. "The law is clear and on my side. Besides, I'm happy to swear to the King's right to supreme reign over England. That may be enough."

"You know as well as I do that it's not enough."

"We shall see." He looked over at Owen . "And who have we here, Elis? You've been rude by not introducing us."

"There's no time for frivolity. What will you do?"

"I might ask you the same question, my dear friend." He walked over to Owen. "Let me guess. You would be the young scholar Owen ap Madoc of the Bristol Greyfriars, am I right?"

Owen bowed slightly. "Yes, my Lord."

"We should sup together and discuss all these letters you've had the onerous task of translating. Well done, son, well done."

Owen wanted nothing more than to let Sir Thomas More know how much he cherished his work, his logic, his mind, but his tongue worked against him. He only managed to say "Thank you," and he bowed again.

They heard loud banging through the hallway; then a drumming of footsteps that rattled the walls. The chamber door flew open. A dozen men in knee-length leather coats with red crosses splayed across their chests pushed their way over the threshold. The infantry lined up, swords at their sides, and made way for the Chief Minister. The jowly man strode into the room. All went silent.

"Ah! If it isn't Thomas Cromwell who darkens my door," said Sir Thomas More calmly, as if he were asking his mother to tea. "So thoughtful of you to pay a visit on such a dreary evening. You honor me by coming yourself rather than sending only your entourage," he added, indicating the soldiers.

"You know why I come."

"Yes, I've been expecting you."

"So you still deny the rights of the Crown?"

"I deny the rights of no one."

"Who are these men," Cromwell said, eying Owen keenly.

"They're my friends, who have also showed me their kindness by visiting on this cheerless night."

Cromwell looked down his nose at Sir Thomas, and the flesh of his neck pinched in his collar. "Do you think I'm an idiot? I can see that they're friars." He turned to Owen. "Tell me, boy. Who do *you* serve?" he barked. "The King or the Pope?"

The guards stood at attention. Owen could feel their stares bearing down on him.

Father Elis stepped out of the shadows and crossed the room. He stood in front of Owen. "Dear Sir, we serve no one but God almighty."

Cromwell clasped his slender hands behind him and circled Father Elis. "And the Pope?"

Father Elis's voice remained calm, but his eyes were filled with fury. "The Holy See is God's representative on earth."

Cromwell's smiled dryly, a cat toying with its prey. "Do you swear to the Crown's supremacy over the Church of England?"

"I do not."

"Arrest him!" Cromwell shouted, pointing a bony finger.

The guards moved in. Father Elis turned his back to them and faced Owen. "Go," he whispered. Father Elis flailed the men, swinging his arms and kicking his legs, giving Owen his chance. While the men thrashed and tumbled, Owen crept along the shadowed wall and escaped through the door.

The house matron grabbed Owen's arm and pulled him down the hallway to the back of the house where the coach stood ready. She tossed the coachman a package and hurried him into the carriage. "Take this lad to Bristol Greyfriars. Godspeed, man!"

Two of the soldiers came running around the house and blocked the causeway. "Halt!" they demanded.

The coachman snapped the reins. The stallions lurched forward, bearing down on the soldiers.

"You are under the King's orders to stop!" they shouted, swinging their swords.

"Yah!" shouted the coachman. The horses picked up speed and barreled straight into the soldiers without breaking stride. Owen heard their swords clatter to the ground and their bones snapping under the weight of trampling hoofs.

They flew down the causeway, passing the sodden gardens and orchards to the road that ran along the River Thames. The carriage turned sharply west, listing fiercely as it headed through the dark toward Bristol.

Owen was thrown about violently inside the coach as the horses stampeded down road. He was numb. He tried to block thoughts of Father Elis and Sir Thomas at the hands of the soldiers. It was no use. He leaned back and closed his eyes.

The pounding of hooves continued without ceasing. When Owen thought he could endure it no more, the coachman shouted, "Whoa!" The horses snorted and shook their manes. Out the window, the rain had cleared but clouds still shrouded any light the sky might have offered them. Owen could hear the rushing water of the Thames, but the dark night obscured the river completely.

"Brother Owen!" the coachman called. "Are you all right?"

Owen leaned out the window. "I am. At least I think so."

"May name's Willie. These are strange times, Brother. Strange times."

"Did you see what happened back there? Cromwell was going to arrest us! Did Father Elis escape?"

"I don't know, but we can't dwell on that now. We need to keep our wits about us. We've still got a long road ahead of us, and we're not out of danger yet. I'll not be going by way of Oxford, that's for sure. It's likely that Cromwell's guards have taken over the whole city by now. We'll stay on the back roads."

Owen shook his head. "I can't believe this."

"Neither can I. But there's no time to fret over it. Here, Brother," he said, tossing Owen the package the matron had given him at Beaufort House. "Katerina thought you'd be needing these."

Owen opened the package. Inside were breeches, leggings, and a coarse shirt that laced at the neck.

"Change into those and hide your robe in the bushes. Then come sit up here with me. I got no mind to be carrying a friar anymore."

It had been five years since Owen had put on the clothes of a layman. The nettlecloth shirt and hemp pants were rough but softer than his robe. It felt good to be wearing them again. He jumped out of the cab and stuffed his cassock under the briars that spilled out and over the edge of the road. Then he climbed up next to Willie.

Willie pulled off his wool cap. "Take this," he told Owen. "We won't be fooling anybody unless you cover that bald dome of yours."

Willie clicked his tongue and snapped the reins, and the horses started up again. They maintained a steady trot the rest of the way, stopping only to let the horses drink. By daybreak they'd reached the outskirts of Bristol.

Up the long steady grade that flatted to a plateau, they were greeted by a spectacular sky. Reds and oranges penetrated the scattering clouds, painting their undersides and illuminating the lands below. By the time they reached town, the wind off Môr Hafren had swept the sky of clouds, and the morning light fell generously upon Lewin's Mead.

Small clusters of what looked like fog pocked the pastures and hovered in strange patterns throughout the valley.

"Do you see that, Willie?" Owen asked. "What is it?"

Willie's face was hard. "I don't like it." He stopped the horses and jumped from the rig. "Stay here," he said and he disappeared over the hill.

Smoke was rising in great plumes across the borough. Farther off, Owen could see similar pyres, some reduced to smoldering ash after their long burning. Willie returned, his face wet with tears.

"She's gone, Brother Owen. All gone!"

"What are you talking about?"

"The abbey. The abbey's gone! It's Cromwell's men who done it. They've burnt her to the ground."

"My God!" Owen stepped back and stumbled. "We've got to get to Greyfriar. We've got to warn the vicar. And Brother Michael, and Brother Dan!"

"No, Owen. I could see Greyfriar from the abbey. It's empty. It's been spared the burning, but no one's there. If they catch you there now, they'll kill you."

Owen was stunned. Just yesterday, he sat in the warmth and comfort of Father Elis's quarters in Oxford. Today all the land from London to Bristol was thrown into the burning arms of hell. "Willie, what should I do?"

"No doubt you'll be recognized if you ride with me. You may be a friar, Brother Owen, but you were a shepherd first. Keep cover and follow the sheep runs on the farthest pastures and find your way back to Bentley. You haven't got much time. GO! And for God's sake, Owen, keep that bald head covered!"

Owen pulled the cap down over his ears. "Goodbye, Willie. I'll never be able to repay you."

Owen knew his way from Lewin's Mead to Bentley Manor better than anyone. He had traveled that route so many times with his grandfather, and later to visit his Uncle Seamus down at the docks. It was a long hike but an easy one, and he was careful to stay hidden under the cover of the forest.

It took him all day to move as silently as he could through the underbrush, picking his way up and over one hillock after another and dodging the trails that led to open pasture.

By dusk, he had reached the outskirts of Bentley Manor. He crossed the lowland marshes and passed the bog where, what seemed a lifetime ago, he had saved little Lizzie's life. He climbed the gentle rise that led to the fields where he and Grancha walked together those countless mornings as they led the flocks to pasture. His heart ached at the sight of it. Finally, he reached the edge of the drive that led to the manor house. He thought about Grancha as he retraced the steps he took that miserable day he carried his grandfather home in his arms.

The night sky was bejeweled with stars when Owen stepped into the manor house yard. The door to the kitchen cracked open, allowing a beam of light to bleed out onto the ground. It was Peter hauling a pail of garbage to the rubbish pile.

"Peter," Owen whispered.

"Who goes there?"

"Shhhh. It's Owen," he said stepping into the light.

"Dear God! Is it really you? You shouldn't be here, Owen. The King's men are searching for you everywhere. It isn't safe."

"I've got nowhere else to go."

Peter bit his lip. "Come with me then."

He followed Peter through the scullery and into the kitchen. It was late. Aunt Beatrice had already gone to bed. They went up the dark stairs to the grand room. Peter knocked on Master Blazer's door.

"Who is it?"

"It's Peter, my Lord."

"Why do you come to me at this late hour?"

Owen opened the door.

"Holy Mother of God," the Master said, jumping out of his chair. "Owen, I thought you'd been killed!"

Owen closed the door. Standing across the room under the shadow of the window was another man.

"Uncle Seamus!"

"Owen!" Seamus threw his arms around him. "It's no less than a miracle!" he said, smacking Owen on the back. "You're alive, my boy, really alive!"

"I am, Uncle. But I need to know what's going on. I'm tired and confused by all that's happened. Last night, at Beaufort House, Cromwell tried to arrest me and Father Elis. Sir Thomas, too. I barely escaped with my life. What's happened to Father Elis?"

Master Blazer laid a hand on Owen's shoulder. "It's too soon to know, my boy. I only got word this morning. The moment I heard that the King's Treason Act was enacted, I sent Peter to get Seamus. Your uncle has spent all day and night trying to get the Greyfriars down to the docks to find them passage out of here."

Owen turned to his uncle. "Do you mean that Brother Andrew and Brother Dan have been saved?"

Seamus nodded. "Yes, Owen. And the others, too. By now, they're well on their way to Porta Magna. I've only just returned to report back to Master Bentley."

"Looks like you've got one more friar to stow away, Seamus."

The sound of horses charging down the drive came through

the windows.

Peter opened the door. "They've come, Master."

"Go, Peter. Keep them at bay as long as you can. Seamus, go out the back way and wait outside until you hear from me. Cromwell's men have no business with you. They shouldn't give you any trouble."

Seamus nodded and walked out.

Master Blazer ran over to Lady Bentley's portrait and threw the latch. "Get over here, Owen. They'll be here any moment now."

Owen stepped inside the hidden buttery, and the Master closed the door and locked it. All went dark. "Keep our dear boy out of harm's way, my darling," Owen heard him say to the painting.

Moments later, Owen heard the scuffling of boots on the floor. Men were marching into the room and lining up, the way they had at Sir Thomas More's.

"Master Blazer. We come under orders from the King," said the officer.

"You barge into my home and storm my private quarters in the dark of night? What orders are these? I'm within my rights to hear them," the Master said, pounding his fist on the table.

Owen heard him walk up and down the row of men, and the slow and deliberate stomping of his boots shook the floor. "Look at you," he said. "You have the nerve to call yourself soldiers. Ha! You blush like women. Step forward into the light where I can see you."

The men didn't move.

"Ah, yes, that's why you linger in the shadows. Cowards! Did you think I wouldn't recognize you?" He tapped his fingers on the desk. "I know who you are. You should be ashamed of yourselves. Lieutenant! Are you aware that some of these boys were my own servants? And now they have the gall to come back to accuse their Master. Is this the justice you serve, Lieutenant?"

The men shuffled uncomfortably.

"You!" he barked. "Jonathan, am I right? On what grounds am I accused?"

Owen heard Jonathan step forward. "We have been sent by Sir Thomas Cromwell, Master." Owen felt chilled to the bone.

"Is this true, Lieutenant?" Master Blazer demanded.

"Yes, my Lord, I'm afraid it's true. We're under the authority of the King who has given Sir Thomas Cromwell orders to arrest any man who sides with Sir Thomas More or any other traitor. Under the Treason Act enacted by His Highness this very day and year of our Lord, any man who sympathizes with those who oppose the King and his supreme authority under God is to be arrested and tried. We are obliged to also arrest those who would harbor such traitors."

"You call me a traitor?" Master Blazer seethed. "Must I remind you, good men, of my long service to the Tudors. Ha! His Highness commands it, you say. While our young Harry still wore his breeches in his native Wales, I was the one who took up the cause of his father. I was the one who was first to throw my gold into the voyages to the new worlds, not once but twice, and before Sir John Cabot even thought of setting sail. Both expeditions were sanctioned by the King himself. Did you stop to think of that? Without me Cabot would be nothing. And now he collects the fame that should be mine! The man was neither English nor Welsh but a Roman by birth! It was I, not he, who understood the wishes of the Tudors, and I upheld them to the letter. Now you have the audacity to stand here in my own house and say I'm a traitor! Jonathan, what do you have to say for yourself?"

"The indictment is not for you, Master." The boy's voice was shaking.

The Lieutenant spoke next. "We seek one Owen ap Madoc who has allied himself with the traitors Elis Bowen and Thomas More. We have word that he's hiding here."

The Master ignored the Lieutenant. "Jonathan, Jonathan. You of all people would accuse Owen ap Madoc? Have you no shame? You played together when you were knee high. When you grew old enough, you worked side by side with him. Christ, Jonathan, you even ate at his mother's table. Now you accuse him? By God, Jonathan, You are no soldier, you are a Judas!"

"It is not he who accuses, but the King," reminded the Lieutenant.

Master Blazer's tone was deadly. "Look at me. All of you." He moved among them, pacing and stopping to examine each one. "I ask you, do I look like a religious man who would throw himself at the feet of any vicar or bishop?"

The men laughed nervously.

"Go ahead and laugh. You may wear the King's colors, but you don't fool me. I've known the lot of you since you were babes at your mother's tit. Go and tell Cromwell who I am and who it is I serve. My interest is in gold, not God. Give unto Caesar what is Caesar's but you can be sure that I'll take my share first."

The Lieutenant piped up. "My Lord, it's also true that you throw your gold to the Greyfriars, where Owen ap Madoc was ordained. So how can you claim that you're not allied with the Pope rather than the King?"

"Who are you, man, that you would continue this line of questioning? Your name!"

"My name is Lieutenant Graham, sir."

"I will remember it, Lieutenant Graham. For your information, Owen was never ordained. Look it up for yourself. And it's no secret that I am the founder of Greyfriars. Is that Cromwell's test? To accuse me of allegiance to the supremacy of the Pope because of my investments? Let him come here himself if he wants to know what has become of the friaries and the monasteries. These Houses of God have turned into places of wanton greed. Who here has seen a monk who lacks anything? Fat and happy, they are. That's not religion, my boys, that's good business. I own that friary and hold the land it sits on. You tell Cromwell that when he's ready, we'll strike a deal. But I'll give not one shilling more to those so-called holy men. Good riddance to their spoil and waste."

The room was tense and heavy and the men squirmed and scuffed uncomfortably. Master Blazer sat down at his desk, raking his chair across the floor, taking more time than he needed. "I'm no fool. I see what Cromwell's up to. He sends the youngest of his ranks to test the waters of Bentley Manor. Is that it?" he grumbled. "Not one of you is old enough to grow a hair on your ass." He sighed. "Listen up, men. I'll show you what allegiance means."

He pressed an iron key into the lock of a gilded box that sat on his desk. It sprang open, and he rifled through its contents until he extracted a red velvet purse. He loosened its drawstring.

"Give me your hands." Owen heard his master say. Then he

heard the clinking of a few coins being poured into each waiting palm. "This I know for certain about our dear King Henry," his master continued. "He wouldn't want me to send you away with empty pockets, now would he? Take it young men, and if these spoils are somehow lost on your travels home," he said, with a shameless wink, "no one will be the wiser." He began slapping the soldiers on their backs as he led them to the door. "Go now, my accusers, or permit me now to call you my protectors. Let our good King Henry know my alliance is secure. I serve His Majesty as I served his father."

The men rushed for the door. "In closing, my fine soldiers. If Owen ap Madoc were at Bentley Manor, surely you would have found him by now." He guffawed and slammed the door, then waited until they mounted their horses and rode through the manor gates.

"You can come out now, Owen," said Master Blazer unlatching the lock. He threw open the door, and Lady Bentley rattled on her hinges. "And bring me a bottle of rum."

Owen stumbled out squinting in the candlelight.

"Could you hear them in there, my boy?"

"Yes, Master, I heard everything."

"Then you know you must hurry. It won't be long before they figure out where you are. Next time you won't be so lucky. Go through the buttery. Take the stairs on the other side that lead to the scullery, then sneak out the back door. Take care that no one sees you. If the fates are with us, then Seamus will be waiting for you. *The Mary Margaret* sails tonight. You'll go with her.

"But my mam. May I see her before I go?"

"No, Owen, I'm sorry. To see her now would be her death sentence. You are to see no one and to be seen with no one until you hit the high seas. Do you understand?"

"Yes, my Lord."

"Go." But before he could leave, Master Blazer grabbed him by the shoulders and kissed him on both cheeks. "Farewell, Owen ap Madoc."

Uncle Seamus was waiting on a mule-drawn cart. "This is a fine mess you've gotten us into, Owen. Get yourself under the straw, and don't come out until I say. Not a word from you, mind you."

Owen did as he was told, and Seamus pulled out. Owen braced himself for a careening ride. Instead, the mule plodded along at a snail's pace. They went along this way, up and down the hills until they ever so gradually flattened out as they neared the shore. The day dawned through a briny mist that rolled in from the bay by the time they reached Môr Hafren.

"All's clear, Owen," Seamus said. "You can come out now."

Owen emerged from the pile of straw and picked the chaff from his hair. "Why so slow, Uncle Seamus? I thought they'd catch up to us any minute."

"Nothing draws attention like a runaway wagon. They've got no business with ordinary peasants pulling a load.

Owen climbed up next to his uncle and shivered. He was bone weary and ready to collapse.

"Peter's told me all you've been through. Don't waste your energy talking, Owen. We're almost to Bristol."

Uncle Seamus drove the wagon onto the path that ran by the docks. He pulled up to his hut by the wharf and helped Owen out of the wagon and inside the door. A pile of ash smoldered in the hearth. Seamus stoked the coals and added wood.

Owen plopped down into a chair and held his head in his hands.

"Eat this, Owen. You'll feel better," his uncle said, handing him some soup.

Owen wasn't hungry, but he sipped at it anyway.

"I hate to tell you this, Owen, but we haven't much time. The crew is waiting for me. I'm late getting back, and I know they're wondering where I am. Here's what we're going to do."

His uncle proceeded to tell him his plan. They would sail out of Môr Hafren this morning. They'd pass the tip of Ireland, then head southwest in search of Hy-Brasil. Then they'd change course and take a northward tack to the trading posts at New Found Land.

Owen closed his eyes.

"I know it sounds impossible, especially after all you've been through. But the Master's orders are clear. You can't stay home. It's too dangerous. You're to sail with us. Are you strong enough to make it to the ship?"

"I think so," Owen said in a daze.

Owen was able to walk out of the hut without help, and slowly they headed down the path to where the *The Mary Margaret* was docked. But when they boarded the ship, he felt his uncle grab his arm as they made their way across the gangplank.

Owen felt the alarmed stares of the crew who remained silent. Uncle Seamus led him across the gangway and down the steps to the captain's quarters below, where Owen collapsed on the cot.

"Are you okay, Owen?"

He nodded with his eyes closed.

"Good. You'll stay here and rest. I'll send Renny down in a little while to check on you. The truth is, Owen, we are out of time. I'm needed at the helm. We need to set sail immediately."

Owen threw his arm over his eyes, as if that would block out what his uncle was going to say next.

"Hy-Brasil waits for no one," Seamus began. It had been seven years since the last appearance of the fabled island. Seven years since that fateful day when Owen's father, Madoc ap Morcant, was lost to her mysterious realms. According to his uncle's calculations, they only had a few weeks before she showed herself. "We've still got a chance of getting there in time to see her rise again," Seamus said. He started out the door and then turned. "I'm bound by oath and duty to find your father, Owen, no matter the odds. And with you with us we've got a fighting chance. It's no accident that you fell into this mess when you did. You've got the grace of God upon you, Owen. You're our lucky charm."

They shoved off and Owen felt anything but lucky. He spent the first two days with his head hung over the deck rail. No matter how hard he tried, he couldn't keep his stomach from listing and churning and rocking along with the ship. Unlike his father, he was a landlubber through and through.

His uncle climbed the stairs to the small quarterdeck at the ship's bow. "Any better today, Owen? I've brought you some salty stock." He handing him a steaming cup. "Logan says you'd best drink it down whether you want to or not. It's his best concoction for hangover, so it should work for the seasickness too."

Owen's stomach rebelled at the smell of it. "Ugh, what is it?"

"I have no idea, but I'll attest to the fact that it works. Drink."

Owen took a sip. The salt felt good on his tongue. Another sip and his stomach began to settle enough to work up a thirst. "Thank you," he said wiping his mouth with his sleeve. "I'll thank Logan myself when I can find the strength."

"You're a sorry sight, for sure, but you'll get your sea legs soon enough. Better that you're here on the ship even if you're sick as a dog. Otherwise you'd be standing on old Cromwell's chopping block. You had a close call, nephew."

"I know. It all still seems unreal. Wait!" he said, grabbing his uncle's arm. "Uncle, did you learn what happened to Father Elis?"

Seamus's face fell. "I'm sorry, Owen. I hate to tell you, but it didn't turn out well for Father Elis."

Weak from sickness, shock, and fatigue, Owen couldn't hold back his tears any longer. He buried his face in the crook of his arm.

"Best you know the truth than believe a pack of lies. God rest his soul. I'll leave you to your sorrow. Get some sleep if you can. You've had a hard time of it. It's a following tide today with a smooth sea. Stay here under the foremast. That sail will cast some shade on you for a while yet. I'll have Renny check on you later."

Owen fell into a fevered sleep where sight and sound were a blur. Time stretched and twisted, twirling about his head like a pinwheel, colors blending and frothing and igniting into shades he had never seen before.

He heard birds—or were they angels? The whistle of their wings cut the air as they dove into the sea. They beat the sky, breaking the water's surface with their feathers, lit and glowing and rising up and up into the cloudless heavens. The sun shone straight into his eyes throwing a drape of brightness over him. Now he could hear them—a thin ringing, heavenly and ethereal. The sun, the sound, and the birds became one, and the whole host started to spin. Owen watched as the world widened its radiance with every turn. The horizon and the ocean, all taken up in the eternal spinning. The water began to swell—a funnel taking on weight and substance until it, too, became a living thing that carried him on the crest of an enormous wave glowing fantastically beneath swirls of foam. The angels sang louder and louder as they circled the sun. The sea began to froth and boil, blowing steam and spray. A wall of water surged in all directions revealing an island in its midst. She was magnificent! He saw the tops of sharp mountains. Then came the shapes of rounded hillsides, networks of stone. From the depths of the ocean, Hy-Brasil rose up in full glory, dripping in her baptismal water, gold and silver and shining with brilliant majesty, her shores awash in jewels and crystal. Owen could see figures moving about in the hovering mist, but they were so distant that they soon disappeared into the brightness of the landscape. Though he was dreaming, and he knew he was dreaming, he called out. "*Tad!* Father, is it you? Are you there?" But his voice made no sound. The more he tried to shout, the more his elation turned to despair. He looked away, and when he did, he began to fall from that mighty wave. He watched himself plummet through an empty sky until he plunged into the deep and endless sea.

His dreaming went on like that for days. Several times, he came out of a relentless fever only to feel a soft stream of warm liquid Renny was pouring down his throat. "There, there, Brother Owen," he heard him say. "You've got a powerful ague, but the angels won't be taking you yet. Not while I'm on watch." And off went Owen again into his land of dreams.

Nearly a week had passed before his fever broke.

"Where am I?"

"You're below deck, Brother Owen," Renny answered. "Here, you need to drink more of this."

He choked down more of Logan's swill and talked Renny into helping him to the main deck. He sat on the worn planks next to the limp square sail. Only then did he notice that the ship wasn't moving.

"We've been in the doldrums, Brother Owen," Renny explained. "Not a breath has touched these sails in two days."

The morning was pleasant enough, and he inhaled the rich cool spring air. He didn't know what the doldrums were. At least the ship had stopped rocking, and for that he was grateful.

"How long was I out?"

"With fever, you mean? I've been turning the glass for the Captain, Brother Owen, so I know. You've been in a terrible way for six days straight."

He shook his head. The dreams and night terrors were still fresh on his mind.

"After the first day when the sickness came on hard, we brought you below deck where I could keep a better eye on you. Soon you were rolling and shaking something awful. I had to strap you to the cot to keep you from hurting yourself. I wasn't sure if the good Lord intended to take you right then. You do look a mite better right now. A couple days on the cook's rations have done you good. Honest to God, Brother Owen, you were looking straight down death's dark throat for a moment there."

Owen held out his hand, and Renny shook it. "Thank you, my friend. I see how much trouble I've caused you. You've saved my life."

"Well I was glad to do it, but to tell the truth, it was the captain who was responsible. He said, 'Renny, my nephew is in your hands. If he dies, your hide will pay.' And he wasn't joking neither."

Owen laughed. "I'm no stranger to my uncle's threats. I'm in your debt, Renny."

"Oh, you don't owe me a thing, Brother Owen. But I wouldn't mind if you'd put in a good word for me from time to time when you're praying to the good Lord above. I've got a good deal of forgiveness to collect before I'll be able to pass through those great and pearly gates." His face was earnest and grave.

"Rest assured, Renny, I'll do everything I can."

The watch from the crow's nest shouted down to the deck.

"What's that?" Owen asked looking skyward.

Renny shielded his eyes and craned his neck. "It's Niall calling from his perch!"

Atop the main mast above the limp sail, the lookout shouted again. "Captain, starboard side. I see something along the horizon. Looks like a riptide's forming. A line of clouds dark as pitch are gathering behind it! Can you see it?"

Seamus answered from the stern castle. "I can't see it from here, Niall. Is it a reef?"

"Can't tell, Captain. Seems like it's something else, but I suppose it could be the tide against a reef."

"Not this far out to sea unless we're closing in on land. Is it still stirring, Niall?"

"It is, Captain, and gaining strength. You best come up here and see it for yourself."

Uncle Seamus gave the helm over to first mate Tulley and raced down the quarterdeck steps. He scaled the main mast and climbed onto the lookout. Shading his eyes from the glare of the sun on the water, Seamus looked out across the ocean. Something was wrong, Owen could feel it. Then his uncle dropped his gaze and slapped Niall on the back. "Good work, man. Keep this up and you'll make first mate in no time. Keep watch and let me know if anything changes."

"Yes, Captain," said Naill. Seamus climbed back down the mast and passed the drooping yardarm sail. He landed on the deck with a thud and stopped in front of Owen.

"I see that your strength is back. Follow me to the cabin." He turned on his heels and headed belowdeck. Owen stood, surprised that his legs felt sturdy and strong, and followed after him.

Now that he was in a state of mind to notice, Owen could see that the captain's small quarters were amazingly well equipped. Located beneath the stern castle, the space accommodated a spacious oak table, a line of shelving overflowing with maps and relics, a few padded benches that opened to storage, and a small nook where a bed and nightstand spanned a dark wall. The ship, a Caravel, was beautifully crafted. Paneless windows stretched across three sides of the cabin, allowing ample daylight into the quarters and onto the captain's table.

"What's the matter, Uncle Seamus?"

His uncle sat in his chair, tapped his fingertips against one another, and stared out across the still waters. "I don't like it, Owen," he said, swinging around to face his nephew. "You've had a hard time of it, I know. But I can't say we are done with it yet. Niall's right. The water does roil out there, and I don't know why. I want to show you something."

His uncle began fidgeting with a drawer tucked under the lip of the black varnished table. He turned a series of wooden slats and levers hidden in the veneer. "Now that your father's gone, you and I are the only ones who know about this drawer. When these slats are moved in sequence, they spring the lock." Owen heard it pop and his uncle slid open the drawer. "Look here. It's built for the sea, watertight." He reached into the drawer and pulled out the scroll. "Remember this?" he asked.

Owen recognized it right away. It was the Turkish map his uncle showed him the day he told him the truth about his father. Seamus unrolled it onto the table and weighted its corners.

"See this?" He pointed to the middle of the ocean where the conspicuous island loomed far to the west. "We're right here, Owen. The stars confirm it. I suppose the disturbance could be something else. Each time we see it, it looks different. There's no way to know for sure."

He rolled up the map and carefully placed it back in the drawer. "What troubles me more is the sky. Here we sit in the dead doldrums, while out there darkness brews. It's a cold sky with a greenish cast. That means a storm's hatching. The last time we saw a sky like that, we scarcely made it back home to tell about it. I don't know whether to cut clean of Hy-Brasil and head north, or keep to it. I'm asking your opinion as a holy man who should have a clear line to God's intentions. Are you a believer, Owen ap Madoc?"

Owen didn't know how to answer. Did he believe in what? A God who allowed men, women, and even children to suffer needlessly in this old and tired world? A savior who favored some but let others slip away? What of Father Elis? What of Grancha Hywel? Were their lives snatched out of compassion or neglect? He couldn't say which and tell the truth. So instead he said, "Uncle, I've had a dream. One that seems different than the others. A few days ago, when I was belowdeck and in a fever."

Seamus leaned in, his voice low. "Was it God-given, son?" he asked.

"I don't know. But in it I saw the island. It was Hy-Brasil. I sat on top a huge wave and watched her rise in all her glory and magnificence. When I saw her and all her light and shine, I called for my father, as if he were over there and could hear me. But my voice didn't carry. Then I tumbled into the sea and woke up. I don't remember anything else."

Seamus stared at Owen and slapped his desk. "Owen, you've had a vision! You've been sent to this ship by God above to let us know we should carry forth. God is with us, Owen ap Madoc. We'll find your father yet!"

His uncle rushed out of the cabin before Owen could say another word. Now he regretted telling his uncle anything. But it was too late. Uncle Seamus would not be diverted. The weight of uncertainty fell on him with such force that all he could do was sit at his uncle's desk, his father's desk really, and cry.

Owen saw dark shadows march through the cabin windows fanning out across the room until he could hardly see. Outside, the sky grew angry, and green clouds kicked up long trails that spun toward them at an alarming speed. In one unannounced blow, the wind hit the starboard side like a cannon and the ship tipped precariously. The table slid across the floor and pinned Owen to the wall.

Owen heard his uncle barking orders. "Turn about! Turn about! Bow to the wind, men. NOW!" The men's footsteps clattered above as they crossed the deck. He heard them drop the sails on the forward mast and raise the lateen on the mizzen, and it groaned miserably at the pulling force of the squall. He'd been told *The Mary Margaret* was built for speed and maneuver, and she didn't disappoint. She came around instantly just in time to receive a gigantic wave on her bow. Water broke over the quarterdeck and threw half the crew on their backs.

"Come down from the lookout, Niall, or you'll be knocked down for sure!" Owen heard the yardarm lines beat ferociously against the mast as Niall hurried down. He landed on the deck with a thud just as another wave hit the ship.

Owen fell to the floor. The table slid portside and blocked the door. Another wave slammed the hold, spilling through the windows.

His uncle called from above. "Here she comes, men! Don't panic. Hold your positions. Tie yourself to the rigging if you must, but wait it out. The storm will blow over soon enough, men. You're not likely to see a vision like this ever again."

Across the cabin, Owen had a clear view through the windows.

Another peal of thunder echoed through the chamber, and a blade of white-hot lightening struck the water. The wind spun around and around, and a whirlpool appeared. The spout took up water at an astonishing pace. As it did, its vortex stretched and widened. All at once, it hit the ship and threw her from the turbulence into the quiet eye of the storm. In an instant, the clouds were swept away revealing a deep and penetrating blue sky. A full moon hung eerily from the heavens, its celestial light shining upon them even though it was early in the day. The sight of it was terrifying. Owen felt something warm trickle down his face. He dabbed at the scratch across is forehead to stop the bleeding.

He looked out the window. "Holy Mother of God."

Then the water came alive again. Giant sheets of froth and foam gave way, revealing sharp peaks of mountaintops rising in the churning waters. Hundreds of them, no thousands, each wet and translucent in the strange and steady moonlight. A mist ignited over the water, a veil of light illuminating the island. All was aglow. Hy-Brasil had risen.

An unnerving quiet settled in the storm's eye. Owen heard a splash behind him. He turned to see that the ship's cockboat had been lowered, and his uncle was climbing aboard. Tulley dropped him a small cask and sack. His uncle gripped the oars and rowed furiously toward the island.

Owen flew to the door still blocked by the huge black table. He pushed with all his might to move it, but it was hopeless. He ran back to the window.

"Uncle Seamus, Uncle Seamus!" He tried to climb out but couldn't break through the lattice. "Uncle Seamus!" he called again. "Take me with you!"

Seamus rowed relentlessly and flew out across the sea toward the island. He turned to Owen and waved just before he vanished into the mist.

Owen looked at the sky. The moon was gone. The other side of the storm was coming. He heard the crew scramble chaotically above, bracing for what was just ahead. The green and lashing wind returned with a vengeance. Lightening struck the ship with deafening thunder. The tide rose and the island disappeared in the torren-

tial rain. A rogue wave hit hard, and the ship lurched to her starboard side. Another hit, and she tipped dangerously, throwing Owen
portside.

He tried to stand but was knocked down again.

The cabin was taking on water. "My God," he said. He fell to
his knees and prayed. In an instant, that familiar pillar of light filled
him to the core. He had found that place within, where no manner of
storm or threat could harm him; that place where even rising islands
of glory held no meaning. Whether he lived or died, he knew that all
of it, life and death, were the same in the mind of God. Eternity was
passing over, around, and through him. He walked upon this earth
for only an instant, having been called from the great halls of endless
time that had harbored him before he was born, and when his last
days on earth were fulfilled, he would be called back again into the
comfort of that welcoming eternity.

Owen got up off the floor and walked over to the window in
time to see the high wall of water crash over the ship.

NUSHÈMAKW

✠

1534 CE

FISHING MOON

A month had passed since her father's death and still the grieving shook her to the bone. Alone on Little Turtle Island, she was at least able to hold onto her loneliness in a way that brought her peace now and then. It felt good, this loneliness, an empty feeling, uninterrupted, spent and worn, a deep hole. She hoped the hole would never fill. If it did, if her grief would find a way to leave her, then her father would be gone forever. This was the life the Great Spirit gave her, and she would honor it in the traditional way, by blackening her face with cinder. At night, she lay awake, with time slowing to a crushing pace, and the dark and heavy sky closing in on her. During those periods of impenetrable solitude, she offered prayer and song and burned kelekenikàn as she was taught to do. After awhile, she felt lifted up, not into the higher heavens, but from the lower worlds where she had fallen. She sensed the presence of Earth Mother Kahèsëna Hàki. Just as in the stories her father told her, the Mother of All Things provided solace and gave Nushèmakw encouragement. She wasn't troubled by the fact that her Guardian Spirit, the one revealed to her during her initiation, hadn't reappeared on the island since the time of the great fire. Nushèmakw knew that Kahèsëna Hàki would send Maxkwe to her when the time was right. Then, her spirit bear would guide her and give her counsel for the rest of her life.

Blackpaw was a true godsend. Every evening at dusk, he would return from trolling the island, and they would spend the long nights together in front of the fire. He would sleep beside her, his warm coat and steady breathing a comfort. Of all who could have accompanied her to the island, she was glad that Kahèsëna Hàki chose Blackpaw. Blackpaw was the only other living soul who understood what she was going through. No one else would be coming to Little Turtle Island, not until the year of mourning had passed bringing with it a new spring. Chief Kitakima and Uma wouldn't be coming. They respected her sacred path and her year of exile that honored her father's death. The rest of them wouldn't dare come. They saw what happened to her father at the hands of her Onondaga enemy, and they wanted no part of it.

During the weeks that passed, she kept herself busy building out her camp. When she and Blackpaw first arrived, she spent a good deal of time choosing the place to raise her wikwam. She settled on a spot in the island's basin downhill from the giant white pine that had protected her during the fire. The hill faced south and fell off gradually to the creek that divided the basin floor. Here she would receive the full benefit of the sun's warmth as it arched its path across the sky, and the ridge that circled the island would shield her from the strongest winds. The basin was larger than she remembered and more beautiful. On the opposite side, an old growth forest towered in the distance, huge white oaks flanked by smaller sweet bay and swamp maple trees. Closer by, she discovered a clearing of stone and moss at the edge of the creek where a lone tree stood proudly. It was a nushèmakw, a mother tree, her namesake. This she knew was a gift from Kahèsëna Hàki, and she spent many afternoons watching its beautiful cascading limbs dance in the breeze.

The air was chilly at dawn. She relit the fire and warmed her hands. Tossing in some red cedar and bearberry, she gave thanks to the new day. Her moccasins were damp with clinging dew as she headed down to the creek. She knelt down and sank into the lush gray moss that covered the banks. The cold water looked reddish brown, stained by the leaching roots of old cedars as the creek meandered past. It tasted good and clean, leaving a refreshing tart flavor on her tongue. She walked over to the mother tree and patted her trunk. "I'll need a few more today," she said, snapping off several pliable branches. "Thank you, mother tree," she said, careful to show her gratitude.

Beside the warmth of the fire, she began repairing a large mat that had torn in the middle while she was dragging mud up from the creek. Tying off the last knot, she held it up, admiring her work.

Downhill from her wikwam closer to the creek, a small, unfinished structure stood next to her sizable pile of mud. Only a little taller than Nushèmakw, the dome was built of vertical limbs bent toward its center and lashed at the top. The sides were plied together with tightly woven reeds covered in chinking. It was a *pímẽwakàn*, a sweatlodge, and it was almost done. She spent the morning spreading the wet mud over the reeds layer by layer until she was satisfied that the walls were thick enough to hold steam from the sacred fire that she would build inside. She slapped handfuls of it in place, splattering her arms and face. She worked it into the crevices, smoothing the round walls as she went along. One more pass and she'd be finished.

Blackpaw burst through the brush at the crest of the hill barking and whining. His coat was covered in burrs, and his feet were thick with the fishy muck of the marshes. He barked again and shook violently, and salt water went flying everywhere. When she reached for him, he pulled away jumping and crouching. Then he nipped at her skirt and pulled her in the direction he'd come.

She followed him back up the ridge and down the other side to the marsh. Here the island emptied into a soggy lowland, a maze of thin peninsulas with long rushes and cordgrass growing between the marsh's soft fingers. The dog had trampled the weeds, laying them flat, forming a narrow winding path down to the sea.

Beyond the dunes, a pale overcast sky hung over the ocean. Turkey vultures wheeled round and round above her, their wings spread full. Blackpaw led Nushèmakw into the murky wetland. She cringed when her moccasins sank into the rank mud. It stank of warm dead fish, something she never got used to after a childhood in the pristine mountain waters of Onondaga. Each step made a thwack-thwack sucking sound when she lifted her feet. She regretted that she had left her small canoe at the village. It would have passed through these shallows with ease. Thankfully it was low tide, and the distance to the dunes was slight. She dove in and swam across with Blackpaw paddling beside her.

The dog scaled the dunes and was on the other side by the time Nushèmakw reached the top. A strong wind blew in off the water and through her dripping hair. She glanced up the beach and saw nothing but the vultures probing the shore. Blackpaw barked from the other direction. Hopefully, whatever he'd discovered hadn't been dead too long.

She saw something long and flat floating in a shallow tidal pool. As she got closer, she could see that it was made of wood. Not driftwood, but something built with dark planks lashed together and covered in pitch. A canoe, maybe. It was a thick and clumsy thing, more like a raft, but this one had posts fastened to each corner. One of these had broken off.

"*Èchei!*" she gasped. There was a body lying on the other side of the raft at the edge of the pool. A still and lifeless figure. She rubbed her eyes to make sure she wasn't dreaming. No, it was real. She approached the thing. Blackpaw barked and wagged his tail, proud of his accomplishment. "Good dog," she said. "*Ontiendakkna*, now sit!" and he sat on his haunches and was silent.

It was a man. He lay on his side naked and covered in salt. His skin was bright red in places, and a constellation of blisters pocked his back. "What has the sea done to you?" she whispered shaking her head. The sun had not only burnt his skin but bleached it white and had turned his hair orange in places. He had a peculiar fringe of hair around his scalp and some stubble across his crown. There was no lack of hair on his body. This creature was covered in it, all over his jaws and chin, across his chest, and down his torso and legs. "Has Kahèsëna Hàki sent me a *yakwahe*, the horrible naked bear of old?" No, she decided. This wasn't *yakwahe*. Kahèsëna Hàki would never send her a fearsome beast.

Besides this was no monster. It was a man, and while he looked strange and malformed, she sensed that he was harmless. She bent over and lowered her cheek to his nose, a wide round nose with coarse hair sprouting under it that at another time would have made her laugh. She stilled herself and listened. Air was passing from his nostrils faint but steady. Although he lived, she wasn't sure for how long.

She touched the medicine bundle that hung around her neck. "What should I do?" she asked. All at once, she remembered the last of the prophecies she had received from Wemahtekënis, the Keeper of the Forest.

A new darkness will come upon you. When it does, return to your island and face it. This time it will blow in from the east, and in time it will reveal your destiny.

Could this be what Wemahtekënis meant—a man, washed ashore from the east? Should she save him—heal him if she could? She looked down at the stranger. He was in awful shape: weak, wounded, and barely alive.

Then from the root of her being, a clarity of purpose opened before her. That light, that spirit that dwelt within her, the one she had carried with her into this life, the one that had been a constant source of comfort and refuge—it was that light that now became a wellspring within her. She sat on the shore and looked out over the endless sea and felt its outpouring of goodness and wisdom and truth fill her to the core.

Her destiny was certain: she would heal this man. She was a healer, a medicine woman. Like her mother. Like her Aunt Sarhak. As long as she lived, she would heal everything she could in this wounded and suffering world. She knew now that this pale, weak being before her was a gift from Kahèsëna Hàki. Whatever he was, whoever he was, he was a gift.

She jumped up, ran to the other side of the pool, and plucked a broken mussel shell out of the sand. Eelgrass choked the water, its tendrils furling around her legs. She cut fistfuls of it with the shell's sharp edge and threw it onto the raft.

"We will take him home, Blackpaw, and see what we can do."

She pushed the buoyant raft over to where the man was lying. The condition of his back took her breath away, his sunburn red and inflamed. "I've seen worse," she told herself, although she wasn't so sure. She was grateful to see that the sky was overcast. At least the sun wouldn't ruin his skin today. She rolled his limp body off the bank and into the pool, holding his head above water while she cleaned his sores of sand.

She whistled for Blackpaw. "*Tonín*, come here!" She led the dog onto the edge of the raft. "*Ontiendakkna*." He sat obediently, and his weight tipped the raft into the water just enough to cuff the man under his side. She whistled again. When the dog jumped off, the man was levered onto it. She rolled him over, and he flopped face down into the nest of clean eelgrass.

While she waited for the tide to come in, she set to work gathering deer tongue where it had overwintered along the dunes. She braided the grass into a harness for Blackpaw. By midday, the tide was returning, bringing with it thicker clouds that looked like they held rain. She moved quickly, lashing one end of the rope around Blackpaw, and the other to the posts on the front of the raft. As the tide rose, and the pool began to fill, they drifted inland. With Blackpaw pulling the lead, they floated through the narrow break in the dunes, across the salt marsh, and into the channels that led back to Little Turtle Island.

They reached the island before the rain. When the raft would go no further, she ran it up the narrow beach and untied the dog. The poor man looked no better, but no worse either. She snapped her fingers at Blackpaw, who gently climbed onto the raft and lay down beside him. She dashed up the hill. Out of breath, she quickly made her way over to her camp. The coals in the fire pit were still warm. She threw on some wood and fanned the flame. To quiet her thumping heart, she tossed kelekenikàn into the fire and inhaled its sweet aroma. Next, she grabbed her woven mat still covered in the mud she was using on the sweatlodge, and shook it clean as best she could. She hurried down to the creek, the mat flying behind her. She pulled up sheets of soft damp cedar moss, soaking them in the creek before tossing them onto the mat. When the mat was overflowing, she pressed the whole thing down, rolled it up, and raced back down the hill pulling the mat behind her.

Blackpaw was right where she left him. The limp creature still lay there motionless. Nushèmakw unwrapped the mat and spread it on the beach careful to keep the moss bedding clean. With the eelgrass under him, the man slid easily off the raft and onto the mat. She tucked the moss all around him and across his back, knowing that its healing ways would begin to draw the anger from his wounds.

She secured the harness around the mat's frame, and she and Black-paw pulled their stranger home.

Night came on while a gentle spring rain fell. Nushèmakw sat with the stranger, who was still prostrate on the mat. Raindrops sizzled on the hot fire that was keeping them both warm. She watched the moss that covered him drink up the rain, sending life and healing into the man's deadened skin. She warmed her hands on a cup she had fashioned from an elbow of wood and sipped on broth of mussels and fiddleheads. The sky cleared and the Star Path appeared. She hoped her father and Snow were traveling safely on its many spiraling trails. The air took on a chill, and she covered her shoulders with her feathered shawl. Soon the day's events took their toll, and her head bobbed with sleep. She lay down next to the stranger and dreamed of her childhood home in the mountains.

A thin red line was hugging the horizon when Nushèmakw woke. The stars were fading. Even *Ansísktayèsàk*, the Seven Sisters, had left the sky to travel the heavens until darkness fell again. Blackpaw was already off hunting. The stranger was motionless under his blanket of moss. She started a fire and said her thanksgiving prayers before heading down to the creek for water. Once there, she filled her water pot to the brim. It was heavy, but she was able to lift it and make her way back up the hill to camp.

While she waited for the water to boil, she walked over to her wikwam and drew aside the grass curtain that covered the door. The fresh spring air flooded inside. The door faced west away from the harsher winds. Although a little of the morning light fell through the chimney hole, the room was still in shadow. The wikwam was tight and holding well, and she was proud of her work. Domed like the sweatlodge but larger, its cedar bark shingles smelled sweet, and the pleasant scent permeated her home with their healing and spirit essences. She swept out the old ash pile from the center of the room, and lay in fresh kindling. Under her bed, which stretched along the southern wall, she removed two strips of dried squirrel meat and a duck egg from a clay pot.

She would deal with the man soon, but first she needed to eat. She walked over to the fire pit and carefully lowered the egg into the boiling water. She skewered the squirrel flesh onto a green twig and propped it over the coals. As the sun crept over Little Turtle Island, she ate quickly licking the yolk that stuck to her fingers.

She knelt beside the stranger and checked his breathing. Still weak but steady. Bit by bit, she began to remove the moss careful not to further injure his damaged skin. She uncovered his eyes, hoping to see some relief from the burn. The flesh was puffy and red, and his eyes were still swollen shut. His back looked a little better. The sores, although wet, weren't as inflamed. She pulled a small, hinged clam-shell from her bundle and rinsed it in the pot of hot water to rid it of debris. Then she began tweezing out the remaining bits of sand and silt that doggedly clung to his wounds.

Pleased with the results, she stepped back to examine him in whole. That white skin disturbed her, and she could see that he needed to dry out. Maybe that would help his color return. The sun was blazing, flooding the camp in warmth and light. As pleasant as it felt to her, it would be the stranger's ruin. She had to get him into the wikwam.

She shouted for Blackpaw. "*Tonin!*" but he didn't come. He was too far out in the marshes to hear her. Inhaling deeply, she prayed for strength and courage, then grabbed the mat and dragged the man into the wikwam.

"This is going to hurt," she told him before thrusting her arms around his chest and pulling him up and onto her platform bed. Not a sound came from him, which worried her more than if he had screamed.

She struck a flint, lit the kindling in the center of the room, and added a few pinecones. The fire spit and flared as it licked the sticky sap. From her medicine bundle, she pulled a pinch of red cedar and the last of her bearberry and sprinkled it over the flame. With three eagle feathers she stroked the smudge-smoke that rose lazily from the coals, directing its fragrance over the man, opening the channels of healing that she prayed would come upon him. She sang and she shook the turtle rattle, and she danced around the fire, while the sun warmed the cedar walls of her new home.

As the day wore on and evening descended on the island, she saw improvement in the stranger. His badly swollen tongue had shrunk somewhat. Still too far gone to swallow on his own, she placed wet compresses of soaked moss into his cheeks, hoping the nourishing moisture would revive him. It worked better than she expected. Soon, she was able to pour a trickle of tea down his throat, a concoction of thistle and nettle root she had gathered along the creek. It was well into the clear and moonlit night when exhaustion overcame her. She fell asleep leaning against the bed.

Spring burst forth in all its splendor the next morning, and the forest responded in full. A cool breeze blew across the yard, the warming sun drying the dew-laden grass. With her stores getting low, this was a perfect morning to collect the plants and herbs that were pushing up from the cold ground all over the island.

The stranger fared better today. The slightest flush was beginning to creep into his face. Her prayers and remedies were working. She dipped a bit of moss in the nettle tea and placed it over his badly swollen eyes. She turned him on his side and gently covered him with her soft deerskin blanket, careful to keep it off his sore back.

She grabbed her basket, exhilarated by the prospect of a day in the woods. The forest always smelled best in the morning, fresh and pungent and clean. The birds were already busy. She could hear the chewink, its loud *tow-hee-tow-hee* resonating from the underbrush. The bright goldfinch chirped and pranced along the cedar canopy looking for a mate. She crossed the creek and followed the deer path further into the woods, startling a flock of blackbirds. Their emblazoned shoulders caught the sun as they flew away. Along the bank, a rush of violets bloomed, and she picked their delicate blossoms. Further along the path, she stopped to dig up the tender roots of a sassafras tree. The fiddleheads were still tight under the shady canopy, and she gathered as many as she could. She passed the familiar swamp maple with its knotty trunk, and checked the pot she'd left hanging from a wound in the bark. Nearly full of sap, she would carry it back to boil down when she returned to camp.

Closer to the marsh, a stand of shadbush was already in full bloom, heralding the arrival of the shiny silver shad that would soon run up the creek to spawn. Leatherleaf spread along the underbrush, with white blossoms hanging from thin stems like tiny rows of teeth.

As the day wore on, she crossed the island, reaping all that she needed. Blueberry and pyxie bushes abounded with new growth, and she gathered their tender stems. She was on the hunt for the ingredients to make kelekenikàn—the sacred blend of bark and herbs she was taught to mix with her tobacco before offering it to the Great Spirit. Red sumac had just sprouted leaves and was easy to collect, as was the bark of the young alder, chokecherry, and the bright red branches of dogwood. The last thing she needed was bearberry, so she headed back toward the creek where she'd seen some. Along the sloping terrain, the forest floor grew spongy and dampened her moccasins. The woods opened to a dark pool where slivers of light sifted through the cedar ceiling and onto the water. She picked her way over soggy ground for a better look and was greeted by a spectacle she had never seen before. All across the sparkling pool, tight clusters of glowing pink flowers stood on top of tall green stalks that towered out of the water.

"Swamp pink!"

She'd heard of swamp pink but had never actually seen any. Along the sides where the cascade of flowers thinned, mounds of golden club floated lazily over the quiet water. She would collect their roots before she left to dry and grind into flour.

The sun broke through the trees blanketing the pond with white light. A pair of painted turtles lolled about on a floating log, basking in the warmth of early spring. Nushèmakw stayed in that magical place well into the afternoon. When the sun dropped behind the trees, she hoisted the straps of her basket over her shoulders and started for home grateful for her bounty. Rather than take the deer path home, she decided to stay closer to the creek, where the bearberry bush was abundant.

Up ahead she spotted a tremendous white oak, its width surpassing even the girth of her giant pine. Its central branches were torn to splinters, and close to the ground, it was burnt to the core.

"A lightning strike," she guessed, laying her hands on the gray bark. The tree lived on. The ancient sap had found a way around the injury, feeding the newer growth above it. She set down her basket and began to sing. Her song returned to her, an echo almost beyond hearing. It reverberated inside the oak, and she realized that it was hollow. Over endless years, the massive thing had been transformed into a chamber of sound. Who else had been here, she wondered. Certainly the Forest Keepers, but she sensed that others had been there too. She pressed her ear against the rough bark. Like the voices that inhabit the ocean's empty whelk shells, so did voices inhabit this tree. She could hear them, or almost. She imagined she could hear the voices of her people, her Onondaga and Minisink and Kechemeches. She hummed a sacred song, and the tree received it. Now her voice would be an echo among the rest.

She turned to leave, and the tree spoke. "Listen" it said. "Look." Pressed into a fold in the gnarled bark was a burrowed hole, a carving left long ago by the oak's old friend, *papaxès*, the woodpecker. She peered inside.

The last rays of the setting sun fell over the tree and into the hole, catching on his fine pelt, turning his black coat to gold. His fur shimmered as it slowly rose and fell with each breath. She stepped back. It was her beautiful Maxkwe, her Black Bear, her Guardian Spirit. He never left the island after all. It was still the time of his long sleep, and just as the island was awakening with spring, so would he.

"Dream on, my Guardian. Soon we will meet again."

Nushèmakw returned to her camp to find Blackpaw gnawing contentedly on some gruesome carcass he had dragged home, maybe a red squirrel or what was left of a small beaver. She built up the fire and started some water boiling. Digging through her basket, she tossed in some roots and herbs and would add the rest of her dried squirrel a little later. She poured water into her cup and went to check on the stranger.

He had wet the bedding, a good sign that he was coming round. The sores were healing quickly now, no longer angry and with new skin growing over them. Ever so carefully, she removed the moss from his eyes and was glad to see the swelling was almost gone. Gently she placed a finger to his lid and lifted it.

"Èchei!" she cried. She dropped the cup, and splashed water all over the floor. She backed away then took a deep breath. Slowly, she bent over the man again. Bracing herself, this time she lifted both lids. "Oh my," she whispered shaking her head. "Poor, poor man." By now Blackpaw had entered the wikwam, curious and sniffing about. "Blackpaw," she said, "our poor stranger must be blind. Just look at his eyes. The sea has turned them blue!"

OWEN

1534 AD

MAY

The first thing Owen saw was smoke. All around him, white billows tumbled and swirled and wound their way up to a light that
hovered above him. He lay on his stomach, head to one side. His
back felt like it was on fire. In front of him was an opening covered
in mesh. Light bled through it and mixed with the hot churning air.

He tried to remember where he was but nothing came to him.
He thought of home, and his mother, and their cottage at Bentley
Manor. He thought of Grancha. And then he remembered that
Grancha was dead, and he started to cry. Soft sobs went on for a long
time, and still he didn't know where he was.

I have died too, he decided. *I've gone to hell and will lay here for an eternity in this lonely place of brimstone.* He began to cry again. The heat was
unbearable. Sweat poured from every pore of his body. Then he realized that the mist that fell all over him wasn't smoke after all, it was
steam. He inhaled it, and the moisture drifted up his nose. This was
not the rank stink of hell's burning rot; it smelled like cloves or maybe sage. Encouragement crept into his heart. *Am I in heaven?* He closed
his eyes and tried to move, but it was hard. He opened and closed his
hands. Then he moved his toes, and they dipped into something like
sand. His body was sore and weak, but with a shaky arm, he managed
to turn on his side. He breathed deeply and opened his eyes. Now
facing the light in the wall, he realized that it was a covered door. *I'm*

in a cave, he thought, small and tight and barely as long as he was.

He heard singing. *What's that?* A woman's voice, soft and low, a soothing chant that filled him to the brim. The singing stopped. Now she was chanting. Now she was silent. Then came the slow pulsing of a rattle. He reached for the door and pulled back the drape.

"*Diar!*" he cried. "My God, she has wings!" Her back was to him, and he could see the white feathers falling over her shoulders as she shook the rattle slow and steady. He rubbed his eyes and looked again. "This must be heaven because God has sent me an angel!"

The woman heard him and spun around. She stared back at him, her face brown but painted black. His mind knotted up. "*Diar!*" he cried again right before he fainted.

He woke in the middle of the night, not in the cave of smoke, but in a hut, one that carried a familiar scent. He'd been in here before. A fire smoldered in the center of the room, and a few small stars shone through a hole in the roof. He pulled off his covers and sat up. His back felt better, but his limbs were weak. He looked down to see that he was wearing nothing but some sort of strange loincloth made of thin suede. On the floor to his right lay the black angel, asleep and still covered in her feathered wings. Now that he could see how young she was, she looked harmless. Next to the door sat a big white dog, a sentinel who eyed him top to bottom. His long pink tongue hung from the side of his mouth, and he panted gently. Owen held out his hand, and the dog came over and sniffed him. He was a fine animal with a thick white coat and pricked ears. Both his front and hind paws were tipped with black. He'd never seen a dog quite like this one and suspected he was part wolf. He scratched the dog behind his ear, and the dog licked his hand.

"*Ontiendakkna*," came a voice from across the room, and the dog sat down immediately. The woman stood and looked at Owen but unlike the dog, her stare unnerved him. He froze when she approached. Without making a sound, she leaned toward him so close that their noses nearly touched. Out of the black paint that covered her face, her two dark eyes bore down on his with relentless concentration. Then she backed away and began waving her hands frantically in front of his face. He leaned back. Now she was coming at him with a pointed finger, and his eyes crossed. Round and round her finger went, and his eyes followed until he was dizzy.

"*Gatkattaacli!*" she hollered, and the dog barked. She was overjoyed.

"*Kulamàlsí hàch?*" she asked, but it was lost on him. He shrugged his shoulders. Now he could see that her feathered wings were not white after all, but silver and brown. He pointed to them, "Are you an angel?"

She tilted her head, perplexed.

"Your feathers," he said again pointing.

She patted her shoulders.

"Yes. Your wings, I see that you have wings!" he shouted, as if shouting would make her understand.

"*Ouaga?*" she asked, tapping her shoulders. In one swift movement, she took off her feathered shawl and tossed it to Owen. He gasped, surprised to see that her wings were nothing more than a cloak. He blushed profusely at his mistake, and that made her laugh. He managed a laugh, too, although nervously. He could see that behind the black paint was not a celestial being after all, but an earthly woman with a warm smile. He was alive!

She went out the door, and the dog followed. While Owen sat there, the sun crept into the hut saturating it with dim light. She returned with a bowl of broth. "*Cherha,*" she said, handing it to him. He nodded his thanks and gazed out the door, backlit and radiant. What had become of him? He closed his eyes. When was the last time he'd prayed? He didn't know. He opened his eyes, and the woman was still scrutinizing him. She pointed to the bowl in his hand. "*Cherha,*" she said again, and he drank it all.

She blew on the embers in the middle of the room and reached into the leather pouch that hung around her neck. She pulled out some dry herbs and held them to his nose. They smelled like pine and something else vaguely familiar, and she sprinkled them over the fire. The lazy scented smoke hovered over the flame. The woman closed her eyes and chanted words he had never heard. They were a prayer. It fell on his ears with such tenderness that he filled with sadness all over again. Now she held three feathers between her fingers and began to fan him, first across his arms, then his back and legs and head. She kept fanning the smoke, chanting all the while, and coaxing it up through the roof where it disappeared into the morning sky.

She looked him over, then grabbed his hands, pulling him to his feet. His legs were wobbly and suddenly they looked thin as rails. She held him by the arm and helped him outside to a central yard where a fire pit was laid. He sat on a log and watched steam rise from an earthen pot that smelled like meat. His stomach growled shamelessly. She filled the bowl and handed it to him, and he ate it all.

"Thank you," he said as she served him a second helping. "What's this?" he asked picking out a cube of meat from the soup. "This, what is it?"

She pointed to a line tied between two straight cedar trees. From it hung the pelt of some peculiar animal. It looked like a giant rodent with reddish brown fur and webbed hind feet. He popped the morsel in his mouth. It was delicious.

"*Tëmakwe*," she told him, as she served herself a bowl.

"Tow-ma-qua," he repeated, and she laughed.

When they finished, she went back into her hut and got the deerskin blanket to place over his shoulders.

He took it off. "No thanks. I'm hot."

She put it on him again. Patting his back, she pointed to the sun. He saw that she was worried about sunburn. "Thank you, but no. I don't need it," he said, and he took it off again. With the same perturbed look that he had seen cross his mother's face many, many times, she grabbed his hands and pulled him up. He followed her to a spot near a creek, where the cedars shaded the mossy banks. The creek was beautiful. It reminded him of the moors at Bentley, and his heart ached. Exhaustion began to take over again, a warm and peaceful feeling. He couldn't resist closing his eyes. He rolled onto the deerskin she'd laid out for him and fell into a deep sleep.

He woke with the sound of the woman calling to him. He popped up. Something was happening down at the creek, where she was running back and forth and motioning for him to come. He wiped the sleep from his eyes and stood on legs that felt stronger. Up the creek, the water was roiling and whipping over rocks and fallen logs. Where the woman stood, it slowed remarkably forming a vast pool still as glass.

"*Tonín!*" she called again. Owen rushed down the bank. She was elated, and now he could see why. Where a huge mound of sticks and debris dammed the current, hundreds of silver fish swarmed, their scales glistening through the water. She dashed up the bank and returned with a large braided net that she threw into the creek. Stones weighted the corners. When it sunk, she pulled it across the water, and it filled with the squirming mass. She tugged harder and harder, and the fish flipped and flailed. The catch was so heavy she had trouble dragging it up the bank. Owen saw her struggling, and he grabbed hold, too. Together, they were able to haul it to dry ground. Owen plopped down on the grass completely spent. The woman opened her arms skyward and said a prayer.

Back at the camp, he helped her gut the fish with one of her sharp flint tools. Some she boiled in the earthen pot, and some she fried on a hot stone slathered in grease that he guessed was rendered from the strange rodent hanging on the line. "*Tëmakwe?*" he asked. She nodded, visibly satisfied with his pronunciation.

They sat under a tree and feasted. It tasted better than anything in the world, and he couldn't get enough. With a pile of bones beside him, he leaned back against the trunk and sighed.

"What's your name?" he asked. "Your name?"

She tilted her head.

He pointed to the rodent pelt. "*Tëmakwe?*" he said. She nodded, yes. He pointed to himself. "Owen." She nodded again.

Then he pointed to her, and she said, "*Nushèmakw.*"

"NEW-shimawk?"

She shook her head. "*Nushèmakw,*" she repeated, this time slowly. "*Hakchínna Nushèmakw.*"

"New-SHEM-awk."

This time she nodded. Now it was his turn. She pointed at him. "a-WÈN?"

He shook his head. "No, OH-win."

"Owen."

"Yes!"

She laughed and returned to the fire to stir the soup.

While he lay comfortably against the tree with his stomach full and body rested, he began to remember. It came on quick. At first, it was a jumble of memories hard to sort out. Then they slowed and fell into place, and he lapsed into an overwhelming grief. He remembered everything. Master Blazer and the night he learned about his father's plight. The day he arrived at Greyfriar, and he touched the top of his head where the hair had nearly grown in by now. And then there was Oxford and his work with Father Elis. He looked at his hands. What had happened to all the manuscripts? Then he thought of Sir Thomas More and that stormy night when he barely escaped, and learning of Father Elis's fate at the gallows. He closed his eyes against everything that came flooding back. His harrowing ride back to Bristol, the abbey up in flames, Greyfriar empty as a tomb, Master Blazer hiding him in the buttery and protecting him from Cromwell's men.

Then he remembered Uncle Seamus, and he leaped to his feet. He yelled to the woman.

"Nushèmakw, Nushèmakw!" he called to her. "Is my Uncle Seamus here? Please. Is there another man? A man, a man white like me, but old." He saw that she didn't understand any of this, and he sat down and buried his head in his hands.

She sat next to him. "Owen," she said, touching his shoulder. She began scratching in the dirt. She made a stick figure with a skirt and long hair and pointed to herself. Then she drew another, this one with a breechcloth, and she filled in the lines with a little white ash and pointed to him.

Next to them, Owen drew a third person, a white man with pants and a shirt and yellow sand for hair. "Have you seen another man?"

She looked at him sadly and shook her head. No, and she erased the man with yellow hair. It was just the two of them. He lay on his back and covered his eyes with his arm. *The Mary Margaret*, his seasickness, he remembered it all. He was locked in the cabin with the captain's table wedged against the door. The storm came, and then the sea calm, and the island rose from the depths. Uncle Seamus rowing the cockboat toward the island was the last thing he saw before the wall of water hit him.

Without opening his eyes he asked, "Am I on Hy-Brasil?"

When she didn't respond, he sat up, and started drawing again. This time he drew England with Ireland next to it and tapped his chest.

"This is where I'm from."

He made a row of waves, and underneath he scratched a long line ending at a small circle in the middle of the ocean. "You," he said. "Is this where you are?"

She took the stick from him and drew another circle, this one larger. She divided it into thirteen parts; four squares on each side and five down the middle. She added four webbed feet, a small head, and a short pointed tail.

"*Tulpehakink.*"

She had drawn a turtle.

NUSHÈMAKW AND OWEN

✺

1534 CE, JUNE

STRAWBERRY MOON

Nushèmakw and Owen spent the weeks that followed trying to understand each other. As the days grew longer, they passed the evenings playing their stick game, scratching and drawing in the dirt. They started with the objects they shared, words like "tree," "squirrel," "rock." Then they tackled things particular to their own worlds. Owen learned "wíkwam, skunk, maize" and Nushèmakw "castle, hedgehog, wheat." They soon moved to phrases and then sentences. She spoke mostly in Onondaga, but sometimes in Unami. He used Welsh sprinkled with English. They were equally adept at learning languages, and soon they developed their own pidgin dialect that was a mix of them all. By summertime, they were able to converse passably. But there were other stumbling blocks to overcome.

It was the beginning of summer, and Nushèmakw couldn't believe Owen's reaction when she headed out into the blazing hot field without her blouse. He turned as red as a strawberry and asked her why she was going outside naked. "What do you mean?" she asked. "Look, I've got my skirt on." He cringed and told her that in his land it was shameful for women to go without a blouse. She thought that was a silly custom and ignored it. But he became so distressed that finally they agreed to both wear shirts in the hot summer sun and be equally miserable sweating under the clinging suede.

She was surprised, too, at how uncomfortable he became when

she tried to talk to him about Wemahtekënis, the Keeper of the Forest she had encountered during her rite of passage. In fact, everything about her ritual journey seemed to bother him. Her cleansing at the wiktut, the ceremonial songs and dances that her father and Chief Kitakima bestowed upon her before her ritual fast, Grandfather Thunder. She puzzled over this while they finished planting the last hill of tobacco with seed she'd brought with her when she fled the village, a stash that all the medicine women carried in their bundles. She stood next to Owen and examined the newly planted mounds of earth.

"If Kahèsëna Hàki smiles on us this season," she told Owen, "and if Grandfather Thunder brings the rain, then we'll have enough tobacco to carry us through the winter."

Owen became quiet and walked away. She shook her head. What was it that caused him such distress? His people knew about the Creator. He told her that. And she'd seen him pray. Nothing about this man made sense. She knew she should be patient with him, but it was hard. And now that she was busy from sun up to sundown tending her plots and foraging for food, there was little time to probe him for answers.

She watched Owen cross the field with an armload of long branches. *He'll finish it soon,* she thought. He was building his own wikwam, and even though it was a square of logs rather than a bark-covered dome, she had to admit he was doing a fine job. As soon as he was able to get around on his own, he had insisted on his own place, saying it wasn't right for them to sleep under one roof unless they were family. She agreed with him. Besides it was making him stronger and distracting him from all his worry and grief.

Such an odd man with his curly red hair, which thankfully had filled in on top. And it turned out that the blue of his eyes had nothing to do with blindness. Apparently his people have many colors of eyes and hair, and he told her that his mother's eyes were actually green! How is that possible? She learned, too, that his pale skin was not a sickness after all, but the way all his people looked. Still she was glad when he was able to spend some time in the sun and his skin gained a little color. He insisted, too, on removing his beard, which did improve his appearance. It had grown in thicker than anything she had seen before. Unlike her uncles, who plucked the sparse hairs from their faces, Owen had to use her flint knife to shear his face and neck.

Something caught her attention. Not a sound but a feeling. She raised her hand to shade her brow and searched the length of the creek.

"Ah," she whispered.

There he was. Maxkwe had finally returned! Her Guardian Bear stood in the distance on the opposite bank grand and beautiful. How long had he been waiting for her? She ran to the creek to greet him, but by the time she got there he was gone. She crossed the water and found his huge prints leading back into the forest. Then she saw his reason for coming. A large buck lay slain beside his tracks. A fresh kill, a gift. Her black bear knew that there were two of them now, and they would need more meat to survive the winter. He had provided for them.

"What happened?" It was Owen calling from the top of the hill.

"Owen!" she said waiving for him to come. "Maxkwe has been here. Come! You can cross where the oak has fallen."

She was surprised at the ease in which he dashed down the bank and across the wet log.

"Look," she said, kneeling by the carcass. "He left this for us."

"Who left it?"

"Maxkwe, my Guardian Bear. I saw him. He was waiting for me. See his prints?"

Owen looked at the dead deer, then at her, and his face filled with concern. "This bear you speak of. He's not a man, yet you talk as if it were."

"I know he's not a man, Owen," she said, feeling the heat rising in her face. "Do you think I'm stupid? He's the Creator's spirit helper. Like the angels you talk about."

"A bear is not an angel."

"How do you know?"

He had no answer for her, and instead remained silent while they dragged the deer home. They spent the rest of the afternoon dressing the meat and carting the offal away from the camp where the turkey vultures would find it. She was thankful for his help, but at the same time it made her uneasy to have a man do all of this women's work.

✶

1534 CE, JULY

GREEN BEAN MOON

She left Owen at the camp the next morning, and told him she would be gone for five days. It was her moontime, she had said, and she would stay in the wiktut she had built in the forest by the pond. That was all the explanation he got except that she would bring back a store of shadbush berries if they were ripe, and more bearberry, sumac leaves, and red cedar for the sacred smudging.

Owen shook his head. What was he to make of her with her dark skin and, of all things, her tattoos! He had seen black people at the docks at Bristol, the free Africans and the awful condition of the ones the English kept in chains. He'd seen the Turks and the Chinese that traveled with them. But she didn't look like any of them. Her hair was black, long, and straight, and she wore it rolled into a bun at the nape of her neck. Some days she let it fall loose around her shoulders; other times she braided it or tied it back with a beaded leather lace. Thankfully she only painted her face black when she performed her strange rituals, a practice she said she did to honor her father who met a violent but honorable death only a few months ago. She was so healthy and strong for a woman, yet the softness in her face showed him that she could be no more than sixteen or seventeen years old.

For someone so young, she was amazingly knowledgeable about everything on the island and could answer any question he asked. She was a healer, a medicine woman, she said, and he didn't doubt it. After all, hadn't she brought him back from the dead? It was a miracle even if she did it with her mysterious chants and herbs and smoke and prayers. She prayed about everything. She was a heathen with beliefs more blasphemous than anything he had ever encountered. Yet she was sincere, and in many ways, more religious than the friars back home. It was an odd combination, and it confused him. She was pious and profane at the same time, in one instance singing so beautifully it would melt the earth, and the next talking like a sailor about the ways of copulation without a trace of inhibition. It was scandalous behavior, especially for a woman.

But she could be embarrassed too and by the most unlikely things. He noticed the way she could hardly look at him when he carried water up from the creek or helped her weed the maize. It was a woman's job to do these things, she said, and he realized now how unmanly she thought he was acting. "Can you hunt?" she asked more than once and was relieved when he nodded yes. He could build shelters and clear land, too, which lifted her opinion of him, if only a little.

Now she was gone, and he had five days before her return. He stood up and began to prepare for a journey across this strange island to see if there was any way to get back home.

It was afternoon when he crossed the creek, heading in the opposite direction of the pond where Nushèmakw was staying. A narrow sandy path wound westward into the forest, and he followed it until the sun went down.

After taking a long drink from the cedar creek, water that tasted as good as any he had ever had at home, he sat on the mossy bank and rested. He pulled a biscuit from a leather pouch Nushèmakw had made for him. The bread was good, chewy and moist, made from dried roots she'd ground to powder. They would taste better, she told him, when she could mix in the berries and seeds that she would gather later in the summer. It tasted delicious anyway, and he munched away.

He looked up at the multitude of tall straight cedars that sprang from the banks. Oaks and maples grew in the gaps between them choking most of the light with their thick canopy. By the size of their leaves, Owen guessed it must be the middle of June, yet this beautiful copse stayed cool and breezy beneath the trees.

Something in the brush caught his attention. He sat quietly and watched. To his astonishment, a small creature flew up and out of bushes spiraling straight up into the air. The dusky sky shone behind it making it hard to identify. Maybe it was a bat, but bats didn't live so low to the ground. It was a bird, he decided, and he could barely make out its bulbous shape and long tapered beak. Up and around it flew, whistling all the while, before plummeting into the brush, chirping loudly. Up it flew again whistling away, a male for sure. Owen knew a mating dance when he saw one. He couldn't help but laugh at this crazy lovesick bird and wished Nushèmakw was here to see it.

When the sky grew dark, he left the path and made his way to the edge of the forest so he could see the stars, and immediately, his legs were snagged in briars. The tangled hedge was impenetrable, and he searched for a break where he could get across. He moved slowly, careful not to catch a thorn on his bare feet. In the clearing, a new chorus fell on his ears with a resounding *quonk-quonk-quonk*. They were frogs, but these were calling from the trees rather than the ground. Was there no end to the mysteries on this island?

The clearing led to a sandy cliff that fell sharply to the water below. He had reached the western limits of the island. On top of the sandy soil lay a thick covering of needles, and he leaned against a large pine and stared into the sky while it filled with stars. There was the Great Wagon constellation pointing to the northern lodestar just as it did at home. He thought about his mother and what torment she must be going through watching these same stars fan across the horizon as she searched for the *The Mary Margaret*.

He would get back home to her if he could find a way, but for now there was nothing more to do until daybreak. Without moonlight, it was hard to see how expansive the water was below him. The reflection of stars twisted and turned on the waves near the shore, but further out, there was only a black dark mass. He hoped it was land.

Soon an answer came as a light twinkled along the landscape, then another, then another. It was the light of small campfires shining through the trees, and he realized he must have found the village of Nushèmakw's people. He watched the horizon for a long time comforted by the scores of fires that warmed the hearths of her family across the water. He would ask her to take him there when he got back to camp. But before that, he wanted to see what lay on the other side of the island.

In the morning, he started a small fire and roasted a fish he had skewered in the creek. He searched the thicket where he'd seen the funny dancing bird the night before. The hen was sitting staunchly on her nest barely moving, and he reached under for a few eggs. They were small but good scrambled on a hot stone. Full enough for now, he put out the fire before making his way south down a path that ran along the shoreline. The view was spectacular, and he could now see clearly the landmass across the bay where the Kechemeches lived. The distance between them was substantial. Unless there was a strait further north that broached the divide, he couldn't see how Nushèmakw made it across, especially without a boat.

Out from under the shade of the forest, the sun shone brightly. The sandy cliffs slowly diminished, opening to wide beaches plush with wildflowers. Vast carpets of low-growing vines with yellow blossoms sprawled everywhere over the dunes and up the sides of the sandy banks that skirted the woods. Here, the dunes retreated, engulfed by large brackish pools, where masses of purple flowers swayed atop tall green stalks. As the day wore on, the air became hot and stagnant, and he spent much of his time swatting at the mosquitos that bit incessantly, and praying that they wouldn't give him marsh fever like they could at home.

He continued hiking well into the afternoon. To his disappointment, there appeared to be no end to this stretch of beach that held a straight course south. The Unami villages he had seen before seemed even further distant as the bay expanded between them. He was hot and thirsty and had lost sight of the creek. Seeking shelter under a scrubby maple, he sat to rest. It was foolish of him to have left the path near fresh water, and he only hoped he could find it again before nightfall.

A crashing sound came over the dunes. Blackpaw galloped merrily toward him, breaking through the grasses and splashing through the shallows, his tongue hanging out the side of his mouth.

"Good dog," Owen said, "Am I ever so glad to see you!" He sat down and let the dog lick his face. The dog made him feel like he was back home, and he loved him for it.

"*Tonín,*" he said to him, which he had learned was "Come" in Onondaga. They climbed up the sandy banks and disappeared into the protection of the forest.

The island was larger than he had imagined. Even with Blackpaw's help, it took them two days to reach the other side. He sat on the dunes and looked across the ocean, while Blackpaw gnawed on a fish carcass that had washed ashore. It was here on the beach with the sun low behind him that he realized he was not going home. Not now, not ever. It wasn't just the endless and infinite water that stood between him and England, it was that still small voice from deep inside. He wept. One last time for all that was lost: for his mother, for his brothers at the friary, for Father Elis who found heaven too soon, and for the boy Owen once was. He was twenty-two, yet he felt like an old man.

Nushèmakw would be back by now, he guessed, and he stood to go. He called out her name, "Nushèmakw," and Blackpaw responded by leading them over the dune and into the marshes. They were heading home.

It was just before sunset when they reached the marsh that led to the ridged basin when something strange caught his eye. Hidden in the grasses along a sandy knoll was a large black platform partially submerged in the mud. It was the raft Nushèmakw told him about; the one she used to carry him across the water when he was marooned. The raft with four posts with one broken off. It was just as peculiar as she had described.

He cocked his head. "It can't be!"

This was not a raft at all. It was a table. A desk turned upside down. It was a captain's desk, Uncle Seamus's desk, his father's desk! He ran his hand over the flaking varnish and peeling paint. Everything was beginning to make sense. The desk had washed out to sea with him, and somehow, it had carried him all the way to this strange, strange island. Nushèmakw's Little Turtle Island.

Could it still be there? His heart started to pound, and he checked the corner buried in mud. Nothing. The other side sprang up from the water, and he raced around. He felt under the molding. There it was. The sealed drawer hidden in the desk. He fingered the wooden slats hidden in the frame. Surely nothing could have survived the cruel battering of salt and sea. The first lever was swollen and warped and broke off in his hand, but it cleared the way for the second, which had suffered less damage and fell into place with little effort. He pushed the third lever and then pulled the fourth. When the last slide gave way, he heard the lock pop. The drawer slowly opened.

Lying in pristine condition inside the drawer's enameled walls were three items that had survived the scourge of the ocean. A package of sewing needles, a small jeweled dagger, and a tightly rolled map.

❧

1534 CE, JULY

BLUEBERRY MOON

He seemed at peace now and Nushèmakw was grateful. Ever since he returned from his trek across the island he was friendlier and less withdrawn. She was able to learn more about him in the weeks that followed, and she was glad that he was willing to learn more about the ways of her people.

She was astonished at how much he had suffered before the Great Spirit brought him to her. It was if he came from an under-world where violence, betrayal, and sickness always prevailed. But he was a kind man, and he spoke often now about a savior spirit, not an animal like her Guardian Bear, but a man who shined the light of truth and goodness upon the earth and died a hero's death to save his people and bring peace into the world.

He spoke with such raw sincerity that she knew he walked in that truth. Yet she still had so many questions about this savior. If he came many, many years ago to bring heaven to earth as Owen said, where was the peace? Not on his island called England. He told her that much. Certainly not on her own Great Turtle Island. From the northern lakes of the Haudenosaunee, down through the Susque-hannock territory, to the grandfather lands of Lenapehokink, strife and conflict were increasing.

She refrained from saying too much about the sacred ways of her people, even when he prodded her. It wasn't winter yet, the time for storytelling, and she didn't want to bring harm upon them by telling the stories out of season. They would finish the harvest first. When Grandfather Winter covered the ground with frost, then she would teach him her father's ways. He would learn the ceremonies that please the Great Spirit, and they would tell their stories in the traditional manner.

Owen walked across the yard wearing a smile and carrying a strange box. He was a good-looking man she decided given all things, and when he was happy his blue eyes lit up like the sky.

"What is it, Owen?"

"I have brought you presents," he said.

They sat on the ground, and he placed the box between them. "Open it."

She lifted the lid and reached inside. A small bundle of thin shiny sticks were tied together with twine. She carefully turned them over in her hand. "What are these?"

Owen struggled to find the word. "They're needles, Nushè-makw. For sewing. Like the bone awls you use to make clothes only these are made of metal and are much stronger."

"Thank you, Owen. You're very kind. This is a fine gift. These needles are heavy," she added, weighing them in her hand.

"Like I said, they are made of metal. Something strong like stone but easier to shape. They will last a long time. My uncle used the large ones to mend his nets. The smaller ones were for patching clothes. Look, there's more."

She pulled out the scroll from the box and examined it. "You're full of mysteries today, Owen. What is this? It's much too smooth and fine to be an animal skin."

"In a way it is an animal skin. It is something called vellum made from the hide of a calf, a young animal common in my country. We use it to write on."

"What do you mean?"

"We draw letters on it and pictures. Something like the drawings you and I make on the ground, but our people draw on vellum so it will last. Open it."

She unfurled the scroll and Owen weighted it down with stones. It took her breath away with all its bright colors and finely etched lines.

"This is a beautiful thing," she said as she ran her hand across it. "I'm sure my people have never seen anything like this. What do you do with it?"

"It's a map, Nushèmakw. A map of my world and a little of yours, I think. I was hoping we could study it together and see if you know where we are."

"But I know where we are, Owen. We're on Little Turtle Island. My village is over there," she said pointing west, "and our Lenapehokink extends a long way past it. And far, far away over there in the mountains," she said pointing north, "is where my Onondaga family lives."

"What I mean is, where your home is on the map and where my home is on the map. I thought if we put our minds together we could figure it out."

"Yes, we can try, I suppose, but only after we smoke the kelekenikàn." She hoped the tobacco would also help her understand more about this strange man. "Anyway, it's a beautiful gift. Thank you."

"There's one more thing."

She reached in the box and drew out the dagger.

"Èchei!" She jumped up and threw it on the ground.

"What's wrong?"

"I've seen this knife before," she said with her hand to her mouth.

"What do you mean? How can that be?"

"I've seen it in a dream. This exact knife. It holds a bad spirit. I'm sure of it."

She turned to Owen. "Where did you find it? You had nothing when I found you on the beach. Where'd you get it?"

"It was in the raft, Nushèmakw. I found the raft where you left it down in the marshes when I returned from exploring the island. It isn't a raft after all. It's a table. A platform that stands on four posts. It was on my ship when it sank. It has a drawer made to keep the water out. These things were in the drawer."

Nushèmakw considered all of this carefully. "Owen, you are a good and generous man to offer me these beautiful gifts. I'll find many uses for the needles, and the map will give us many hours of amusement, but I can't keep the knife. I won't even touch it."

Owen picked it up, "But why?"

"In my dream I saw this knife with all its pretty stones. But its beauty is a mask. In truth, it's full of lies. Its greed is insatiable, and it's proud of the suffering it causes wherever it goes. Whose was it?"

"I don't know," he said looking at the thing in his hand. "I thought it belonged to my Uncle Seamus or my father, but I don't know for sure. The stones are from another land and maybe the knife is too. Maybe it belonged to a stranger."

"It doesn't matter. We must not keep it or it'll bring us trouble for sure. If the people who own such knives come to our shores, they will surely be coming to destroy us."

Owen grew pale and sat down.

"What is it, Owen?"

"You're right, Nushèmakw. There are many Englishmen I've met who would come to these shores just to ruin everything they could get their hands on. I've seen the awful things some of them do." He tossed the knife on the ground. "What should I do with it?"

"You must bury it under the giant white pine, and I'll pray that the Great Peacemaker of my Onondaga people will come and break it in two."

1534 CE, AUGUST

GREEN CORN MOON

Owen followed Nushèmakw to the beach the next day. She had insisted that they go.

"If we waited any longer," she had told him, "the quahog will no longer be good to eat. And who knows, maybe we'll find some *chíkolale*."

"What's quahog?" Owen had asked.

"Quahog is a clam with a beautiful purple and white shell."

As they crossed the tidal pool to the dunes, she told him that the beads made from the quahog and whelk were valuable. The purple and white strands of wampum she would make were especially prized by her Onondaga family.

"And my new needles will make the beadwork go a lot faster."

Clamming was something Owen knew about. Since he was knee high, he and his Grancha would go out into the lowlands during the summer months, and at low tide, they'd fill their buckets to overflowing with tasty cockles and mussels. It was a relief to be able to take charge for once. He was tired of being so dependent on Nushèmakw for everything. She seemed to enjoy watching him dig the sandpit and line it with stones. He gathered dry grasses and driftwood and laid them in a pile on top. Striking a sharp flint against a rock, he sent a spark into the duff, and gently blew on it until the grass caught fire. It would take some time for a the wood to reduce to a fine bed of coals, so he waded out into the ocean feeling for the humps of the *èhĕs* in the sand, which he plucked up and pitched to shore.

"Do you think that's enough, Nushèmakw?"

She smiled and nodded. He climbed out of the water to check the fire. The coals glowed brightly, and the stones were red hot. He tossed in a load of seaweed. Immediately the steam began to rise. The clams went on next, topped by more seaweed and an insulating layer of grass. Nushèmakw smiled. He had impressed her.

They sat on the dunes while the clams steamed. The ocean was calm, and the tide was coming in. A few thin clouds scudded across the sky. "The tide will put the fire out for us in a few hours," Owen said.

They watched Blackpaw splash through the water, scaring the gulls that floated on top of the gentle waves.

"Owen," she said, "this may be the best day I've had since I returned to the island."

The possibility that he had made her happy thrilled him.

"Just look around us," she continued. "The blue sky on the dark water, the warm sun on our backs. And we have a feast before us! I can already smell the clams cooking. And now I have you. Not a stranger anymore, but a friend."

Owen was at a loss as to what to say. He was afraid he'd spoil this precious moment. He took a chance anyway.

"I'm so glad you consider me a friend," he said. He was too nervous to look at her so he stared at the water. "You mean a lot to me, Nushèmakw. More than I can say. Not just because you saved my life, but since then you've been so kind. You didn't have to help me, but you did. I'll never be able to repay you for what you did—for finding me out here that day."

Nushèmakw blushed. "You know, Owen, in a way, you've saved me too." She spoke slowly and thoughtfully. "Before you arrived, my heart struggled and grieved until I was nearly torn in two. I had Blackpaw, yes, but there was nothing I could do to keep from drowning in my sadness. I missed my father so much. It felt as if my world was falling apart. It helped to be alone on this island, honoring my father with the year of mourning, and I prayed that he would show me what to do." She brushed away a deerfly that nicked her arm.

"Then you came. This strange man, all alone. I saw then how large the universe is, and how many secrets it holds. I could see the whole world spinning under the heavens. We walk the earth for only a short time, Owen. One day, whether we live to grow old or not, we'll join the Great Spirit and finally live in that peace we're always searching for."

"What's become of us, Nushèmakw? We're living impossible lives, yet here we are. You've traveled enough to see that violence and suffering are everywhere. So have I. We've seen the evil men can do, but we've seen the good too. When I first arrived here, I thought I'd landed on Hy-Brasil, that paradise from old. But I see now that this isn't paradise. You struggle the same as I do, and none of it's fair. I'm coming to believe that Little Turtle Island is purgatory, not heaven or hell but a place in between. Maybe we've been chosen, you and me, to travel in this mysterious realm, a place where we are being tested."

"We shall see, Owen. These are hard questions that deserve the proper ceremonies to help us understand." Her eyes were so filled with deep and fathomless mysteries, it took his breath away.

"What is it, Nushèmakw?"

"Are you willing to stay?" she asked, looking at the ground. "If you'll stay with me on the island through the winter, until the end of my mourning time, I think we may come to find our answers."

Owen thought his heart would burst. "I'll stay," he said too quickly.

Blackpaw came racing over the dunes with a piece of driftwood in his mouth. Owen wrenched it from his jaws and threw it into the ocean, and they watched the dog chase after it.

"Let's eat," Owen said and he walked down to the pit to dig out supper.

After they stuffed themselves, Owen buried the fire, and Nushèmakw gathered the shells she'd bring back home.

She jumped suddenly. "Do you hear that?"

The tide had come in. Owen was dragging the table off the bank and into the tidal pool. "No, what?"

"Listen!"

Then he heard it. A chatter followed by a string of low caws.

"It's the storm crow," she told him. "He only calls when thunder's nearby. Hurry up, Owen, hurry! We've got to get home before it rains."

He saw how upset she was getting. "What's wrong? It's only a rainstorm. A little thunder and lightening won't hurt us."

She became very quiet and dragged the basket of shells over to the raft. Owen grabbed her arm. "What is it? Something's bothering you."

"Yes. It's the thunder. It brings back bad memories." He didn't ask her to say more but she did. "I have an enemy, Owen. His name is Guiarasi. He's my cousin from my Onondaga home. When we were young, I came upon him torturing an animal that he had bound to a tree. I saw an awful light falling all around him, and I knew he was consumed by a bad spirit. He thought that if he could finish this unspeakable act it would earn him praise from our Chief. But I stopped him. I had to. I threw a stone and knocked him out. Then I released the animal and her young. A shameful thing for a woman to do to a man, but I had no choice. It was a black bear, like my Guardian Spirit, but this one was a she-bear, a mother trying to protect her cubs!"

Her face was flushed, and tears welled in her eyes. "He had no right to do it, and I stopped him. In the end, he had nothing to bring back to the tribe to prove his manhood and to claim his rights as a warrior. He blamed me. He swore on that day that he would bring revenge upon me for as long as I lived. He was becoming like the Tadodaho of old, the ancient chief who had snakes in his hair and was possessed with nothing but violence. That's why I had to leave my Onondaga village."

Owen couldn't believe someone so young had suffered so much, and his heart ached for her. "But that was years ago and so far away, Nushèmakw. How do you know he's still trying to kill you?"

"He's not trying to kill me. Instead, it's his mission to make me suffer by harming those I love. I know he's still hunting for me, Owen, because he's the one who killed my father."

Owen felt like he'd been stabbed. "My God, Nushèmakw. I'm so sorry. I didn't know."

"After I saved the bears, Guiarasi returned to the village and vowed to destroy me. Just as he took his final oath, thunder clapped across the sky, and the rain began to fall." She brushed at the flies that swarmed around her head. "I'm not afraid of Guiarasi anymore, not like I used to be. But he's still dangerous."

Thunder rumbled in the distance, and they stood to go.

"Look, Owen!" she said, grabbing his arm.

Owen strained his eyes over the water where she was pointing. Way out where the edge of the sea met the sky, something rocked and bobbed on the ocean, moving ever so slowly northward.

"What is it, Owen?"

As he watched the ship disappear over the horizon, a feeling of dread came over him. Not because it was sailing away, but because he was afraid that it wasn't. They both stared in disbelief.

"Your people?"

"Maybe. If they're not English, they could be Spanish or Dutch."

"Will they come looking for you?"

"I hope not," he heard himself confess. "I pray they don't find this place for a long, long time."

꧷

1534 CE, OCTOBER

HARVEST MOON

They sat in Nushèmakw's wikwam while torrents of rain blew over the island. Water dripped from the roof hole and sizzled in the fire where a pot of squash soup was simmering. She watched as Owen picked roasted corn from his teeth and tossed another cob into the flame.

"How about some more soup?" she asked. "We have plenty."

By the time they finished their meal, the storm had passed, leaving the island crystalline under a sparkling sun. They had spent the last two months harvesting everything they could. The tobacco came in early. It took Nushèmakw weeks to carefully spread their broad leaves in the sun to dry.

"We'll have more than enough kelekenikàn to last the winter," she said.

She packed dried blueberries into a leather sack and placed it next to the others in the dirt cellar Owen had dug next to the wikwam. He had built her a smokehouse, too. "Like the one we had in England," he told her. She loved it. Now it made quick work of preserving the flesh of fish, beaver, turkey, and deer.

"Are you sure we'll need this much food?" he asked her.

"We'll bring whatever we have left back home when we return at the thaw," she said, and he helped her carry baskets of colorful shelled beans and orange rings of dried squash into the cellar.

The blue maize kernels were beginning to harden. Nushè-makw braided and hung them from the rafters to finish drying. Up there she had already tied every kind of plant and herb imaginable, a stockpile of medicine swinging from the ceiling.

"A perfect afternoon for picking *pakím*," she declared. "The ground is too damp to harvest anything else today."

She whistled for Blackpaw and the three of them trekked east-ward through the woods in the direction of the marshy bogs.

Only a few months before in the springtime, when she had taken him down to the bogs for the first time, the entire forest floor was a sea of white blueberry blossoms. Owen told her then that it was the most beautiful sight he'd ever seen.

"Wait until you see the *pakím*," she said. "You won't believe it."

Just before they got to the bog, she made Owen close his eyes. She took his hand and led him the rest of the way. "Now open them," she said.

The cranberries were ripe and the bogs where flush. Huge beds of the fiery orbs spilled out across the edge of the forest and into the sunny lowlands. He stood gazing, awed at the spectacle.

"I wish my grandfather were here to see this," he said quietly.

"I wish he were, too." She handed him a basket and they stepped in.

The next day broke in a splendor that felt like home. Owen had spent many mornings like this one walking the moors across Bentley Manor. He loved it. The first frost had not yet come, but it was close. The chill in the air, the clear and deep blue sky, the daz-zling display of stars still visible under a pale sliver of moon that would soon disappear behind the warming light of the sun.

He was down at the sweatlodge repairing the walls that had washed away in the rain, replacing the clay with bark shingle that would last through the winter. Ever since that first day when he woke in the sweatlodge, confused and frightened, he realized how cleansed he had felt afterwards. So he continued to use it. Nushèmakw would prepare the sweat by pouring water over the heated rocks and burn-ing the herbs and kelekenikàn that would mingle with the heavens to heal not just the body, but the mind and spirit as well. He would take the holy sacrament, juice from the red cranberry and a wafer of pone, in place of wine and bread, to ready himself for his purification. He would enter the lodge while she danced around the fire pit, performing the ritual songs and shaking the sacred rattle.

He secured the last shingle and rehung the drape over the door then stood to stretch his body and breathe in the crisp air. He headed down the deer path to explore the woods. The edge of the forest was ablaze with color. The height of autumn was upon the island, and the crimson, gold, and orange leaves of the oak and sassafras pressed through the dark cedar and pitch pine. He found a rock bathed in sun and sat in the wonderful solitude, watching the animals scratch and flit throughout the woods, diligent in their winter preparations. Across the dunes, the sea stretched to eternity.

In the penetrating peace of the forest, he thought about this beautiful place and the animals and plants largely unspoiled by mankind. The moors in Bristol were beautiful too, but there was a difference. No one owned Little Turtle Island—no king, no lord, no chief. Nushèmakw told him it was the same way throughout all the Unami lands and across all of Lenapehokink and the Haudenosaunee Longhouse. The bands and tribes had hunting territories, boundaries that were ancient and well known. When Owen asked her who owned the land, she didn't understand what he was talking about. When he tried to explain, she finally said in exasperation, "How can a man own the land? It's as ridiculous as if he could own the sun."

So many gaps to fill, so many things between them still foreign and misunderstood. Yet they were making progress. He began to feel that even though he had suffered the loss of home and family, these events had come upon him for a reason. He was here in this realm, a world apart from everything he had ever known, to finally awaken to his purpose in life. After all his doubts and questions and denials, he came to understand in the quiet shelter of the woods that, once stripped of all he possessed, not just his cassock and sandals, but of everything he clung to, that he was a man of God after all. He laughed at this realization. He was not a Greyfriar like the ones at Bristol. He was a Franciscan of old, a man who owned nothing and thus discovered joy. A man thankful to walk this great and good earth, where all of creation sang God's praises, a world that he, like his St. Francis of Assisi, knew and adored.

Deep from within, he felt a stirring so profound it shook him to the bone. He fell to his knees and faced the sky. The spirit of light, his true abiding, swelled and poured in and around him, and he willingly surrendered to it. Soon from the core of his being, he began to chant, his voice low and full, and the song sailed into the shining light that filtered down upon him. Up went his offering into the blazing trees, where the squirrels leapt and the birds fluttered. The sound came through him but was not him, and he knew he was in glorious communion with his God, as he sang over and over again the good saint's Canticle of Brother Sun.

Acorns lay in piles everywhere and Nushèmakw was in the forest collecting them to sweeten in ash water before she ground them to flour. At the crest of a gentle rise that dropped off toward the ocean, she heard it. A low and throaty sound, like the wind through a flute. She realized it was Owen. She followed the sound of his voice, stepping silently through the underbrush. It was a magnificent sound, filled with beauty and honor and humility. She spotted him sitting on a rock overlooking the sea. She stood quietly some distance away to listen and watch.

It was not the language he had taught her, but some other tongue, and it fell on her ears like water over smooth stones. A hush had descended upon the hollow. The forest and all it contained were listening to the sound of Owen's soulful voice. Birds were gathered in the branches above him, still and attentive—the robin and the goldfinch, the catbird and the red-winged blackbird. A great blue heron flew low, hugging the shore and landed in a tidal pool perched on one leg, its eye trained on the singing man. From across the woods, where a wide bog saturated the forest floor, Nushèmakw saw the silhouettes of two large figures floating across the pond. Two dazzling white swans glided into view and settled close to the bank to listen to the man's call to worship. These were the migrating swans of the tundra who had just arrived from the north country. The female had a small spot of yellow at the base of her black beak, an odd and distinguishing shape that Nushèmakw recognized.

"It's you, Mother Ice, back from my childhood home," she

whispered to the creature, who had provided so much comfort during her spring of sorrow. "Do you bring good tidings from my Onondaga aunts and uncles? Listen now. Listen to this man send the light of the Creator over the whole island."

Owen finished his canticle and reached for the sky, offering one last prayer of gratitude. After his benediction, the birds and squirrels began to chatter and scratch again, resuming their busy lives. He turned and saw Nushèmakw wiping tears from her eyes.

He ran toward her. "What's wrong, Nushèmakw? Are you hurt?"

She shook her head. "No, Owen, I'm not hurt. I've heard your sacred song. So have all of *Kishelëmùkònk's* creations. Look how Mother Ice still lingers at the edge of the pool!" she said, with a sweep of her hand. "I cry because the Great Spirit is so pleased. These are tears of joy. You have filled me with hope, Owen."

The light in his eyes was penetrating, and for a moment they looked like they carried the whole ocean. "With what we have seen and lived through, Nushèmakw, I'm surprised that I feel hopeful, too. That alone is a miracle."

They stood together in silence relishing the penetrating beauty of the forest. Then out of nowhere, Owen became tense and edgy. Nushèmakw looked at him, not sure why he was acting so strange.

"What's wrong, Owen?"

"Will you sit down, Nushèmakw? I've got something I want to ask you." He took a deep breath and cracked his knuckles. Then he said it. "Nushèmakw, I want you to marry me. Will you?"

She leaned back and smiled. The question didn't surprise her. She'd sensed that he was working up the courage to ask her for quite awhile. She stared back at this impossible suitor, this foreigner who knew so little about her people and their ancient ways. Here he sat, his face as open as the sky, asking her to be his wife. The longer she hesitated, the darker his expression became. She could feel his disappointment rise. "Look at me, Owen. I have a question too."

"Yes?"

"If we marry, it will be difficult. You know it's true. I'm not so worried about how my Kechemeches brothers and sisters will react to it. They're generous people, and I expect they'll welcome you as my husband. But there's something else." She took his hand. "As I've told you, Owen, I have an enemy. A dangerous one. If we marry, he will seek your life, just as he seeks mine. Are you prepared to risk that?"

"If Guiarasi is possessed with evil as you say, then he's no match for the God that lives in both of us. Yes, I'm prepared for him."

"How can you be so sure when I'm not? I believe as you do that the Great Spirit will protect us." She looked at him and began to cry. "But what would I do, Owen, if I lost you? I don't believe I'd survive."

Owen hugged her and wiped away her tears. "Together we'll face anything that comes our way. I've never been more certain of anything else in my life. Together we are stronger than anything, even Guiarasi."

Nushèmakw took a long deep breath. "You're right, Owen. I know you're right. So yes, I'll marry you. It pleases me and it pleases Kahèsëna Hàki."

She never saw a smile so big. "I've got a gift for you, a gift to celebrate this special day." He handed her a small package wrapped in suede.

She opened the soft folds of deerskin. In the center lay a slender wooden comb with delicately carved teeth running along a tooled spine. "Do you like it?" he asked clumsily. "It's a comb for your beautiful black hair."

"I can see it's a comb, Owen," she laughed. "It's the most beautiful comb I've ever seen. How in the world did you ever carve it?"

"It took a long time," he said proudly. "I used a limb that fell from the nushèmakw down by the creek. I thought you'd like a gift from your mother tree."

"Owen, you're the most thoughtful man I've ever met," she said, hugging him. "I love this comb more than any other gift you've ever given me because you created it with your own hands. I'll cherish it always."

They were surprised that the sun had crept so low in the sky. He took her hand and they headed home.

1534 CE, NOVEMBER

HUNTING MOON

A cold snap finally descended on the island, covering the ground with white rime. The season's first frost had arrived. Owen spent the morning traversing the creek collecting firewood to add to their mountainous piles. By afternoon a strong north wind blew in through the hollow as he carried the kindling back to camp. The wind picked up when he approached the yard, sending leaves and debris sailing through the air.

"Nushèmakw!" he called out, but she didn't answer.

Something was wrong. Her pestle lay on the ground. The maize in her log mortar was being carried away in the gusts, something she would never allow to happen. He whistled for Blackpaw, but he was out of earshot. He called for Nushèmakw again and again. There was no answer. He checked her wikwam and his cabin to no avail. He crossed the yard and started up the rise toward the giant pine. Then he saw her.

"Stay away," she shouted. "He's waiting for you!"

The wind blew brutally, and he shielded his eyes from the pummeling sand. She was leaning against the pine tree at the top of the hill. A man stood in front of her with his brown face painted yellow and red. His tangled mass of black hair flew about unfettered by the feathered band he wore across his brow. His arms were poised with a loaded bow, and the arrow was aimed at Nushèmakw. He saw

Owen and smiled maniacally.

"We shall see how brave you are now!" he shouted to Owen in Onondaga.

"Leave, Owen, before he kills you."

"*Tíliotieriu!*" Guiarasi shouted. "Silence!" He lifted his bow and aimed it at Owen.

"Don't do it, Guiarasi," Owen said in Onondaga.

Guiarasi looked surprised. But only for an instant. He quickly regained his composure and drew the bow.

"You shame Tadodaho by doing this," Nushèmakw said.

He struck her, and she fell over. "I *am* Tadodaho," he shouted. Owen started toward her.

"One more step, and you're a dead man," seethed Guiarasi. Owen kept moving.

Guiarasi's face darkened and he released the bow. The arrow sailed through the air. Owen lunged forward to dodge it, and the arrow went right through his hand.

A sudden and deafening roar ripped through the woods, an awful monstrous sound. Guiarasi spun around to see what it was. Out of the forest burst the Great Maxkwe, who was charging up the hill at a frightening speed. In seconds, the giant black bear reached the summit and stood on his hind legs towering over the intruder. With one powerful swipe with his mighty forelimb, he bludgeoned Guiarasi, raking his razor claws over the man's bare chest. Guiarasi fell to the ground. The Guardian Bear roared ferociously and disappeared back into the forest.

Owen was stunned. Somehow he managed to clamber up the rise, pressing his wounded hand under his arm. By the time he reached Nushèmakw, she was kneeling beside her nemesis.

"Is he dead?"

She shook her head. "No, not yet."

Owen had never seen eyes that held such sorrow. "We must try to save him," she said.

"I'll go for water," he said. "What else do you need?"

"Let me see your hand."

He released his thumb from the clean cut, and blood pooled into his palm. Nushèmakw tore a strip from her skirt and tied it tightly around his hand.

"Bring back some moss for his wounds and yours, along with the water," she said, removing the medicine bundle from around her neck. "Everything else I have here."

He stood to leave.

"One more thing, Owen. I will need my comb."

By the time Owen returned, she had built a small fire and was chanting over Guiarasi. She fanned him with her three sacred feathers, coaxing the scented smudge smoke across her unconscious enemy's prone body. Owen handed her the water pot, and she placed it over the fire between two stones. She took the moss and saturated it, and began to wash Guiarasi's wounds. When they were clean, she turned to Owen.

"How's your hand?"

"It'll heal."

She examined the flap of skin that lay open on his palm. "You'll have a scar." She sponged it clean and squeezed water over it until it ran clear of blood. She pressed the moss into his palm and tied it with a fresh strip of hide.

"Will he survive?" Owen asked.

"No, he doesn't have long now. Did you bring the comb?"

He gave it to her. She placed her hand gently across Guiarasi's forehead. "My cousin," she said, "no more must you live the life of the Tadodaho of old. He too was possessed with a violent and crooked spirit. He too caused misery wherever he went. He too had snakes in his hair. Soon you will be called to the great Star Path, where Keeper Grandmother guards the door to the highest heaven."

She carefully removed the band of feathers from across his crown. "While there's still time, my cousin, as Ayonhwathah did before me, and as the Great Peacemaker taught us, I, too, will comb the snakes from your hair."

And in this greatest act of kindness Owen had ever seen, Nushèmakw gently combed the hair of her enemy until he breathed no more.

❦

1535 CE, MARCH

SUGAR MOON

The winter months passed peacefully. Soon after they were married, they moved into Owen's cabin. He learned that weddings were not a tradition among her people, that agreeing to live as husband and wife was all that was required. Owen loved the simplicity of it. They used her wikwam for storage, and she would go there during her moontime when the deep snow made it impossible for her to travel to the pond.

Nushèmakw taught him how to play snowsnake, a game from her childhood home in the mountains. He built a sled like the one he'd made for little Lizzie back in Bentley Manor and dared her to soar down the icy hill with him. They ate well, gobbling up the stews and dumplings, the pancakes with honey, and all the other rich and satisfying foods they had harvested that fall.

It was finally winter, the season for storytelling. Every evening, while the snow fell over the island, they exchanged tales. They shared pipes of kelekenikàn to help their thoughts mingle in the smoke that blended and curled and drifted up and out the roof hole and into the cold sky.

Nushèmakw started by sharing the legends of the Lenapeyok, the stories of the Sugar Maple and Woodpecker Papaxès. She told him about the Mastodons, those terrible beasts that roamed along the Great Namès Sipu River, and about the giants that lived among them.

"Our people have giants too," Owen said. He told the old Welsh tales, about the court of King Arthur and his exploits slaying giants, and about the story of David and Goliath, the boy who slung a stone that killed the giant and saved his people.

"Do you still have giants in England?" she asked.

"No, it was a long time ago, thousands of years past."

"When I was a girl traveling from Onondaga to Lenapehokink with my father, I came across a man who looked like a giant. He was a Susquehannock. A fierce looking man more than two heads taller than my father, who was a tall man, too. He turned out to be my father's friend, and he helped us travel in safety. He told me that long, long ago, his people lived among giants and some of them married. That was why so many of the Susquehannock were taller than most men."

There was plenty of snow during those cold months to the delight of Blackpaw who felt as if he had returned to his native land up north. The snow kept coming until it completely banked the north side of the cabin, insulating them from the coldest wind. The low winter sun shined on the south facing walls, keeping them snug and warm.

The night was relatively mild, and the crusty snow glowed under the bright full moon. After they finished their evening meal, Owen prepared their pipes for the ritual smoke that they would take by the fire burning outside. When the rich aroma of the pipe smoke reached his nose, a thought struck him, something he had all but forgotten.

"Nushèmakw," he said. "I just remembered the first time I saw you."

"I remember, too. It was that day you woke up in the sweat-lodge."

"No, Nushèmakw. It was before that, before I came to Little Turtle Island. I was sitting in the chapel at Greyfriar, where tall windows of colored glass covered the walls. It was the end of vespers, one of our holy ceremonies, when the priest lit the incense and the smoke filled the nave. I wondered at the time why the priest burned such strange incense because it smelled unlike anything he'd burned before. Now I know. It was kelekenikàn," he said tapping his pipe.

"I'm sure of it. It was a premonition. I must have fallen asleep after that or else a trance came upon me, because when I regained my wits, I was alone in the chapel. The sun was low and shining through an image in the glass. Beautiful beams of colored light fell all over me, and I was filled with a peace of heart and mind I can hardly describe." He was silent then, and she waited. "Nushèmakw, the image in the window was of you. I've only now realized that it was a message—a way to let me know that if I found you, I would be on the true path. Is that possible?"

"Of course it is. You had a vision, and now you know it's true," Nushèmakw reassured.

Their pipes grew cold, and the fire died down to embers. "It's getting cold, Owen," Nushèmakw said. "Let's go inside."

She rekindled the coals in the cabin hearth, and soon they were warm and comfortable. They watched the soft, dancing flames.

"Shall we roll out the map?" Owen asked. It was their own ritual, an amusement they indulged in at the end of the day.

"Who was the man who created this beautiful thing?" Nushè-makw asked.

"His name is Piri Reis. That much my uncle told me. And I can see for myself that he was an accomplished scribe as much as he was an artist." He pointed to the finely drawn scrollwork and the labels identifying known lands in their Latin names. The compass rose was masterfully laid, its arrow pointing due north, while mighty ships with their billowing sails crossed vast oceans.

"Do you miss it, Owen? The writing, your life as a scribe, to do work such as this?"

"Sometimes, but not as much as I imagined I would." He opened and closed his wounded hand, the scar on his palm still angry but healing. "It's a good thing, too, because now it may be impossible for me to ever write again."

"We'll see about that." She pointed to the corners of the map. "I recognize these," she said, studying the cherubs blowing through clouds. "They're your Spirit Grandfathers. We have them too."

It went on this way during those many winter nights. As they poured over the map, they began to piece together their own stories. It was this map that showed Hy-Brasil much further west than any other map. Once she got her bearings and understood that the map had them looking at the earth as the crow flies, she was able to show him a few things.

She knew nothing of the world to the east, where this map-maker had etched in minutia the continents of Europe and Africa, where Turkey and the Arab nations and the lands of the Far East stood out in spectacular relief. Instead, she lingered over the left side of the map where everything west of a vaguely drawn coastline was largely empty except for the fanciful embellishments by the artist.

"Your people know nothing about us, Owen," she said laying her hand on the vellum. She expected to see the Namès Sipu cutting a line north to south through the middle of her homeland. "They haven't even drawn our Great Turtle Island. We're the people who have lived here since time began, yet I see nothing. Your people should know our stories."

Owen nodded, feeling both awe and dread. "You're right, Nushèmakw. But I'm exhausted. It's getting late. Let's go to bed."

They woke the next morning to the first inkling of spring and a warm breeze that passed over the island. It was the last throes of winter when the sun crept higher and higher with each passing day, gaining strength. Soon the season of ice melt would begin. More nights of freezing temperatures would keep the ground solid for a while longer, but not much longer. So they decided that tomorrow was the day they would leave Little Turtle Island.

They'd been out to the isthmus—that narrow neck of land on the northwest side of the island that stretched over to her village. In the winter, deep snow prevented passage; in the warm months, it was flooded. They could cross now, but not for long. The spring melt was coming on fast. They had little time before it was under water again.

A quiet settled between them. They packed their things. She'd spent her year of mourning well, respecting her father and her tradi-tions. She was rewarded with the gift of her husband, and the greater knowledge of the spirit world that first broke her heart and now found a place to soar.

Owen felt the pang of loss again, too, sad that he would no longer have Nushèmakw to himself. It was selfish of him, he knew.

But all that was meaningful in his life—his awakening to all that was sacred, and the discovery of his life's path and purpose—came about in her presence. He decided to trust God as he promised he would, and he turned his attention to the task at hand.

"The sled is full, Nushèmakw. I don't think it could hold another thing."

"We shouldn't need anything else," she said. "What we can't carry ourselves, we'll load in Blackpaw's packs."

The dog jumped and nipped at Owen, sensing their melancholy. "Yes, Blackpaw, there's still a little time to play."

They took the dog up the hill. Owen played fetch with him, while Nushèmakw sat quietly by the giant white pine. "Thank you," she said. It was her goodbye, since she didn't know if she would ever be back. "If Maxkwe comes looking for me after his long sleep, let him know that I'm well."

They crossed to the other side and said goodbye to all of it— the marshes and the dunes, the great herons and the gulls, the sand and the sea. On their return, they pushed their raft with its broken leg off the bank and watched it float out on the tide. The last goodbye came when they passed Guiarasi's grave, marked with his arrows broken in two.

Night fell over their camp. When they finished their stew, she wiped clean the pot to pack with their other belongings. They sat by the fire pit, and lit their pipes for the last time.

They had saved their creation stories for this last night.

"In the beginning," they said in unison, and they both laughed.

"You go first, Owen."

He spoke softly. "God said, 'Let there be light' and there was light." He told her how God created the dome of sky over the water and the land across the sea and the plants and seed and fruit that grew upon the land. And the two great lights, the sun to rule the day and the moon to rule the night, and the sky was filled with stars.

Owen stirred the fire and sparks flew into the sky. "God filled the land and sea with a multitude of creatures and said, 'Let us make humankind in our image according to our likeness.' And so it was. And on the seventh day when the heavens and the earth and all they contain were created, God rested. Now God beheld all of creation and blessed it and made it holy."

They sat quietly in the moonlight and listened to the crackling flame.

"It's a beautiful story, Owen. You honor your people by telling it."

Owen nodded, "I know. There are many more I can recite from memory, but I'm forgetting some of them, too. But it doesn't matter because they're all written down."

He could see that this bothered her. "What's wrong?"

"You're always talking about these books. The countless words that you put on paper. How you captured all of your sacred stories and pressed them on sheets. Piles of them, like the map you gave me."

"Yes, that's right. In many languages and in many forms, the Bible is being spread across my home in England and across the continent, too, and into far-reaching lands. It's a miracle that the sacred word can now travel so far."

"You call it a miracle, but we'll see," she said lighting her pipe again. "If all of your sacred stories have been written down as you say, like this map, then I worry that the stories have died, killed by your own hand, like a harness on your tongue."

"What do you mean? The stories haven't died. The opposite is true. Because we've written them down, people can read them anytime and not have to wait until someone tells it to them. We're keeping them alive."

She was angry now. "You showed me this map and the way to see it as the crow flies. And I do see it. I see the lines and the ink and the color. But these shapes and forms are not Lenapéyok or Ononda-ga. They're dead things lying on the page. So it is with words. Words only come alive when they're spoken. It's the voice of the storyteller that gives them life. It's our breath that carries them to the heavens where the Great Spirit hears them and is pleased. Your own creation story talks about the god who spoke and so it was. He didn't write, Owen, he spoke."

He'd never thought about it this way before. They were both quiet for a long time; she to calm down, he to consider what she was saying.

"I'm afraid of something, Nushèmakw," Owen said, finally.
"I'm afraid that what you say is true. I spent so much time learning
how to write, and I did it well. I can write in four languages. I've finished entire books without speaking a word of them." He looked at
her. "I'm thinking about my grandfather. Grancha could read words
in English as well as write them. He could read the Latin verses too.
But he never showed me how to write in Welsh, my mother tongue.
He refused to. Now I see why. He felt the same way, I'm sure of it.
We call it a tongue for a reason. The old Welsh tales came to me not
by books, but in the warmth of the fireside, like we're doing here,
with our voices carrying all the way into our hearts. Did you know,
Nushèmakw, that the Welsh have no creation story?"

Nushèmakw stared in disbelief.

"Grancha could recite the story of Genesis the way I just did.
We all could. But it's not my origin story. It's the creation story that
came to us many thousands of years ago from the Hebrews, a tribe
far east of England. My own tribe either forgot their creation story
or were forced to."

"How's that possible?"

"England is a brutal place and has been for as long as anyone
can remember. Wars raged endlessly. They still do. Not just from
foreign invaders, but among our own people, too."

Nushèmakw nodded. It was happening between her tribes as
well.

"There were eons of battle. Nations upon nation rose to
mighty heights, and fell to nothing just as quickly. We were con-
quered time and time again. It took a toll on my people. So many of
the elders were taken out that eventually no one remembered our
traditions or even our own beginnings. That's what my grandfather
told me." He lay on his back and sighed. "Nushèmakw, we do live
in the stories we tell, but what a curse it is when we can no longer
speak."

Nushèmakw sprinkled kelekenikàn on the fire. "I pray that
your people will find their stories again."

Owen propped himself on his elbows. "Tell me your creation
story, Nushèmakw."

"This is how Grandmother Uma told it to me." She spoke

slowly the way her father had taught her. "In the beginning there was only endless space, and therein dwelt *Kishelëmùkònk*, the Creator. *Kishelëmùkònk* had a great vision, and he saw the endless space filled with stars. He saw the sun, the moon, and the earth. On the earth, he saw mountains, valleys, lakes, rivers, and forests. He saw the trees, flowers, crops and grasses, and the crawling, walking, swimming, and flying beings. He saw the birth of things, their growth and death, and other things that seemed to live forever. When he thought about his vision, it started to happen."

Nushèmakw's eyes were pools of light. "In the vision, *Kishelamàkânk* saw things of opposite natures and so created light and darkness, hot and cold, above and below, good and evil. Many laws were woven into the creations of *Kishelamàkânk* for the wellbeing, harmony, and balance of all things. These laws governed the movement of the sun and earth, moon and stars, the cycles of life, birth, growth, and death."

She told Owen about the giant turtle that rose from the water and the tree that grew on its back. She told him how the tree sent out a sprout that grew a man; and another sprout that grew a woman – the first human couple.

She stirred the fire as she moved from her Kechemeches stories to the origins of her Minisink and Onondaga families.

She finished with the story of the Great Peacemaker who, long ago, traveled to the land of the Haudenosaunee in the stone canoe, spreading his message of peace, and uniting the great Longhouse of the Five Nations. She told how his disciple Ayonhwathah returned the brutal treachery of evil Tadodaho not with revenge but with forgiveness, and so healed his enemy of his crooked ways.

The fire had gone out. Neither of them spoke as they doused the coals and got ready for bed. In the comfortable warmth of the cabin, they slept a peaceful sleep, and the Star Path glittered above them, shining across the heavens.

The morning was warm and the birds called out from the forest. Rills of water carved through the snow etching furrows down the hill and into the creek. Nushèmakw packed the last of the biscuits and dried squirrel they would eat on their travels. Owen checked the wikwam and cabin for anything they might have forgotten, then secured the hides over the doors. He tied the bundles to Blackpaw, two bags on either side of his shoulders held together with a leather harness. Nushèmakw was waiting with her pack on her back.

"Are you ready, Owen?" she asked.

He swung his pack over his shoulder. "I hope so, Nushèmakw. I pray to God I am."

They turned and walked over the hill, across the ridge, and into the lowlands, leaving Little Turtle Island behind them.

ACKNOWLEDGEMENTS

Writing this novel has been a remarkable journey across winding trails that sometimes led into uncharted territories. As is the nature of long passages, the way is often marked by welcomed respites at opportune times. For me, they have come in the form of my friends and family, for whom I am enormously grateful. I am more than fortunate to have two gifted daughters who reviewed early drafts and greatly improved my work: Liza for her meticulous scrutiny of grammar and syntax; Josie for examining each scene for continuity and context. To Todd for believing in dreams. To Shawn for the long hikes that brought clarity to my thinking. For Frances, a wellspring of encouragement, who nudged me to keep going just when I needed it most. For Eser whose enthusiasm and support always enriched me. For Judy whose belief in the creative process propelled me. For Jo who helped me see the dips and turns that slowed down the plot. For Elizabeth who helped me shape my first draft into a cohesive whole. For Eliza who was my sounding board. For Vickii who helped unravel the knots. To Linda for her uplifting faith and humor. To Amy and Lois for their unending support. For the librarians and curators at American Indian museums and resource centers and their commitment to advancing the knowledge and understanding of Native cultures. And finally to my husband, Dave, who read through each and every draft (and there were many!) with a steadfast willingness to help me see this journey to its end.

ABOUT THE AUTHOR

Linda Johnson has been a freelance writer, painter, illustrator, and designer for 30-plus years. She lives with her husband on a little piece of heaven on the Front Range of northern Colorado, where its abundance of natural beauty is a never-ending source of inspiration.

ABOUT *LITTLE TURTLE ISLAND*

Little Turtle Island is about first encounters and how two individuals deal with the myriad misunderstandings that transpire as they reach across the chasm between their cultures. The novel takes place in the early sixteenth century right before European contact on the Mid-Atlantic shores—a moment that opens an opportunity to explore the complexity of what was happening in both cultures at that time.

It is the author's hope that *Little Turtle Island* is seen as an invitation to further the difficult conversation about race, culture, class, and religion in a way that is beneficial and inspiring. By taking a deep dive into the histories of the Northeastern Woodland Tribes and Tudor England during the early 1500s, readers are able to draw easy parallels between the struggles of that period and our own.

THE HAUDENOSAUNEE LEGEND OF
THE PEACEMAKER

AN ABBREVIATED VERSION OF
THE WHITE ROOTS OF PEACE (WALLACE 1946),
PUBLISHED IN DEAN R. SNOW'S THE IROQUOIS (1996).

It was a time when war was the normal state of things. North of Lake Ontario there was a young Huron woman who lived apart from her mother. Although still a virgin, the young woman became pregnant. Her mother dreamed that the child was destined to do great things. In due course the child, a boy, was born. The child was named Deganawida and accepted by his mother and grandmother as a truly gifted child.

Deganawida grew quickly to become a handsome young man. He had a natural gift for speaking, and preached to the children of his community. Eventually he clarified his message of peace through power and law. But he came up against the doubt and jealousy faced by all prophets in their own countries. After announcing his intention to depart, he built a stone canoe, and launched it with the help of his mother and grandmother. He came to the country of the five Iroquois nations, who were then fighting each other as vigorously as they fought other nations.

He passed from west to east through Iroquoia, urging the hunters he met along the way to take his message of peace back to their chiefs. Eventually he met a woman, who lived in a small house along the trail, where she fed hunters who passed by. She was the first to accept his news of peace and power, and he renamed her Jigonhsasee, "New Face."

The Peacemaker moved on, stopping among the Onondagas and gazing through a smoke hole into the house of Ayonhwathah (Hiawatha). He quickly converted Ayonhwathah from cannibalism, and charged him with converting Thadodaho (Adodarhonh), a particularly malevolent Onondaga shaman with snakes in his hair. Leaving Ayonhwathah to convert Thadodaho by combing the snakes from his hair, the Peacemaker left to travel to Mohawk country.

He went to the place of the great Cohoes Falls near the mouth of the Mohawk River. There he climbed a tree over the gorge and waited. The Mohawks felled the tree into the torrent, but the next morning they found the Peacemaker sitting by his fire. The feat convinced the Mohawks of his power. They accepted his message and became the founders of the League.

Meanwhile, Ayonhwathah's efforts to convert Thadodaho had met with failure. Worse, the shaman had killed each of Ayonhwathah's three daughters. Devastated by grief, Ayonhwathah left his village, following the trail eastward toward Mohawk country. Along the way he came to a lake. A flock of ducks flew up to allow him to pass dry shod, carrying the water with them and revealing a lake bottom strewn with shell beads. These Ayonhwathah collected and put in a buckskin bag. Some he strung on three strings as symbols of his grief. Wandering aimlessly, he eventually encountered the Peacemaker. Deganawida took the strings of shell beads and made more strings from the beads collected by Ayonhwathah. Laying the strings out one at a time, he uttered the words of the Requickening Address for the first time. With fifteen strings he wiped away the tears, removed obstructions from the ears, cleared the throat, dispelled the darkness, and dealt with the other eleven essential matters of condolence. The ritual cleared Ayonhwathah's mind of grief, and together they sang the Peace Hymn, the Hai Hai.

The Peacemaker and Ayonhwathah taught the ritual to the Mohawks, and accepted adoption in the Mohawk nation. With the essential ritual now in hand, they traveled westward, accompanied by Mohawk chiefs. The Oneidas joined the League quickly, and were called younger brothers by the Mohawks. Beyond the Oneidas were the Onondagas and evil Thadoaho. They bypassed this obstacle to approach the Cayuga, who joined as easily as the Oneida had done. They also took the side of the younger brothers. The three nations then returned to the Onondagas, all of whom save Thadodaho also joined, but as older brothers on the side of the Mohawks. Then, with the chiefs of the four nations, they went to the Senecas, who also joined as older brothers, completing the League.

With the power of the chiefs of Five Nations behind them, the Peacemaker and Ayonhwathah returned to the lodge of Thadodaho.

There, with the greatest difficulty, his mind was made straight, and Ayonhwathah combed the snakes from his hair. The Peacemaker made Thadodaho first among equals in the role of the fifty League Chiefs, placed antlers on all their heads as signs of the authority, and taught them the words of the Great Law.

THE LEGENDARY ISLAND
OF HY-BRASIL

THE CHARTING OF HY-BRASIL

Excerpts from the Preliminary Sketches for the Reappearance of HyBrazil,
by Sean Lynch in Project Muse: The Johns Hopkins University Press

The island of HyBrazil [with no connection to the country Brazil] first appeared on sailing charts completed by cartographer Angelino Dulcert between 1325 and 1339. Based in Genoa, Dulcert asserted that HyBrazil could be found in the Atlantic Ocean, to the west of Ireland. The island continued to remain on maps and charts for several centuries, under various pseudonyms such as Insula de Berzil, Illa de brasil, Ui Breasail, or Brazil. It existed as a kind of terra incognita: within reach of sailors on the Atlantic, potentially visible from high cliffs on the west of Ireland.

HyBrazil continued to appear, as in Paolo dal Pozzo Toscanelli's 1457 chart, which was used by Christopher Columbus on his 1492 voyage. Other islands such as Isola des Demonias, Frisland, Buss Island, Antillia, and the Islands of Saint Brendan frequently accompanied it.

In July 1480 Bristol merchant John Jay sponsored a ship to sail westward in search of the Isle of Brasil. The nine-week expedition did not find the island, and the ship was forced back to Bristol by storms. Several other attempts are reported. In 1496 an Italian merchant, Giovanni Caboto, arrived in Bristol. Known locally as John Cabot, he obtained a Royal Assent from Henry VII "to find, discover, and investigate whatsoever islands, countries, regions, and provinces which before this time were unknown." He sailed for HyBrazil but never returned; his five ships and three hundred men were almost all lost at sea. Some returned to England to tell the story, after first reaching Newfoundland. By 1498, Pedro de Ayala, the Spanish envoy to London, reported that two to four ships a year were being sent from Bristol, all with the expressed intention of finding the island.

WHAT IS HY BRASIL

Excerpts from History Ireland, *Issue 4 (Jul/Aug 2008), Web. June 2017.*

Legend tells that somewhere off the coast of Ireland there was an island, always covered by intense fog and only seen on very rare occasions. Every seven years the fog would fade away, revealing this fabulous land. Mountains, green fields, and a glowing city were briefly visible. This Celtic land was the home of fairies, magicians, and wizards. Legends and myths of ancient Ireland contain many references to heroes who, attracted by this fantastic vision, launched into the sea in search of it. Anyone able to touch the island would achieve eternal life in a delightful paradise. But every time they approached it, the island disappeared again below the sea.

St. Barrind's Story

Excerpts from the Voyage of St. Brendan the Navigator, *900 AD*

I [St. Barrind] was brought by my son to the seashore facing west, where there was a boat. He said to me, "Father, embark in the boat and let us sail westwards to the island which is called the Promised Land of the Saints which God will give to those who come after us at the end of time."

We embarked and sailed, but a fog so thick covered us that we could scarcely see the poop or the prow of the boat. But when we had spent about an hour like this a great light shone all around us, and there appeared to us a land wide, and full of grass and fruit. When the boat landed we disembarked and began to go and walk round that island. This we did for fifteen days—yet we could not find the end of it. We saw no plants that had not flowers, nor trees that had not fruit. The stones of that land are precious stones. Then on the fifteenth day we found a river flowing from east to west. As we pondered on all these things we were in doubt what we should do.

We decided to cross the river, but we awaited advice from God. In the course of a discussion on these things, a man suddenly appeared in a great light before us, who immediately called us by our own names and saluted us, saying, "Well done, good brothers. For the Lord has revealed to you the land, which he will give to his saints. The river there marks the middle of the island. You may not go beyond this point. So return to the place from which you departed."

When he said this, I immediately questioned him where he came from and what was his name. He said, "Why do you ask me where I come from or how I am called? Why do you not ask me about the island? As you see it now, so it has been from the beginning of the world. Do you feel the need of any food or drink or clothing? Yet for the equivalent of one year you have been on this island and have not tasted food or drink! You have never been overcome by sleep nor has night enveloped you! For here it is always day, without blinding darkness. Our Lord Jesus Christ is the light of this island."

NORTHEASTERN WOODLAND TRIBES
1518-1535 CE

The map below is intended to give the reader a general sense of the territories of the Northeastern Woodland Tribes during the early sixteenth century. The designations are approximate due to the shifts in population over the course of that period, as well as archaeological discoveries made since the sources listed below were published.

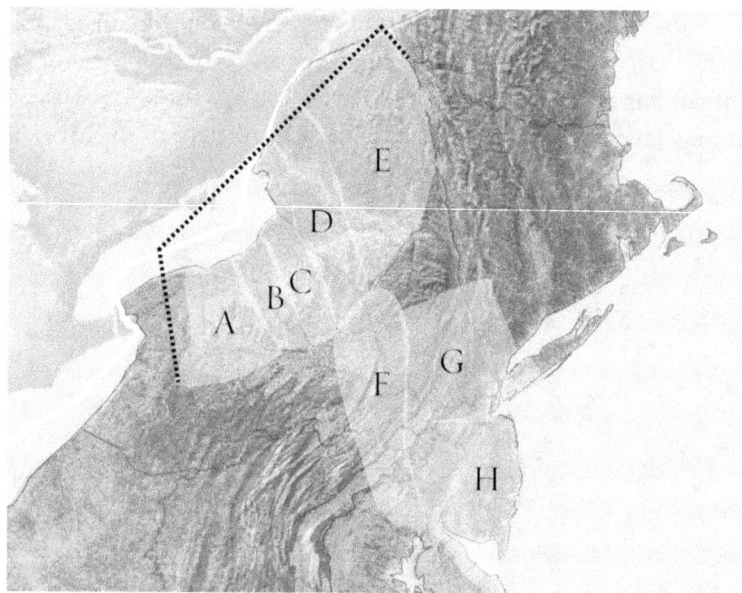

LEGEND

●●●●●● HAUDENOSAUNEE LONGHOUSE TERRITORY (IROQUOIS CONFEDERACY)

A=Seneca B=Cayuga C=Onondaga D=Oneida E=Mohawk F=Susquehannock
G=Lenapé Munsee (Delaware) H=Lenapé Unami (Delaware)

SOURCES

Carol Cornelius. *Iroquois Corn in a Culture-Based Curriculum: A Framework for Respectfully Teaching About Cultures*. Albany, NY: State University of New York Press, 1999.

Kraft, Herbert C., ed. *A Delaware Indian Symposium: Anthropological Series Number 4*. Harrisburg, PA: Commonwealth of Pennsylvania, The Pennsylvania Historical and Museum Commission, 1974.

Snow, Dean R. *The Iroquois*. Oxford, UK: Blackwell, 1994.

Tuck, James A. *Onondaga Iroquois Prehistory: A Study in Settlement Archaeology*. Syracuse, NY: Syracuse University Press, 1971.

Weslager, Clinton Alfred. *The Delaware Indians: A History*. New Brunswick, NJ: Rutgers University Press, 2000.

ABOUT THE MAP

The map in *Little Turtle Island* is fictitious and is a compilation of the two maps shown here. Interestingly, in this Turkish map from 1521, Piri Reis has drawn a mysterious island west of Ireland. His revised map of 1524-1525, combined with Portuguese cosmographer Diogo Ribeiro's 1529 map, is what was given to Uncle Seamus and rediscovered by Owen. The map in the story shows Hy-Brasil much farther southwest, with the territories of the northeastern woodland tribes and nations nothing more than an empty expanse.

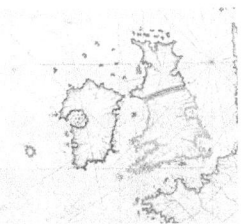

Detail of a 1521 map of Europe by Turkish cartographer Piri Reis from the Kitab-ı Bahriye (Book of Navigation). It was revised in 1524-1525.

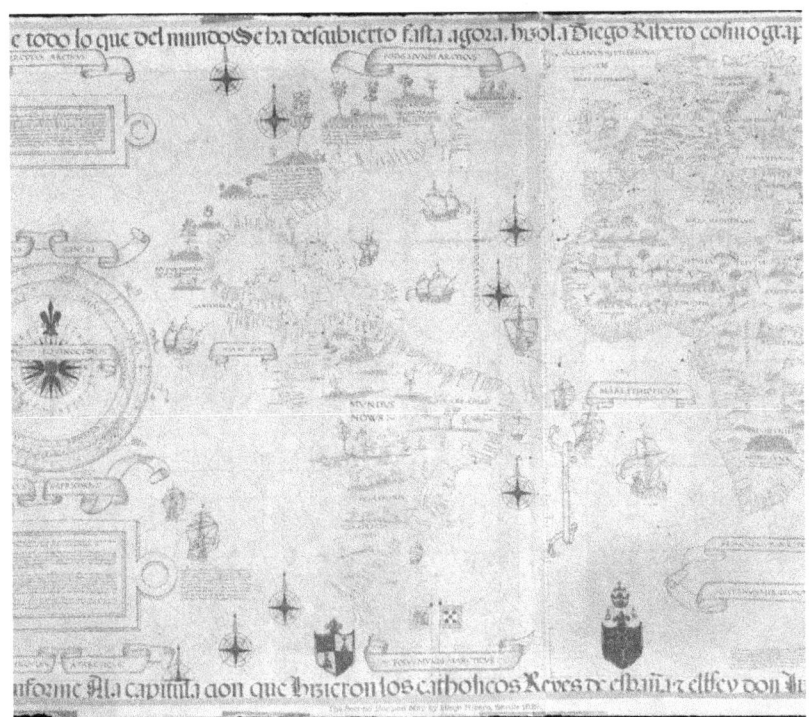

Detail of world map by Portuguese cosmographer Diogo Ribeiro (1529)

SELECTED READING

Baskerville, Geoffrey. *English Monks and the Suppression of the Monasteries.* London: Jonathan Cape, 1965.

Bolt, Robert. *A Man for All Seasons: A Drama in Two Acts.* New York, NY: Samuel French, Inc. 1960.

Boyd, Howard P. *A Pine Barrens Odyssey: A Naturalist's Year in the Pine Barrens of New Jersey.* Medford, NJ: Plexus Publishing, Inc., 1997.

Carol Cornelius. *Iroquois Corn in a Culture-Based Curriculum: A Framework for Respectfully Teaching About Cultures.* Albany, NY: State University of New York Press, 1999.

Kraft, Herbert C., ed. *A Delaware Indian Symposium: Anthropological Series Number 4.* Harrisburg, PA: Commonwealth of Pennsylvania, The Pennsylvania Historical and Museum Commission, 1974

More, Thomas. "Utopia." In *Utopia.* Mineola, NY: Dover Publications, 1997. Previously published in Utopia. N.p., 1516.

Page, William, ed. "Friaries: The House of Grey Friars." British History Online. http://www.british-history.ac.uk/vch/oxon/vol2/pp122-137.

Snow, Dean R. *The Iroquois.* Oxford, UK: Blackwell, 1994.

Tuck, James A. *Onondaga Iroquois Prehistory: A Study in Settlement Archaeology.* Syracuse, NY:Syracuse University Press, 1971.

Weslager, Clinton Alfred. *The Delaware Indians: A History.* New Brunswick, NJ: Rutgers University Press, 2000.

Williams, Penry. *Life in Tudor England.* New York, NY: G.P. Putnam's Sons, 1964.

OTHER RESOURCES

Batsto Village & Wharton State Forest, Hammonton, NJ

Iroquois Indian Museum, Howes Cave, NY

National Museum of the American Indian, New York, NY; Washington, DC

Rochester Museum and Science Center, Rochester, NY

Seneca Art and Culture Center at Ganondagan, Victor, NY

Vine Deloria, Jr. Library, National Museum of the American Indian, Suitland, MD

Waterloo Village, Stanhope, NJ.

❧
LIST OF CHARACTERS

Achimwis Nushèmakw's Kechemeches (Lenapé) father

Atsi a Mohawk friend of Nushèmakw's father

Aunt Beatrice Owen's aunt

Clan Mother Nushèmakw's Onondaga clan mother

Elen Owen's Welsh mother

Elis Bowen Welsh guardian of Greyfriar; also Father Elis and Friar Elis

Thomas Cromwell a real figure in history; Chief Minister for King Henry VIII, considered by many to be the King's henchman during the English Reformation

Grancha Owen's Welsh grandfather, Hywel ap Rhys

Guiarasi Nushèmakw's Onondaga cousin

Hehron Nushèmakw's Onondaga name

Honarha Nushèmakw's Onondaga mother

Hywel ap Rhys Owen's grandfather, also Grancha

Keguenha a Onondaga clan sister of Nushèmakw's mother

Jenkyn boatman at the harbor at Bristol

Kíhkay the Minisink (Lenapé) Chief

Kitakima the Kechemeches (Lenapé) Chief

Lady Bentley Master Blazer's wife; Lady of Bentley Manor, an English estate

Seamus Llewellyn an Irish friend of Owen's father considered an uncle

Logan ship's cook

Madoc ap Morcant Owen's Welsh father

Master Blazer English Lord of Bentley Manor, Lord Bentley

Mistress Lizzie Master Blazer and Lady Bentley's daughter

Sir Thomas More a real figure in history, also Saint Thomas More; an English lawyer and social philosopher; author of *Utopia*

Naill ship's lookout

Njó Nushèmakw's Minisink (Lenapé) friend

Nūmiis Njó's mother, a Minisink (Lenapé) woman who befriends Nushèmakw

Nushèmakw the story's Onondaga/Kechemeches (Lenapé) protagonist; Mother Tree in Unami

Owen ap Madoc the story's Welsh protagonist

Peter Maddock kitchen steward at Bentley Manor

Renny cabin boy on *The Mary Margaret*, one of Master Blazer's ships

Sarangararo a Susquehannock friend of Nushèmakw's father

Sarhak Nushèmakw's Onondaga mother-aunt

Tadodaho a contemporary of Turtle Chief; an Onondaga Bear Chief who holds the position of first among equals among the fifty confederacy chiefs.

Tadodaho from the Legend of the Peacemaker, a malevolent Onondaga chief from long ago who had snakes in his hair. With great difficulty, his mind is made straight, he adopts the Peacemaker's message, and joins the Haudenosaunee Confederacy

Turtle Chief chief of Nushèmakw's Onondaga Turtle Clan; a Haudenosaunee Confederacy chief

Uma Nushèmakw's Kechemeches elder mother/grandmother

Wemahtekĕnis a Unami Keeper of the Forest

Willie Father Elis's coachman

www.ingramcontent.com/pod-product-compliance
Lightning Source LLC
Chambersburg PA
CBHW061323200626
46813CB00017B/2828